LONG
TIME GONE

HELL or HIGH WATER: BOOK 2

SE JAKES

RIPTIDE
PUBLISHING

Riptide Publishing
PO Box 6652
Hillsborough, NJ 08844
www.riptidepublishing.com

Long Time Gone (Hell or High Water, #2)

Cover Art by L.C. Chase, lcchase.com/design.htm
Editor: Sarah Frantz
Layout: L.C. Chase, lcchase.com/design.htm

ISBN: 978-1-62649-061-1

First edition
October, 2013

Also available in ebook:
ISBN: 978-1-62649-060-4

LONG
TIME GONE

HELL or HIGH WATER: BOOK 2

SE JAKES

RIPTIDE
PUBLISHING

For J, N & C, because you've been there from the beginning.

Never love a wild thing . . . the more you do, the stronger they get . . .
If you let yourself love a wild thing. You'll end up looking at the sky.
—Truman Capote, *Breakfast At Tiffany's*

We are all searching for someone whose demons play well with ours.
—Author Unknown

TABLE OF CONTENTS

PROLOGUE: SUDAN

Kasey Coetzee backed against the cold stone of the well's sides, hiding her knife behind her. Abject terror choked her, but she swallowed it.

She would survive, *dammit*.

After being ignored for days, someone was leaning over the side of the well, blocking the light. She wasn't sure which was the more horrifying prospect—being left to die down here or her captors pulling her out.

The last time they'd thrown several bottles of water to her—which had to be more than a full day and a half ago—one of them had called down, "*Jy beter dit werd wees vir jou vader.*"

You'd better be worth it to your father.

Now, a distinctively American voice said, "I'm here to help you, Kasey." She sagged and sobbed with relief. Even if it was the CIA again, at least she would be out of this hole. She saw he was lowering something down to her only when it got close enough to grab, which she did. It was a harness with a pulley and she forced back her tears at the first near-taste of freedom.

"Step into the rig and I'll get you up."

Five days ago, her kidnappers—soldiers from her own country—had trapped her in here by lowering her into the well in a rig just like this, except her hands had been bound in front of her. She'd searched for days for something to cut the rope, which is how she'd found the knife.

And the bones.

The well was fifteen feet deep and both too smooth and too wide to climb. She'd tried, of course, but all she had to show for it were bloodied and bruised hands, her nails jagged and torn. At least it had been somewhat cool, thanks to the depth—that had been the only saving grace over the past few days.

But this man was her true saving grace, and his voice was a rough-and-tumble slide over her nerves. It was deep and low and commanding—a voice she wouldn't have thought to disagree with.

"Kasey, you're thinking too much," he told her now. "Just step into the rig and I'll haul you up. Go on, that's it," he encouraged as she pulled the rope around each leg. It was knotted to hold her around her thighs and waist, and as soon as she felt tension on the rope, she shoved the knife in the waistband of her jeans, grabbed onto one of the knots, and hooked her feet desperately into the smooth stones. She gained a foothold more easily now, thanks to the man's strong grip on the rope.

"Come on now. I've got you." He helped her up the unrelentingly smooth sides, his strength doing most of the work. When she got close enough to the top, she panicked and grabbed for his arms. Her muscles screamed, but he eased her up, making her do as little of the work as possible, and finally, the heat of the midday sun hit her face. She was halfway over the top when he grabbed her around the waist and hauled her completely out.

She remained balanced against him for a second, and even as she blinked to try to get used to the light, she could see a military-looking vehicle coming toward them through the heat shimmering off the sand. It must've been heading their way the entire time, but her rescuer seemed unconcerned as he set her feet on the ground and let her lean against the well. He immediately wound fabric around her head—she assumed it was for camouflage, like the one he wore—and in return, she shimmied the ropes off her legs.

"Can you walk?"

"*Ja,*" she rasped. Coughed. "Sorry, yes."

"Okay. Come on then." His tone was skeptical, but he let her try. She lurched forward, nearly fell face-first into the sand, and he caught her in his arms with a swift, easy movement, and carried her away from the well.

And still, the big green truck came closer. "I'm sorry."

"Nothing to be sorry for."

How he could be so calm when the truck was advancing was beyond her. But it was lulling her into the same state, and she didn't care anymore if it was a false sense of security. She was so tired of panicking. "My father?"

"He's okay."

"Are you taking me to him?"

"No. It's safer not to."

Safer.

She was supposed to have been safe last week, when the CIA had taken her away from her father's house, claiming she was in grave danger. They were the only thing standing in the way of certain death, they'd told her. *There are men who want to kidnap you. We've already got your father in a safe place. He wanted us to come and get you.*

But they'd kept her away from her father, not with him. And not more than two days after putting her in a safe house, the two agents who'd been guarding her had been shot dead, and she'd been captured. Blindfolded, gagged, tied, thrown into a moving car, and brought here.

Now, she blinked and saw a tent. Two trucks were parked alongside it, and several bodies were strewn along the ground like they were made of nothing. Three terrorists down.

More are coming.

He helped her up into the back seat of one of the trucks by the tent and handed her a gun. "Stay down. Shoot anyone who comes close. Except me. Otherwise, just wait here." As if she had someplace else to be.

She did as she was told, lying flat on her belly and peeking up to watch him walk toward the big green truck, his empty hands up in the air. The truck stopped near the other side of the well, and several men dressed in military camouflage got out with their weapons drawn. She instinctively started to raise her gun to save her rescuer, when, in a blur of motion, she saw him suddenly holding a pistol in each hand. With equal parts unmistakable grace and efficiency, he shot and killed the men before they could even register his weapons.

It was the second time in recent weeks she'd seen men killed. But this time, it was the bad guys who died.

She scrambled to the front seat as he jogged to the dead men's now-abandoned vehicle, searched it, and walked back toward her with two bags. He put them into the back of the old Land Rover and got in next to her. The truck started up with a rattle and then a roar.

As he drove, he slowly pulled the camouflaging from around his face, loosening it so it hung around his neck. Ready, she supposed, to be pulled up again quickly, if necessary.

She didn't want to think about that.

She studied him surreptitiously as he drove—there were no true discernible paths, but he didn't hesitate as he maneuvered the truck over the unforgiving landscape.

"Are you hurt?" he asked.

"I don't think so," she said, and how stupid she sounded.

He smiled, just a little. She noticed fresh blood on the sleeve of his T-shirt, but when she gasped, he shook his head as if to tell her he was fine.

"Why didn't they kill you on sight?" she asked.

His mouth quirked to the side a touch. "That's a record. Usually, someone knows me at least twenty-four hours before wanting me dead."

She covered her mouth, but not before the laugh spilled out. A laugh, in the middle of all this shit. He was grinning too, and maybe inappropriateness during times of crisis was what got men like him through.

She didn't think he'd answer her, but he said, "There's a bounty on my head in this country. I'm worth more alive than dead."

"What about me?" she asked.

"Same. But I'm worth more."

"That doesn't seem fair. I think I'm cuter."

He glanced at her slyly. "Life's a bitch." Then he blinked and demanded, "Did you just call me cute in a roundabout way? Because I'm not fucking cute."

She grinned again under her fist. If she didn't laugh, she'd cry, because it was all there, bubbling up underneath the surface.

And God, he hadn't said a word about what had happened in the desert, about the lives he'd taken for her, and why he'd done so. "Did my father hire you to come find me?"

"No," he said bluntly. "He can't do that."

"So who hired you? Because the CIA told me that if I got captured, they wouldn't negotiate for my release. And they said that the South African government wouldn't either."

"Did you see any negotiating?"

"No." She rubbed her arms at a sudden chill, despite the heat. He pointed to the floor by her feet, where a blanket was rolled up. As she draped it over her shoulders, she asked, "You're not with the CIA, then?"

"Fuck no." He glanced at her. "Disappointed?"

"Best news I've heard all day," she managed, and he gave a curt nod.

He was big. Fierce and determined, with gray eyes that were someplace between liquid steel and granite, a gaze that missed nothing when he glanced over at her. Even when he attended to her, he was watching everything around him, including where the truck was headed.

"You know what my father used to do?"

"I know. Nuclear physicists are all the rage nowadays." There was an edge to the sarcasm, and she noted his hands tightened on the wheel when he spoke, but only for a second, and then they relaxed again.

"He'd retired from all of that. He's a high school teacher. We live in Dar es Salaam under new names."

"Forced retirement, no?"

"*Ja*," she agreed. "South Africa stopped its nuclear program and left men like my father exposed." Something she wasn't supposed to reveal to another living soul. Because her father had worked on nuclear weapons, he was considered equal parts pariah and high-value target. She was his biggest liability. "We were well hidden. I don't know how the CIA found us."

Her rescuer snorted. "Yeah, they're good like that."

A swell of panic washed over her. "Did the CIA finding us trigger my kidnapping?"

"Yeah, I think so, Kasey," he said, almost gently. "Breathe."

She drew in a few shaky ones at his reminder. It was as if the adrenaline rush keeping her going until this point had also been stopping the panic. "My father never thought the CIA would try to force him to work with them."

He glanced at her for a brief second, his jaw clenched, but he didn't say anything except, "He was wrong."

"Did they force him by saying they'd turn him over to the terrorists?"

His answer was careful. "The CIA protects their country's best interests."

So then, yes. Fuckers. "They made promises. I followed their rules. That nearly got me killed," she said bitterly.

He didn't say anything about that. Instead, he gestured to the back. "Grab some water. Go slow—I'm guessing they gave you the bare minimum."

She reached over the seat to grab a couple of bottles. She handed him one and then opened one for herself. She did as he said, even though instinct nagged at her to swallow the entire bottle in one large gulp. He had food and water for her. She ate and drank gratefully, was hungrier than maybe she should be after such an ordeal, but he seemed pleased that she had an appetite.

After another half an hour, she was much calmer. He reached toward the radio, but before he touched the button, he said, "Rules are usually in place because they help the people who made them, more than the people who have to follow them. Same goes for people who have questions they want you to answer. Keep some shit just for you. Gives you an edge."

Then he turned the knob and the low beat of the local music filled the truck. That plus the rumble of the truck lulled her to sleep. When she woke, she was in a hotel room. Tucked into bed. Safe.

But she wasn't alone.

The woman who'd been sitting in the room with her introduced herself as Special Agent Lawler and explained that someone had called them with Kasey's location and told them to come and guard her.

"Do you have any idea who that was?" Agent Lawler asked.

Kasey pulled the covers up like a shield. "He rescued me. I don't remember him bringing me in here—I was asleep."

"Did he drug you?"

"No." She actually felt wide-awake, with none of the residual fuzziness she'd had from the initial kidnapping. "He saved me. What will you do for me?"

"You're safe here. There are guards at the door."

Kasey glanced between the closed door and the agent. "There were guards last time too."

Agent Lawler's face tightened, and she ignored Kasey's words, instead asking again, "The man who rescued you—who was he?"

She blinked. "He didn't tell me his name."

"Did he say who sent him?"

"No."

"But he knew about your father."

"He said he did."

Why the man had helped her was a mystery. Why the CIA hadn't been able to find her on their own was another, and they weren't too happy with her when she'd pointed that out. They weren't happy that she didn't expand on what she and her rescuer had talked about either, but Kasey didn't see that it was pertinent.

Later that day, she heard Agent Lawler whispering into her phone, "This is the fourth one this month, and she also won't give any answers about him." Her back was turned away from Kasey. "How the hell does this asshole engender such goodwill?"

Kasey couldn't help but smile. Some people were just born like that.

CHAPTER ONE

From: Tom_B_1@EELTD.com
To: testingpatiencedaily@gmail.com
Subject: Eritrea

It's hotter than hell here. Reminds me a lot of home. You know, my Cajun voodoo home. I used to spend hours tracking my way through the swamps. I could go in there blindfolded and still know where I was. Could lead myself in the dark, based on the sounds around me. The feel of the bark and moss on my fingers. How the ground felt under my feet.

Hint: walk away from the squish or you're headed into actual water. Seems simple, but people tend to panic in the dark. I don't think you would. You take action.

I just fight.

From: Tom_B_1@EELTD.com
To: testingpatiencedaily@gmail.com
Subject: Relationships

I met Cope's girlfriend on Skype. She's very . . . perky. Doesn't seem to fit with Cope. Not that I'm an expert on relationships.

You have to understand why I did it, Proph. I couldn't risk you. With Cope, it's different, and I don't know why.

I know what you're thinking—by that logic, Cope's expendable. But that's not it at all. It's like . . . you took it, Prophet—you took the goddamned curse, and you wrapped it all up in that tornado of yours, and now it's a part of you. Which means that staying away from you will keep you safe.

I keep picturing you, hanging there by your wrists in front of Sadiq. Fighting. Keep thinking that you'd been in that exact position before. I wake up in a cold sweat, not worried about me, but searching for you in that warehouse. I swear I can hear your heartbeat.

Maybe it would've helped us if I could've told you this face-to-face. Maybe you're not getting these. Maybe everyone at EE is, or maybe you're showing them to people and laughing your ass off at me. But that's all right.

From: Tom_B_1@EELTD.com
To: testingpatiencedaily@gmail.com
Subject: Cut the crap

Mick and Blue asked if I'd heard from you. Actually, they asked Cope, and they're pissed and concerned, and I know the feeling.

I didn't know two weeks could affect me so much.

I thought I could walk away from our partnership. I ran. I was scared. <—I almost deleted this line, but what the hell do I have to lose that I haven't already?

From: Tom_B_1@EELTD.com
To: testingpatiencedaily@gmail.com
Subject: Worried

No one knows where you are.

I'm not going to insult you by saying I'm sorry, because that's too simple. I'm not sorry. I'm trying to take care of you.

But I could take better care of you if I was with you. I realize that now.

I've also realized that it's really never too late. For anything.

Tom was losing his mind. He was resolutely ignoring The Weather Channel on the muted TV, but everything he *was* doing was punctuated with the *thunk thunk thunk* of Cope, lying flat on his back on the floor of EE, Ltd.'s Eritrea office, throwing a tennis ball against the ceiling and catching it. Left-handed. A million fucking times.

He'd told Tom he did it because he was right-handed and needed to up his advantage.

When it had started on day one of their partnership, four months ago, Tom swore Cope did it because he knew it drove Tom nuts. That was, until he'd reminded himself that he wasn't dealing with Prophet any more. That Cope was as straight a shooter as it got. That Tom had chosen Cope. Deliberately.

Six months of working for EE and he was already on his second partner, just like normal. Except this time, it was his choice, not the curse that had plagued him his entire life.

The two weeks he'd been partnered with Prophet, they'd fought—each other and outsiders—and Tom had, of course, nearly gotten Prophet killed. Then, just to prove a point, he'd nearly gotten them *both* killed.

Finally, Phil had told him to make a choice—Prophet or Cope.

And here you are.

Tom had texted Prophet only a few times right after he'd chosen Cope as his partner. He'd gotten a couple of short, general answers back that he'd later discovered Prophet had sent out as mass texts to get everyone off his back. And then nothing.

Thunk.

But when he found out that Prophet had quit—or had been forced out of EE, depending on which version you believed—his chances of seeing Prophet again shrank dramatically. What if he never saw the man again?

And that's when the anger had set in.

"He could at least let me know if he's dead or alive," he'd muttered to Cope time and time again.

Cope would tell him that Prophet was fine. "It's not Prophet you have to worry about. He does the killing." A half shrug and a smile. "Granted, sometimes Prophet does things that make you want to kill him, so maybe you should worry."

"Comforting, Cope," Tom had muttered, and Cope had merely shrugged the shrug of a man used to dealing with Prophet for years.

"I'm sure that wherever he is, he's driving someone crazy," Cope offered now, without stopping the throwing-the-ball-against-the-ceiling thing.

Tom sighed, because his first goddamned response was that he wanted Prophet to be driving *him* crazy. He played with the leather bracelet absently, the way he had since Prophet had put it on him, his mind tumbling through the mission, the cage match, the fights, Prophet getting shot . . . "Hey, do you have Mal's number?"

The ball careened wildly off the wall. Tom ducked and caught it as it zinged by.

"Mal, as in . . . *Mal*?"

Tom threw Cope the ball. "Is there more than one? Dark hair. Tattoos. Can't speak. Kind of an asshole. Do you know him?"

Cope snorted and started throwing the ball again. "Fucker's crazy. Like, of all the crazy motherfuckers in the world—and Prophet holds a spot near the very top—Mal is so number one that he's off the goddamned charts, sealed in a fucking box somewhere that's lined with silver, encased in cement, and buried so deep in the goddamned ground, you'd hit China looking for it. That's what I think of motherfucking, crazy-assed, don't-let-him-on-the-same-goddamned-continent-as-me Mal."

Thunk.

"So you don't like him then?"

Cope shrugged. "He's all right." *Thunk.*

Tom sighed. "Can you get in touch with him?"

Thunk. "Not with a ten-foot pole attached to C4."

Tom wondered if Natasha could, but he decided against letting everyone in the office know how pathetic he was. It was already pathetic enough that he'd been emailing Prophet every day, sometimes including scanned sketches like a lovesick puppy.

Thunk.

But writing daily to Prophet since the end of his first week in Eritrea had become the last thing Tom did every night, no matter what. The ritual calmed him and made him feel connected to the man who'd so desperately wanted to disconnect from him.

I might've quit you, Proph, but you quit me first. You just didn't come right out and say it.

He hadn't said that in his emails, though. Not at first. He'd kept them more focused on the job. Cope. His life in general.

But after the first few emails, he'd let himself say whatever the fuck he wanted. Trying to woo the man with words, making promises he might not be able to keep. But what else was new? If working with Prophet had taught him anything, it was that promises were dangerous, especially if they were worthwhile.

But now, after nearly four months without a single email back from Prophet, he knew he'd have to take things further to get in touch with the guy. If Phil ever gave him time off. It was almost as if Phil was purposefully keeping him too busy with constant training in between missions, so Tom couldn't even consider going to find Prophet.

Phil did nothing by mistake, so Tom bit back complaints, continued to prove himself with each and every job he'd been assigned.

Cope liked working with him.

Cope was still alive.

Therefore, in Tom's mind, Prophet had broken his bad luck karma.

Prophet had definitely broken *something*, and goddammit, even though Tom had made the choice, he wanted Prophet to come back and put all the pieces back together.

"The hurricane's looking to be a direct hit," Cope told him now, interrupting his rhythm to point at the TV overhead—he'd been watching it upside down all day, with the sound off so Tom wouldn't worry too much. But the meteorologists had been having a field day with the fact that this hurricane was due to slam directly into New Orleans only days after Katrina's late August anniversary.

Growing up in Louisiana had given Tom a certain perspective on storms. But that didn't mean he wasn't quietly frantic about his aunt. She was just like everyone else in the damn state, even after Katrina. Resilient as hell, stubborn with it, and utterly unwilling to evacuate. But with Della's heart problems and the storm amping up instead of downgrading like they'd said it would, he was worried. And in Eritrea.

But the storm was still five days out. Anything could happen in five days.

From: Tom_B_1@EELTD.com
To: testingpatiencedaily@gmail.com
Subject: Hurricane

I know what you'd do, Proph. Nothing would stop you. I guess that's what Phil's worried about, because he told me he'd fire my ass if I even thought about leaving my post. He called my aunt for me, checked in. She's got her supplies, and he said she'll be okay. And I guess I'm supposed to be all right with that, but fuck it, something isn't sitting right with me. Yeah, go ahead and laugh. I can hear you calling me Cajun or voodoo, clear as day.

The bayou's my home. It's where I learned to fight. Every time I head home, I expect things to be different—and they never are. That's the definition of insanity, right? Doing the same thing over and over and expecting a new result.

It's a dangerous place for me, Proph. But I keep getting pulled back. Maybe Phil not letting me go home's for the best. At least that's what I'm trying to believe.

Otherwise, Cope's fine. I've gone four months without otherwise maiming him or getting him shot. That's a pretty good record, considering how many times we've gone out on small jobs together. He's a good teacher. Patient. Talks about his girlfriend a lot. I have to wear headphones when they have phone sex.

I always think about you during those times, Proph. Other times, yeah, but that's when I miss you the most, and not just because you're decent in bed.

Tom sat in front of his glowing computer screen—with his headphones on—and thought about not sending this one. It would be his one hundred and twenty-second email (and yes, he'd counted) without an answer, but in the end, he let it out into the universe, hoping that it might find its mark.

CHAPTER TWO

Twenty-four hours later

Blue slammed through the half-opened window.

On the fourth floor.

Prophet rolled his eyes. Blue, who wore a rope harness over his jeans and long-sleeved, thermal T—all black, of course—along with a black skullcap, even though it was hot as balls, looked unperturbed about having narrowly missed a table. And possibly killing himself.

"You just took out my screen," Prophet told him. Didn't bother to ask why Blue hadn't used the door, because asking Blue that would be like asking God why he'd created the universe—the answer to both being *Why the hell not?* Which was Prophet's answer to just about everything too.

"*Your* friend's an asshole," Blue informed Prophet as he ripped his cap off.

"Why is Mick *my* friend when he's an asshole?"

"Because—" Blue stopped, pulled out his phone, and dialed. Ran his hands through his wild hair as he waited a beat, then said into the phone, "I just broke into Prophet's place. Fourth floor. And I didn't get a lecture. He didn't say a word about danger. No, I won't put him on. You can call him yourself."

He ended the call and raised his hand triumphantly. "I'm going to get something to eat."

Prophet's cell phone started to ring.

"I wouldn't mind dinner," Prophet called after Blue, then picked up Mick's call. "I hate it when Mommy and Daddy fight."

"If you and Tom had fought instead of walking away from each other—"

Prophet interrupted. "I'm siding with Blue on this one."

"You don't even know why Blue's pissed."

"Doesn't matter."

"Empirically, it matters."

"Did you hurt your back using that big word?"

"Is he using *empirically* again?" Blue demanded as he came back in from the kitchen.

"Where's my dinner?" Prophet asked him.

"I put the water on to boil." Blue motioned for him to hang up.

Prophet did, because he knew it would make Mick mad. "You know he'll be here soon."

Blue shrugged out of his shirt, leaving it like a trail along with the rope and his hat. By the time Prophet caught up to him in the kitchen, he had a Coke and was glancing down at his phone one more time before shoving it into his pocket. "Yeah, I know."

And that's why Blue could run, because Mick would always go after him. Prophet was semi-blown away by the simplicity of the entire situation.

Then again, neither Mick nor Blue came with much baggage. Not compared to him, anyway. "Steal anything good lately?"

"Lots." Blue's eyes lit up like a kid's on Christmas. He turned to stir the pasta he'd put into a large pot. "I made bottled gravy—you don't have any tomatoes."

"Haven't been home in a while."

"I know."

Prophet winced at the tone of Blue's voice, but he didn't say anything. Actually, he was surprised he'd been allowed an entire hour at home to himself.

He padded back into the living room, and after ten minutes, Blue was handing him a dish of pasta, putting the cheese and sodas on the coffee table.

"Nice couch," Blue said.

Prophet gave a nod of agreement, especially because it had taken so much goddamned work to steal the thing the first several times he'd done so. The last time, Cillian had actually wired the thing to the alarm system, the suspicious bastard. But then Cillian had up and gone and given the couch to him.

He wanted to hate the guy. Wanted to be so freakin' suspicious of him that he'd get angry if he thought about him. And he *was* goddamned suspicious. But he couldn't get angry, and he hadn't been able to figure out why yet.

So he'd kept in contact with Cillian, but in a strictly business capacity.

Well, mostly business. He told himself he needed to keep Cillian on the hook—and busy—but he'd be lying if he didn't admit that he felt some kind of pull toward the lying bastard.

Because it would be fucking easy between you two.

Because it would be just sex. *And maybe you trying to kill him.* Or vice versa. There wouldn't be more, not on Prophet's end. But on Cillian's? Who knew?

But Cillian was Mal's job now. Mal was just sadistic enough to enjoy the hell out of it.

Prophet shoved Cillian out of his mind as he and Blue ate in comfortable silence. The spaghetti tasted better than anything he'd had in the past months, especially because Blue had seasoned it. Prophet had basically been eating to live, ignoring taste so he could get proper fuel.

After three bowls of pasta for Blue—who still had the appetite of a teenage boy—and two and counting for Prophet, Blue sat back and said, "So you and Tom . . ."

Prophet gritted his teeth. "There is no me and Tom." Twirled the spaghetti on his fork. "Pick a new line of questioning."

Blue ignored the warning. "He didn't want to be your partner, but that doesn't mean he didn't want to fuck." His gaze took in the sketches that Prophet had printed out and left on the coffee table, since this was his goddamned house, and then glanced back up at Prophet. "Figured you'd like it that way."

"Want me to call Mick back?"

"Mick said you fell hard and you got scared."

"Did he, now?"

"No," Blue admitted, having the decency to look semi-sheepish. "He said that's what you told him happened to him when he met me. Figured it could safely apply to you."

"Go climb the building again."

"Too easy," Blue scoffed. "Are you home because of that spy downstairs or because of the hurricane?"

"Neither." Prophet shifted irritably. "And does the entire fucking world know my business?"

"Only the people who give a shit about you," Blue shot back, and Prophet wondered how such a fucking wiseass could've gotten under his skin so quickly.

And then he remembered: because the kid had risked everything to save Mick, and anyone who risked fucking everything—including themselves—was pretty damned okay in his book. And the kid wasn't a kid at all.

Prophet pushed his bowl away. "Not that you don't already know, since you obviously broke the fuck into my phone, but Cillian's coming here tonight."

Blue raised a brow.

"Not here. Like, to his own apartment. It's his place too." For the first time ever, they'd be in the same building at the same time.

Well, other than the warehouse, but that didn't count.

Blue drawled, "Right."

"Shut up." For the first time, Prophet noticed the trail of sand leading from his suitcase to the edge of the couch. Sand would follow him fucking anywhere.

At least something had loyalty.

He snorted, and Blue looked at him strangely, then asked, "So if it's not for the spy or for the hurricane, why *did* you come home?"

Why did you come home?

His phone echoed from the cup holder in the old Land Rover, his vehicle of choice when he was doing black-ops jobs OUTCONUS. He grabbed it, saw the number, and knew who it was and what they wanted.

"I've got another job for you."

"I'm listening." Prophet watched the specialist who'd been his last mission preparing to board a plane, never to be seen again by his family or friends.

"It's an undercover assignment. You want it, get on the plane too."

Prophet ran a hand over the bandana that he'd wrapped around his head to keep his too-long hair out of his eyes. The Land Rover was suddenly too fucking hot for his liking. "How much?"

The man on the other end of the phone laughed. "More than last time." Because Prophet didn't need the money. The question was inane, a way to avoid the inevitable.

"How long?"

"A year. No contact. Three specialists. You're paid if they're dead or alive."

"What's in it for me?"

"Besides a very large check? This is your way back into the Agency. Once they know what you've been doing—"

Prophet laughed then, and it echoed through the truck, a sound so fucking foreign to him at this point that it made his throat tighten immediately. "I don't want back in. And trust me, they fucking know."

"You must want something, because you keep doing this."

He looked over at the plane—the man he'd brought here safely had already boarded, and the pilot was at the door, pointing between it and Prophet.

In or out?

He'd known this offer was coming—in some ways, he'd been busting his ass just to get the damned thing. But whether he accepted or not wasn't the point. Proving himself—to himself, to the assholes in the Agency, to the motherfucking world at large—proving that he was still the best one to work with the specialists because he had balls, brains, and a goddamned conscience . . . well, that had always been the point. Not the fucking money. Not getting back in.

Waiting in the safe house last night, with his latest mission snoring in the other room, he'd finally read Tom's emails—all eleven billion of them—because he figured they'd be full of excuses or "it's better this way" crap. Reading them was his way of saying good-bye, because, when the offer for the next job came—and he'd known it was coming—he had to be ready to leave everything and everyone behind.

Reading them had been the biggest fucking mistake.

"Decent in bed," he growled into the phone, realizing Tom had gotten the rise out of him that he'd probably been looking for.

The man on the other end of the phone told him, "That's not an answer."

"It is for me."

He blinked and finally answered Blue. "I came home because the jobs were done."

"Uh-huh." Blue crossed his arms. "Not sure why you lie to me, of all people. I'm the first one to admit that I still need to steal. And that I know Mick will chase me."

There was so much truth in what Blue said that he couldn't even look at the guy. And Blue also understood that and mercifully didn't comment further on it. Prophet was pretty sure he'd bring it up again, but he was also pretty sure he didn't like Blue taking pity on him now. "How's working with Mick been? I mean, besides your need to break into other people's houses to prove something to him?"

Blue shrugged. "For the most part, it's pretty fucking cool."

"Yeah, I figured you'd like it." Prophet paused. "Cut him a break, all right? If he didn't give a shit . . ."

"Was he this tough on a regular partner?"

"He never had one."

"Just like you."

"Right."

"Same reasons?"

"We both enjoy working alone."

"Because watching someone else's back makes you vulnerable?" Blue asked, and it was a sincere question.

"Yeah, it does, Blue. But for Mick, I know it's worth it, okay?"

Blue nodded, looking down at his plate, a flush blossoming on his cheeks. He'd had a rough year—lost his sister, nearly got killed, went mostly legit, and fell in love.

Prophet clapped a hand on Blue's shoulder, was about to get up and bring the dishes back into the kitchen when Blue asked, "When are you leaving for New Orleans?"

"I'm not."

"Okay," Blue said agreeably, then muttered, "And if you think I believe you, you're dumber than you look."

"You deserve to get beaten," Prophet told him.

"That's my job." At the sound of Mick's voice coming up from the bottom of the staircase, Blue's shoulders stiffened.

"Shit," he muttered.

"Busted," Prophet told him, but Blue was already up, dressed, the rope wrapped around him with a grace that Prophet couldn't help but admire.

"I'll pay you if you give me a head start," Blue said from the window ledge, his body half hanging out.

"I don't need money."

Blue fumbled into his pocket and tossed a small bag to Prophet. He opened it to find a beat-up gold ring with some kind of green stone with a scarab inscribed into it. "Where the fuck did you get this?"

"You know, around." Blue waved, as if things of that caliber just dropped from the sky.

"This is an Egyptian artifact, isn't it?"

"Maybe."

"Blue . . ."

"Tell yourself it's from the gift shop, if you have to."

Prophet stuck it into his jeans pocket. "He's going to find you."

"Eventually." Blue dropped out of sight, like a tattooed Santa Claus, just as Mick burst into the room.

"I don't ever remember giving you a key," Prophet told him.

"There are a lot of things you have selective memory about," Mick started, and Prophet began to see the benefits of being able to drop out a window at any given time.

CHAPTER THREE

Less than twenty hours after Mick left to chase down Blue, Prophet rolled into the Louisiana sunshine, the dog tags clanking randomly around the floor of his old Blazer. Sometimes they were under his feet and at others, they rattled around the floor of the backseat. Occasionally they'd get caught up under the driver's seat and he wouldn't see them for weeks, and then they'd reappear.

Ten-plus years and they hadn't gotten caught in the pedals once. He'd thrown them into the truck the morning of John's memorial service, and he hadn't touched them since.

Not that he was superstitious or anything.

He had the windows rolled down, the sunroof open, and the sunshine felt good on his face as the breeze ruffled his too-long hair. Music blared, and he dodged slower moving cars at a good clip, all while keeping an eye out for cops, which was how he'd made the normally twenty-one-plus-hour trip in under eighteen.

It also helped that most law enforcement was being pulled in to handle storm-related shit. And that's why Prophet was here after all, running toward the storm, rather than away from it, dragging an inconspicuous U-Haul behind his truck. The U-Haul held two generators. Food. Water. Guns. Cash. Enough to keep them safe and big enough to evacuate if necessary.

The French Quarter was one of the safer spots in terms of rising water. The biggest problems they'd face were loss of water and power. And looting.

The National Guard was directing people out of the city. Mandatory evacuation that half the residents wouldn't follow. Of those remaining, half would call for help when it started to get bad, and more would call when it was too late for rescue.

But a significant number wouldn't call ever. They'd live or die here. Tom's aunt was among that group. Maybe Tom had more family in the actual bayou parish he'd been born in, but this aunt was the only one he'd been concerned with.

Prophet's fingers drummed the wheel as Jackson Browne blared "Doctor My Eyes."

"Got to be fucking kidding me," he muttered, but he kept the song on anyway because he liked it. He'd had his regular check-up with the eye doctor just before he'd left for parts unknown.

Needed to schedule another one, but hell, it's not like the doctors could do anything. The genetic disease that predestined him to some degree of blindness was already progressing, according to his last exam, and Prophet was pretty sure he'd know when it actually affected his day-to-day vision before they did.

When traffic slowed down, he noted the checkpoint, which meant he was right outside NOLA. In between the stop-and-go crawl, he checked his phone and saw Cillian's text.

Did you run from me? Cillian had sent the text an hour after Prophet had packed and left. Because, contrary to what he'd told Blue, Prophet *was* supposed to meet Cillian. In his apartment. On Cillian's couch.

"I ran from *me*," Prophet muttered as he approached the checkpoint. Typed in *Hurricane.*

In your apartment?

Asshole. *In Louisiana.*

You have family there?

Ah, fuck it. *Tom does. Gotta check on his aunt.*

Tom's family isn't your problem. Neither is Tom.

That was all true. "And yet, you're in a truck headed to help a man who gave you away like yesterday's news." Prophet shook his head at himself and dropped the phone into the cupholder without answering Cillian.

A camouflage-wearing Guardsman strode stiffly over to his truck. "You're from out of state," he barked at Prophet.

"Yes."

"Sir, we're not letting any out-of-state residents past this point. Please turn your truck around."

The guy was a former Marine. Even without the tattoo on his forearm of the globe and eagle and snake, Prophet would've known it because of his stance. He thought about pulling the military card, decided against it because he was feeling like too much of a dick. Especially after Cillian's comments.

He flipped his fake FBI ID badge. "Gonna let me through now, son?"

Without waiting for the answer, he jerked the old Blazer through the barricade and gunned it, not bothering to look in his rearview.

Prophet: One. World: Zero.

Then again, Mother Nature was prepping to be the big bitch she was and would even out that score soon enough.

And he'd climbed out of hell for this, using Tom's emails as a lifeline. Maybe just in time too. Because if he'd gone any deeper, he would've been unreachable in a way that no email could fix.

And that's what he'd been going for, of course. Dig deep, forget anything that happened above ground. Even now, he could turn around. No one was actually expecting him up ahead, so he wouldn't be missed. But his conscience wouldn't allow it.

Goddamned motherfucking thing. If he could've cut it out with a knife, he might've.

He'd already argued with himself (and lost, obviously) that he wasn't fit for human company—and by human, he meant civilian—and that's who he'd be facing when he drove into New Orleans and the French Quarter and . . . Tom's wealthy Aunt Della.

Did she know about him?

He didn't know much about Tom's past, beyond the jobs with the FBI and the sheriff's department, but what little he did know made him angry. And he was in a really bad place inside his head to be around people who made him angry.

Who the hell had Tommy been fighting in that ring four months ago? Had to be family. Prophet had seen that same fury too often in John not to know that. And now . . . to have to face someone who had to have known what Tom had been going through as a kid . . .

Another Carole Morse, who saw nothing but an angry son and didn't investigate further.

Another Judie Drews, who couldn't do anything.

He mulled that over as he pulled into Della Boudreaux's driveway but kept the truck running.

The house was old but refined, well tended, and cared for. Obviously, someone with money lived there, because this was one of the wealthier sections of the city. And he sat in his truck in the driveway, unable to get out and approach the door.

He hadn't thought much beyond getting here to help Tommy's aunt. But that was a start. He would help her because Tom's words had helped him.

I'm not sorry. I'm trying to take care of you.

But I could take better care of you if I was with you. I realize that now.

I've also realized that it's really never too late. For anything.

For now, that would have to be enough. He finally shut off the truck, got out, and walked up to the porch.

There was so much opportunity here, but Tom had grown up in the parishes of the bayou, not in the French Quarter. So why would he be so concerned about Della, who could probably afford the queen's security?

He knocked on the door and was greeted by a shotgun to the chest. He stared down at the barrel and then the woman holding it. She was pretty. Cultured. And still somehow fierce, in ways that had nothing to do with the shotgun pointed at him.

And still, you didn't protect Tommy.

He froze his anger, stopped thinking about Tom's scars and his temper. He'd just have to use what anger he wasn't able to tamp down to fuel his hurricane prep. "You're doing it wrong."

"Son, I've got a gun to your chest and you're telling me that I'm doing it wrong?"

"Yes."

"How?"

"Closer isn't better." He disarmed her with a swift motion, then offered the weapon back to her. "Further away you are, the less unpredictable I can be."

Della's eyes had opened wide with surprise, but she recovered fast. Took the shotgun back and said, "Okay. Knock again so we can start over."

"I'd rather spend time getting you ready for the hurricane."

She tilted her head and assessed him. "Friend of my nephew's?"

"Tom and I worked together."

"Think I won't notice you avoided the question?" Prophet raised a brow, and she shook her head. "Tom didn't tell me you were coming."

He held up his phone to show the list of messages from Tom, proof that he actually knew the man well. "My name's Prophet. And that's his work email, right?"

"I thought he was busy with work, but I see he's got a lot of time to send emails," she said coolly. "Nice to meet you, Prophet. Why did you bring a U-Haul? Are you also moving in?"

"Supplies. Unless you'd like to evacuate?"

"Never have. Never will. And I have supplies, you know. This isn't my first hurricane."

"You don't have supplies like mine."

She moved aside to let him in, and, after a brief pause as he realized there had never been any escape, he entered.

The house was just as nice inside. He thought back to Tommy's rental apartment, half an old Victorian near EE's HQ and wondered if that was a conscious thing, if somehow this home pulled to Tommy that badly.

"Is there anyone else who'll be staying with you during the storm?" he asked, taking in the portable oxygen concentrator a few feet away.

"Roger and Dave rent the third floor. They've lived with me for the past ten years, but they're completely useless during storms."

"I heard that."

Prophet had seen the man coming down the stairs before he'd spoken. Della simply rolled her eyes. "Prophet, meet Roger. Prophet is Tom's friend—he's got supplies and he'll get us through the worst of the storm."

"Is that right?" Roger asked.

"I'll do my best," Prophet said as he shook hands with Roger.

He looked to be in his late sixties. A man Prophet assumed to be Dave followed closely behind. Both men were still handsome—Dave was taller and thinner, Roger shorter and mouthier—and Prophet liked that they had no problem holding hands, in front of a stranger or otherwise.

Roger saw him glance at their hands. "We've been together thirty years."

Prophet had known John for nine—best friends for all of it, lovers for four years. Add to that teammates and confidantes. Sometimes Prophet had loved him, and sometimes it had been just the opposite, which he suspected happened in every long-term relationship.

"You didn't ask what it feels like to be with the same person for so long," Roger noted. "Which means either you are or were in a long-term relationship yourself, so you know what it feels like, or you're built for one."

"Please ignore his rambling pontifications—they're well-meaning but totally insane." Dave dropped his voice to a stage whisper. "He's already been drinking."

"Hurricanes frighten me," Roger said.

"We've got him," Dave said, pointing to Prophet. "Does it look like anything frightens him?"

"Well, does it? Wait, don't answer that." Roger held up a hand. "I need more wine."

Yes, they had a great hurricane plan—drink themselves silly. Granted, from where Prophet stood, it seemed like a decent way to go.

"So, you work with Tom," Roger continued. "And your wife or girlfriend doesn't mind that you're here?"

Prophet gave a smile that was harder than he thought to muster because Tom's face flashed in front of his eyes. And then it got easier because Tom would get pissed being associated with the word *girl*. "I'm single at the moment."

They weren't trying to dig—they'd read him as straight. Most did, and Prophet liked it only because he never liked anyone knowing things about him.

He also liked surprising the hell out of people.

Dave sighed. "Before we interrogate the man, why don't we let him get settled so he can save us."

Roger lifted a wineglass in Prophet's direction.

Della had pointed him in the direction of a bedroom on the second floor, and Prophet checked it out quickly. He only planned on using it for scoping rather than sleeping, but he didn't tell her that. Just like he didn't mention the inflatable boat and the power engine and oars he'd keep on the second floor, in case they needed to float the hell out of there.

And then he got to work. He wore his iPod most of the day, blasting lots of classic rock so he could pretend not to hear Della or Roger or Dave trying to engage him in conversation—as he'd predicted, he just wasn't there yet. Back from battle and not ready for civilians. And it would pass, but not before the hurricane hit. And maybe he wasn't good at hiding his thousand-yard stare, because they really hadn't tried to talk to him much anyway.

They did, however, talk *about* him a little, because they thought he couldn't hear, and Della said she was worried about Tom, but other than that, they went about their business.

Mainly, they were helpful and unobtrusive.

It took him the rest of the day and overnight to finish his prep sufficiently enough in his eyes. First, he built the pad for the generator, and while it set, he worked on everything else.

Eventually, the groceries were inside. Prophet's truck was in back, away from the trees and wires, ready for an evac, if necessary. Radios, batteries, just-in-case flashlights, and water were set up.

"Neighbors?" he'd asked earlier.

Della had rolled her eyes. "Most of them evacuated. They like to follow rules."

He knew he couldn't say something like *rules are important* with a straight face, so he didn't bother.

Finally, he installed the generator to the panel, which thankfully wasn't as old as the house, because otherwise the thing would be useless. Still, he only wired for essentials so he wouldn't overload anything.

By then, the rain had started in earnest, the wind picking up quickly, a warning that this hurricane wasn't slowing down.

By 0600, he was sitting at the kitchen table, surrounded by maps and his laptop, making several evac plans, just in case. GPS would be down, and even though—thanks to EE—his was satellite powered and installed directly into his truck, he didn't trust anything to work the way it was supposed to. He'd also gone through Della's medications, making sure she had more than enough, and he'd made a few calls to ensure he could get more in a hurry. Because that shit you couldn't fool around with.

As early morning ambled along, Della wandered into the kitchen. He'd made a full pot of coffee, and she poured herself a cup while he continued to concentrate on what was in front of him.

He didn't look up, not until she slid sandwiches and a glass of lemonade next to him.

"You haven't eaten much since you got here, and you can't live on coffee alone," she told him, and his stomach growled in agreement with her. He'd had a PowerBar at some point, and some soda, but that wasn't exactly the breakfast of champions.

"I got wrapped up," he admitted.

"I'm grateful, but I can't let you starve."

Why'd you let Tom get hit? he wanted to ask back, but even he wasn't that much of a dick. Not when he could stuff a sandwich in his mouth instead.

"You're close with Tom?" she asked delicately.

"We were partnered up on a job." That was as truthful an answer as he could give.

She sat across from him at the table, her shoulders squared as if she'd read him and was expecting battle. "And now?"

Prophet was unable to keep the anger out of his voice when he said, "I've seen the bottom of his feet." It was the first time he'd ever let himself actively think about that, never mind speak about it to anyone. The first time he'd allowed himself to dwell on it.

The majority of Tom's scars were covered up by his tattoos, but his feet . . . There was no way to cover the scars of old cigarette burns on the soles of his feet.

Tom had to know Prophet had seen them. But he'd offered no explanation, and Prophet wouldn't push something he understood all too well.

"I've seen them too," she said quietly, the kind of quiet that held a carefully concealed rage. "I was the one who took him to the ER. But it was too late to stop them from scarring."

He didn't bother to hide his heavy sarcasm. "Right. Can't let them scar." He was tired as hell of concealed rage. Hiding shit was where all the trouble started.

She blinked. "Listen up, boy—don't come in here thinking you know everything."

"I think I know enough."

Della sighed. Muttered something that he was pretty sure were Cajun curses before telling him, "Tom stayed with me on and off his whole life. I'm his father's sister. My brother and I aren't close. He always said I thought I was too good for the bayou. Maybe that's true. Or maybe I just didn't like the violence. Tom's mother didn't fit in there either."

Prophet watched her hands wrap around the delicate teacup in a stranglehold.

"You probably want to know why I didn't just keep him here all the time."

"Or why you didn't call CPS or social services."

She stared at him, anger flashing in her eyes before spitting out tightly, "Prophet, I don't owe you an explanation, but I'll give you one. I was a single woman. Family, yes, but in those days, they wanted a complete family, and that was an extremely narrow definition. Make no mistake about it, I wanted him here. My door was *open*." She tapped on the table. "His father didn't care where he stayed. *Tom* was the one who chose to go back and forth. It was almost like he'd come here, gain his strength, and then throw himself back into the wild."

Prophet stared at the scarred table and saw that he'd unconsciously fisted his hands at some point during the conversation. "Yeah, that sounds like the Tommy I know."

"I've never heard anyone call him Tommy, but I like it." Her drawl was soft. "I don't know why he felt like he needed to take that kind of punishment. I told him he didn't, and I know he believed me."

"He understood it, Della. There's a difference."

He unfisted his hands only when she reached out and covered them with her open ones and said, "Sounds like you two have a lot in common."

"You've got that voodoo shit happening too?"

"No, but you don't hide your anger well."

"Not when it comes to him." He paused. "Voodoo or not, you do know about me. About what happened at EE."

She took her hands off his and pointed to the sandwich. He took a bite and only then did she answer his question. "Yes. He called. He told me that he'd made what felt like the hardest decision he'd ever had to make. I asked him if it felt right, and he said that it hurt, which meant it must be right." She pressed her lips together. "I told him that sometimes it hurts when it's wrong, too, and that he had to start learning how to tell the difference."

"I'm not the easiest man either."

"No shit." She grinned and took a sip of her coffee. "What about your family?"

"There's just my mom. I don't see her often."

"By choice, or because of your job?"

"I blame it on the job." He paused. "Tom's worried about you."

"He's always worried about me. Thinks I'm too alone. But I've got tenants who've become close friends. That's all I need."

Roger stage-whispered into Prophet's ear (Prophet had heard him coming a mile away), "She needs a man, but she never married, because she was too stubborn." Della shook her finger at him. "And she's got this wicked, bat-like hearing."

"I was not stubborn. Connor wouldn't have been a good choice."

"He was hot," Roger said. "Hot is always the good choice."

"That's been going on for thirty years. If it hasn't happened already . . ." Della waved her hand and trailed off.

"Where's Connor now?" Prophet asked.

"I hear from him every once in a while." Della shrugged. "He's a wanderer. And I knew he'd break my heart if I let him. So I didn't."

Prophet saw the pain in her face. His chest squeezed a little, because it was obvious she still loved the guy after all these years.

He excused himself, went out onto the covered back porch, despite the rain and wind that still managed to find its way underneath, and sat with his phone in hand, staring at the number on the screen but refusing to hit Call.

The dread got worse each month, even though he knew what his mother would say. She'd complain about the pills and the hospital, but first, she'd tell him that a man called, looking for him. He hadn't bothered changing her number. Because if they were still bothering her, it meant they were no closer to finding him.

Besides that, he made sure her phone and internet signals bounced off enough towers that they would never be traced back to her. The last thing he needed was his mother in the middle of a ransom war. The facility she was in received similar treatment in regards to their internet systems. His mom's doctors too.

Finally, he sent the call and let the phone ring while he held his breath.

She answered with, "You're late."

"By four minutes."

"Late is late."

He put his head back against the cushions of the wicker couch and didn't say anything. Sweat trickled down his face and neck—the humidity was fucking wicked, and the only way to get his body used to it was to let his body get used to it.

"Now you're not speaking to me?" she asked.

"Never said that."

"That man called again, looking for you."

His gut tightened. "And what'd you tell him?"

"That you weren't here. That I didn't know where you were. Then I told him to fuck off." She sounded so proud.

"That's good, Mom. Thanks."

She sighed, an exaggeratedly exasperated sound. "I don't like it here."

Same thing, every time, but he answered that the same way he always did. "Why not?"

"They won't give me my pills."

At least she was *taking* her meds regularly. He spoke to her doctors weekly to ensure that.

"They give you the pills you need."

"Not always. They forget. You never forgot."

No, he hadn't. And that reminder made him feel worse, not better. "I'll remind them, okay? I'll take care of it."

Because he always took care of it.

CHAPTER FOUR

The rain from the outer bands of the hurricane slammed the house in muted thumps like fists against a punching bag. The world had begun its standstill as the chaos crept slowly in the darkness toward New Orleans.

In the background, The Weather Channel played on a continuous loop. Della had left it on when she'd gone to bed hours before. Roger and Dave had as well, after offering to stay up and keep him company, but Prophet had told them to go on ahead and get their sleep.

Because even though he'd prepped the house, once this monster hit, you never knew what the hell would happen. And the worst would happen toward dawn. Always did. Lines would come down, streets would flood, and there would always be some idiots who felt confident enough to go chasing the storm. And they were all too casual about this. It was like talking to Blue about climbing, and Prophet never did bother with that.

The storm surrounded the house, the windows washing with water, distorting what little he could see outside.

His wrists ached. When they stopped hurting, it would mean the storm had definitely arrived, because when the pressure was high, there wasn't any pain.

Just massive destruction—a typical metaphor for his life.

Restless, he stuck his hands in the pockets of his army green cargos and paced the first floor barefoot. He'd tried to settle in to read, but even his old standbys couldn't keep his attention tonight.

The house shook and lightning lit up the sky, and it was just like being back in the Sudan. For a few minutes, he was frozen in the living room.

Not gonna matter when you lose your sight. You'll be so fucked up by then you won't be fit for work anyway.

He blinked as the lights flickered . . . wondered if that's what it would be like at first. His father hadn't talked about it. Neither had his grandfather. Both killed themselves before it got too bad.

Was he expected to? Drews men always followed the family traditions. And from where Prophet stood, it wasn't a half-bad one.

Tom was better off with the choice he'd made.

But Prophet couldn't deny that it hurt, so instead he'd denied everything else he felt about the man, so he could steel himself to come to this house. Thought of it like a mission, which helped his focus.

Finding peace would be considerably harder and not something he planned on trying to do this trip. It was an impossible feat, really, and Prophet figured that he should probably stop trying. But something inside wouldn't let him, continued to search for it with the rabid intensity of a shark with the scent of blood.

"You know sharks keep moving, even when they sleep?" John told him.

"No," he muttered, refusing to look up to see his personal walking, talking flashback. From the time he'd walked into Sadiq's trap until this point, he'd kept too busy to have them.

Guess you don't need flashbacks if you're living the real thing.

"Yeah, you're peaceful—just like Hal," John continued.

"I really don't need your fucking sarcasm." Prophet stared at the wall in front of him, watching the patterns change depending on the force of the wind on the raindrops.

But John was right about Hal—he'd appeared to be a peaceful guy. Even John had been taken in by him, and Prophet hadn't wanted to give anything away.

"You really thought I didn't know?" John asked now, and Prophet still refused to look in the direction of the ghost of his one-time best friend and lover.

In reality, Hal had been one of the angriest guys on the fucking planet. Prophet couldn't say if he'd been like that before the CIA and FBI started crawling up his asshole, but Hal Jones was one of the few projects the CIA, FBI, and Homeland Security actually played nicely on together. Hal was a specialist, knew how to build nuclear triggers, and that made him something of an asset—or a liability—everyone had worked hard to control.

Up until the whole CIA fuckup, and then everything went to shit. There were guys at the Bureau and Homeland who were still pissed at Prophet for choosing the Agency after that whole clusterfuck. Prophet couldn't tell them that he hadn't had any other choice if he'd wanted his teammates—the men who'd become his friends—left in one piece.

As it stood, they all were, albeit scattered around the globe. Last time he'd checked. Which was a few hours ago. And they were all pissed at him.

So, nothing had really changed, and that in and of itself was comforting. But it wouldn't stop the flashback from coming. And he hadn't even been sleeping. Then again, the sleeping flashbacks were the fucking worst, because if he couldn't control himself when he was awake, he had no hope of it unconscious.

He put his hands out, like if he could put them on something real and stable in the house—Della's rounded sofa or her old Victrola— he'd snap out of it and stop seeing the fucking desert in front of him, miles and miles of sand with no end in sight.

"Four hours," John called back to him. The ground underneath Prophet's feet felt like it was moving, and he tried to tell himself it was the wind and not a moving truck, but it was no use.

He turned his head cautiously and found Hal sitting next to him, his face drawn, obviously done with the entire trip.

Four hours wasn't that bad—they'd made good time, until this point. Until 1543. That's when everything went to complete shit.

"I don't want to do this," Prophet told Hal. "I won't do it."

Hal just stared through him, his eyes watching something in the distance. Gunfire. Cars coming over the rise.

John, firing wildly. Prophet took position and helped cover them but the car's radiator was blown. The rest of their SEAL team—their backup—was gone.

"We lost them," John said, and they couldn't go back, couldn't risk transmitting a signal over the radio.

It was the last time Prophet saw his team in one place.

"It's a setup, Proph," John told him.

Hal grabbed for Prophet's gun, but Prophet pushed him back, pinned him down to the seat. "Don't fucking do that."

"If it's a setup, you can't kill me," Hal yelled. He wasn't ready to die. Was anyone, ever?

If you looked at Prophet's family tree, someone might say yes.

CHAPTER FIVE

Prophet didn't know how much longer he stood there, staring at the desert, the blood and sand, until the sights and sounds of the explosions turned back to booms of thunder and lightning.

Gradually, Hal faded.

Prophet blinked. Saw the desert.

Blinked again, and it was Della's kitchen and his phone beeping. He grabbed it with shaking hands like it was a lifeline, wondering how and when he'd left the living room.

Cillian was on the other end of the text. Not exactly the best flotation device but not the worst. *Now someone's trying to kill me.*

Karma's a bitch, Prophet typed. *Where are you?*

In a bathroom.

Dude, TMI.

I'm waiting for the opportunity . . .

Again, TMI.

To kill the man hunting me.

Prophet snorted. *Oh.*

And that's not TMI. What has this world come to?

A particularly loud burst of thunder shook the house. *Going to hell, man.*

You've been drinking?

No. I'm trying to live through a hurricane.

Prophet could hear Cillian's British accent in his head when the spook typed, *Just duck. And swim. You can swim, correct?*

Little bit.

Here's to reaching shore quickly.

Prophet was about to answer with something about Cillian sticking his head in the toilet when a creak stopped him.

The entire house had been fucking groaning all night, but that creak was different. It was the sound of a storm door opening.

He stilled. Put the phone down and reached for his KA-BAR simultaneously.

Something—someone—scratched at the back door. And since Della's yard was completely enclosed by a nine-foot wrought iron fence with spiked tops, that was no mean feat.

What the hell kind of crazy-ass freak tries to break in during a hurricane?

He blinked and looked around, trying to reassure himself that this wasn't a flashback, but everything looked normal. And flashbacks typically didn't use the door.

He turned his focus back to the door and watched the top lock turn slowly. Someone was using a key. Or a lockpick.

He turned his gaze back around and saw nothing but kitchen and living room beyond that.

Definitely *not* a flashback.

He moved decisively to the door, jerked it open, and slammed hard against whoever was attempting to push in. His adrenaline surged when the person grabbed his forearms. Prophet pushed at the man's shoulders as they both started to fall, thanks to the slippery steps. He landed on top of the guy on the grass. The rain pelted him with fine needles on the bare skin of his arms as they rolled together, grunting and fighting.

He got in a few good punches before a strong arm wound around his neck. He grabbed it as the other guy—because this was definitely a guy—attempted to flip him onto his stomach. Instead, Prophet bore down with his weight, then elbowed the intruder in the stomach. Freed momentarily, he turned and pinned the man underneath him, efficiently and effectively immobilizing the guy—

"Prophet?"

Tommy? "Tom?" Prophet couldn't see much, but he knew that drawl. Recognized the feel of the man's hands as they touched Prophet's cheeks, traced them with fingertips . . . Tom reading him like Braille. As the rain washed over them, the smell of grass and earth and floral spice filled the air. His skin tingled from the electrical currents carried on the storm, and his entire body was in a state of heightened awareness that was almost painful.

He wanted to ask what the hell Tom was doing here, why he'd risked everything—including his job at EE—to come here. Wanted to ask if Tom had somehow known he'd be here. But he didn't.

And he also didn't know how he even heard the man over the dull roar of the wind, but he did, heard Tom whisper, "Yes," against his cheek in answer to his unasked questions and fuck, that could mean so many damned things.

Too many to give a shit about parsing, and in the wet, hot darkness, Prophet's mouth found Tommy's instead.

They both groaned into that first kiss. Four months and more of longing released in a frantic rush that started out fast and rolled into something more, faster than the gathering storm and threatening to do far more damage.

And Prophet didn't give a damn, wasn't able to stop himself from rutting against Tom, the friction of the fabric between them and Tommy's hardness sending shockwaves through his system.

And he was finally alive again. Holding onto his lifeline in the flesh, knowing that it had almost been too late. If he hadn't read those emails . . . Another day, another hour and he would've been buried so far underground he would never have seen daylight again.

He brushed that thought away for what was real right now— Tom's hands in his hair, keeping him close. Tom's thighs spread for him, heavy boots landing on his ass and locking around his lower back so the heels dug in, spurring him to rut harder. Tom, holding him in place from that submissive position. And Prophet was fucking Tom's mouth with his tongue, the way he wanted to fuck Tom. The way he wanted Tommy to fuck him. Tom was matching him kiss for kiss as they alternated between wet and messy, ferocious to lingering, lip-biting to tongue-sucking.

Everything else fell away but Tom. The wet, stinging downpour, the wind, the mud . . . the danger, all were merely physical barriers to overcome. The easy shit.

The fact that Tom was in his arms again meant they'd already dug into the hard shit.

He pulled back from the kissing to bite Tom's neck. Tom hissed, bucked his pelvis up, and a low shudder ran through Prophet. And then he made the mistake of opening his eyes and realized he couldn't see. The electricity had cut out, and it was too damned dark.

He could still feel Tom under him, but that wasn't enough. He started to count to thirty, because that's when the generator would kick on. Panic shook him harder than lust, panic leftover from earlier, Then Tom's hand slid into his pants, along his bare ass, trailing a finger between his cheeks and pressing against the tightened muscles of his hole.

"Mine," Tom growled against his ear and Prophet whimpered—fucking *whimpered*—as Tom kept his finger in place, more pressure than an attempt to gain entrance. He had to know Prophet was too goddamned tense for that, but that started to bleed away when Tom said, "Mine," again.

"Yeah. Yours," he agreed, blinked against the rain, seeing shadows as his eyesight adjusted, and just let himself feel Tom's hands anchoring him.

It didn't matter what happened in the morning, in an hour . . . even in ten minutes. It mattered that Tom was going to make him come in his pants, especially when Tom's finger pushed inside of him and the lights flickered back on.

"Proph," Tom moaned as Prophet dug in and writhed with zero control. Tommy gripped his shoulders tightly, pulling Prophet into him. Prophet buried his face against Tommy's neck and knew what Tommy's face would look like—almost angry that Prophet had gotten to him so easily.

God, he wanted to see that.

And you can.

He lifted his head and smiled. The wind swirled around them as thunder rumbled overhead. Branches creaked, houses screamed against their foundations, and rutting like animals in the mud with Tommy was the hottest thing Prophet could remember. Nothing else mattered, because nature's wrath couldn't compare to this.

As their frenzy grew, so did the storm, as if the hurricane built off their furious energy. Prophet would never look at a hurricane the same way again.

And then it was all touch and feelings and tongue and teeth, and then cum spilling inside his pants. His entire body tightened as the orgasm rode him like a bitch, refusing to let go until it wrung every last bit of fight out of him.

And Tommy held him so tightly as he shouted and came, Prophet knew he'd have marks. Wanted them. Because it would be proof that this actually happened.

"Fuck," Tom muttered.

"Fuck," Prophet breathed in agreement, his cheek pressed to Tom's.

"If I'd known . . . would've shown up earlier."

"Wouldn't have worked earlier."

They lay tumbled against one another, soaked by the storm and too worn out to move. Even when lightning flashed overhead, Prophet could only turn his head to see the sky and marvel how well the storm had both insinuated itself into and reflected what his life had become.

Finally, Tommy pushed at him, murmured something about the "wind picking up" and "getting inside" and somehow, they were up, off the grass, and moving.

He felt like he'd been caught by a flashbang—he could barely see, his ears rung, and walking was more like a stumble and drag between them, because they weighed each other down as they tried to help each other into the house. But neither let the other go, because they weren't done. Just the opposite—they were so far from done, how he'd even considered it was laughable.

"Fucking pathetic," he muttered as Tom pushed him against the nearest wall and slammed the door shut with a booted foot.

"Makes two of us," Tom growled as he bent to unlace his boots and get them off, holding onto Prophet for support. And then he was yanking Prophet's shirt over his head, letting it fall to the floor with a loud *thwack*, as Prophet reached forward to unbutton Tom's jeans and work them down his hips.

Would've made more sense to each strip themselves, but neither of them had any goddamned semblance of sense. There were both soaked and filthy and more than halfway to feral.

"Do hurricanes make people high?" Prophet asked, barely able to drag his gaze away from Tom's cock piercings. "Feel like I'm high."

He tossed Tom's muddy shirt away. He caught sight of the thin leather bracelet still on Tom's wrist and dragged his eyes up to Tom's mismatched ones.

Tom had seen him note the bracelet. The man's gaze dared him to say something about it, and when Prophet didn't, Tom said, "It's the heat. Makes people crazy."

"Jesus." He ran his hands over Tom's naked body, feeling for the nipple bars and leaving wet, muddied tracks on his chest. Running fingertips over where the tattoos were, because he'd taken to doing that in his mind over the past months. Instead of counting sheep, he'd catalogued Tom's tattoos.

He realized with a start that Tom was checking him over too, feeling the barely healed scar on his shoulder, lingering on the bullet-hole-sized scar Prophet had gotten on their first—and only—case together.

Tom smiled against Prophet's mouth, no doubt reading him again with that voodoo shit. He'd been able to from the start, and that probably pissed Prophet off the most. Because he might've actually missed that voodoo shit. During their time apart, he'd forced himself—viciously—not to think about Tom. Barely slept in order to control his dreams, kept himself too busy and in too much danger to worry about much more than basic survival, in the hopes that everything Tommy would burn out and not fade away.

It was backfiring now, though, because every muscle and fiber of his being was intent on licking, sucking, touching, inhaling Tom like a starving man at a buffet. He couldn't stop. He would've been embarrassed to be so goddamned needy, submitting to the man's intrusive touches, if Tom hadn't been exactly the same.

"What the hell did you do to me, T?"

Hadn't realized he'd asked Tom outright until he heard, "Same thing you did to me." Like Tommy had imprinted on Prophet.

Prophet could fuck his way through a million men—and some weeks during the past four months it felt like he'd tried—and he'd never come anywhere close to feeling like this. "Like a fucking spell."

"Like I'd do this to myself on purpose," Tom shot back, before biting and sucking on Prophet's nipple.

Prophet hissed and threaded then tightened a grip on Tom's hair in the hopes the man would do it again. Tom didn't care about his transparency and obliged Prophet over and over, staring up at him the entire time he abused Prophet's nipple, concentrating on the one with his mouth and pressing the other hard between finger and thumb.

Needing someone this much couldn't be fucking normal.

Finally, Tom pulled back, grabbed for his jeans and, when he straightened, held up a condom. Then he pushed himself against Prophet, their cocks and balls rubbing together, chest and thighs sliding together, a perfect fit. Prophet braced himself as best he could, prepared to let Tom take him there and hang on for dear life, and at the same time, knowing Tom wouldn't let him fall.

The man had always been physically strong, but months of merc work had hardened his body more. Prophet recognized the honed muscles that came with target practice, walking miles in the heat, fighting against an invisible enemy to be ready for when it became real.

Tom's hands stroked his shoulders and biceps, every touch firm and sure, a reassurance that Prophet was actually there, and that he was fine.

Physically. Neither of them was fine on the other front.

The wind whipped the house, battered the windows and doors like it wanted in and wouldn't take no for an answer. Tom was that storm, demanding Prophet open to him, insisting on it. Grabbing one of Prophet's legs, balancing it against his hip so his fingers could open him. All he could do, all he wanted to do, was give in.

He found no reason not to.

He heard the rip of the condom wrapper, watched Tom roll it on carefully over the piercings. "Don't have lube," Tom told him. "I haven't needed any."

Prophet processed that for a second, then said, "I don't need it."

"Okay, Proph. I'll go slow."

Prophet wanted to tell him not to bother, but the look in Tom's eyes made his breath catch in his throat. Tom put two fingers together and pushed them against Prophet's mouth. "Suck them, Proph."

Prophet did, as Tom watched and groaned. Prophet did the same when Tom took his fingers out and mixed the saliva with the slick of pre-cum from Prophet's cock. And then Tom leaned in, slid his fingers back along Prophet's ass, then urged, "Come on, Proph . . . that's it. Let me in," as his finger slid inside.

Prophet nodded, closed his eyes, and willed himself to relax at this new assault on his system. Part of him was already floating, flying, but another was listening to the sound of warning bells.

He ignored them, let Tom back in, because he knew he really had no other choice.

Tom buried his face against Prophet's chest as he slid his fingers in and out of his ass, dragging his teeth against the man's skin, then sucking hard, needing his taste. He wanted to leave a mark, so he did, higher on Prophet's neck where everyone could see it. Wanted to give Prophet something to see when he looked in the mirror.

Because the man damned well needed some reminding.

But the damned man was here. And thank fuck Tom had ignored Phil's orders, listening instead to his gut, which had screamed to him that getting on a plane would be the most important thing he'd ever done in his life.

The ground shook from a loud slam outside, and Prophet was shuddering. Tom could see his gray eyes beginning to crowd with too much sensation, too much intensity threatening to close in and overwhelm him.

"S'okay—just a tree down," Tom said as he grabbed for Prophet's hips to push him up further. Prophet's wet feet slipped on the floor, and he grabbed for Tom's shoulders. Wound his legs around Tom's back and ended up holding onto the back of Tom's neck as his cock wept between their bodies.

Being taller made this position perfect—Tom eased his cock inside Prophet, and Prophet hissed and dug his fingers into Tom's neck. But it was a good hiss, because Prophet was attempting to push down and take Tom in, deeper and faster.

He grabbed Prophet's hips and stopped him. Held him in place so he could drive himself inside, loved watched Prophet's mouth drop as he entered.

Prophet was so fucking tight around him that Tom nearly stopped. But Prophet growled at him, and Tom slid in balls deep with a hard push that made them both groan loudly. Then Prophet grabbed

Tom's shoulders hard, dug in, and pushed down while resting his head against the wall.

Surrender. Acceptance. They were both there, and Tom took them and ran with them, steamrolled over them with hard thrusts that had Prophet cursing and moaning.

They were loud, but the storm outside was louder. Their own personal hurricane swirled between them until Tom's orgasm shot through him like a rocket. He pinned Prophet with hands and cock, giving the man no quarter.

He put his hand on Prophet's chest, felt the man tremble with exhaustion and nerves and need. Prophet unlocked his legs and lowered them on the floor, and Tom got down on his knees.

He looked up at Prophet. The hard planes of the man's body were glistening with sweat and rain and cum from earlier. Prophet's head was still back against the wall, his eyes closed, and Tom slid a hand around his hip, reassuring the man that he wouldn't let him go. He licked at the light dusting of hair that led down to Prophet's cock, letting his free hand stroke Prophet's balls.

"Tommy." It was barely a breath. Prophet's body broke out in gooseflesh as Tom lapped at the head of his cock, and Prophet finally moved, putting a hand into Tom's hair. Rubbing. Encouraging. Forcing.

How the man could move from so completely submissive to dominant with a single motion was beyond Tom, but Prophet had done it. And Tom's cock was already half-hard again at the thought of what Prophet would do to him after this.

He took Prophet further into his mouth, sucking and humming, cupping his balls, squeezing his hip to leave another mark. He glanced up again and found Prophet staring down at him, the corner of his mouth pulled into a lazy grin.

It made Tom work harder, both to make the man smile more and to wipe it off and replace it with a grit of teeth.

A contradiction. Just like Prophet.

He moved farther down between the man's opened thighs, mouthing one ball, then the other, sucking gently then harder.

Prophet's legs shook.

Tom smiled.

Prophet cursed at him.

In response, Tom moved back up and swirled his tongue around the soft skin that encased the hard throb of cock, then pushed his tongue into the small opening. Prophet gasped and cursed again and held Tom's hair tightly, to the point of pain. But that wasn't stopping him. He speared his tongue into the entrance harder and harder, finally glancing up again to see Prophet, most definitely unsmiling, a flush spreading along his chest and neck.

"Going to . . . fucking . . . spank you . . . for this," Prophet managed, and Tom laughed around his cock, giving a momentary respite before going back to the same torture.

And then he took Proph's cock down as far as he could. When it touched the back of his throat, he swallowed, and Prophet jerked.

He pulled back quickly to stop Prophet from coming, licked slowly from the root upward, then curled his tongue around the top.

Prophet's body shook. Tom took pity on him, slid the man's cock between his lips as he palmed it as well and used mouth and fist to pump in a steady rhythm. He wouldn't last long—and Tom was surprised he'd made it this far.

He was ready when Prophet spilled into his mouth with a violent spurt and a hoarse howl to match. Swallowed him down as Prophet's climax jerked his body with hard shudders. Kept him in his mouth even after the orgasm stopped. Pulled back and licked and sucked gently until Prophet tugged his head away.

Only then did Tom let go of Prophet's hip to allow the man to slide down the wall.

"Now that's a sight for my old, sore eyes," Dave murmured against Roger's ear as they watched the bodies in the shadows. It was too dark to see much, but it was more than obvious what was happening, the two men moving in unison, one pinned to the wall, the other covering him.

"Young love."

"Young lust."

"Looks like he doesn't need our company after all."

In the dark, Dave reached for Roger's hand as they watched the shadowed lovemaking. "Were we ever that beautiful?"

"You still are," Roger told him. "Maybe we should make the most of the hurricane."

"This was definitely foreplay."

"It's like Tumblr, the live version."

Dave chuckled. "True. But I did *not* see it coming."

"Maybe hurricanes affect gaydar?"

"How much did you have to drink?"

"Enough to pretend we can still have sex like that."

CHAPTER SIX

With Tommy collapsed half on top of him, Prophet lay on the kitchen floor, spent. Sweaty. Unable—or unwilling—to break the almost spell-like silence that covered them like a blanket. He hadn't been this wet or dirty since BUD/S, but BUD/S definitely hadn't felt this good.

Tom was still breathing hard, and Prophet's legs still shook from the exertion. But if Tom wanted more, right now, Prophet would be game.

"You know they watched us, right?" Prophet asked finally, his voice rough as he drew lazy circles on Tom's back with his fingertips.

Tom shivered at the contact, then snorted. "Yeah."

Prophet laughed. And then laughed more, which made Tom laugh.

They both stopped when sideways hail began hitting the window above the kitchen sink. The house creaked, the lights flickered, and then went out.

Prophet blinked and tried to swallow the panic. He started counting as soon as the reassuring hum of the generator kicked in—ten seconds down—and he continued to count, even as Tom nuzzled his chest, then bit his nipple hard enough for Prophet's cock to stir.

He wound his hand in Tommy's hair and breathed, and then the kitchen lights returned.

Tom's head lifted. "You installed a generator in my aunt's house?"

"Someone had to."

Tom balanced his chin on Prophet's chest. "Hope you bolted it down."

"And alarmed the fucker too. And set up a trap to catch anyone who went near it." Prophet paused. "I wasn't going to tell you that before you went out to check the oil."

"Fucker," Tommy muttered. "You didn't even know I was coming."

"You said you couldn't."

"Don't look at me that way—I didn't come here to see you."

"God forbid," Prophet grumbled.

"I didn't know you'd be here, Proph," Tom said, his voice gentler now.

"Cut the innocent act, Voodoo. Unless you always carry condoms in your pocket when you travel."

"Dammit, Proph . . . okay, look, I just knew it was as important as fuck for me to get here. I don't ignore my gut. Not anymore."

Jesus, Prophet didn't want to do this yet. Things were so goddamned fragile between them, and the second either one of them pressed for more, it could all fall the fuck apart. Prophet refused to risk any of it to the threat of reality. Because the indisputable fact remained that he'd come here for Tommy, yes, but Tom had come for Della. No matter whether he'd thought Prophet might be here, Tom still hadn't chosen him. "Things are better when we're fucking. Simpler, at least."

"I'm up for keeping it going."

"You can't even move."

"Neither can you."

Prophet held up a hand, then gave Tom the finger. "See? I moved."

Tom lunged to completely pin him. Prophet was quicker, and they rolled underneath the table and hit the bench. Tom ended up on top, and as he leaned in for a kiss, Della cleared her throat in the most obvious of ways before coming into the kitchen.

They both glanced over and saw her feet, and Tom turned back to press his face against Prophet's chest to keep from laughing. Prophet wound a protective hand in Tommy's hair, and felt the man's heartbeat, steady and strong against his.

"Roger and Dave enjoyed the show," Della said. "I'd have charged money had I known. And nice to see you, Tom. Don't get up. Just let me know if the house starts to float away."

Prophet hooted softly, and Della left.

"She's not pissed," Tom said, and as he lifted his head to stare at Prophet, Prophet let his hand slide down to Tommy's neck and then between his shoulder blades. "She actually sounded . . . happy. How long have you been here?"

Prophet snickered and rubbed Tom's calf with his foot, spreading his legs so his cock touched Tom's. "Long enough that she likes me better than you."

"Such an asshole," Tom muttered, but he shifted, a catch in his breath because they were both getting hard again. "What are they predicting? I couldn't get a report during the last few hours before I got here."

"I don't listen. They're never on target—it's either way worse or not as bad."

"Yeah." Tom's hand slid along Prophet's chest and Prophet was dangerously close to rutting up against him again. And really, he saw no reason to try to control himself, but he did.

He needed a distraction. "Guess you've been through enough storms."

"More than I can count." Tom traced a finger along Prophet's jawline. "Are we really talking about weather?"

"Yeah. Weather." Prophet ran a hand down to Tom's hip, the other cupping the back of Tom's neck.

"Better than fighting."

"Not by much. Fighting leads to fucking."

Tom leaned in to kiss the hollow of Prophet's neck, then murmured, "Weather leads there too," with his lips still against Prophet's skin.

Prophet closed his eyes for a second, secure with Tom's body this close. "I don't want to talk about all the shit we're supposed to talk about. For tonight, let's just not go there. There are other things I want to do more."

"While the world falls down around us?"

"Especially because of that." Prophet paused, then, ignoring his own advice, admitted, "You were . . . unexpected." And not just because he'd walked through the door in the middle of a hurricane.

"You hate that."

"Yes."

"Because you'd rather be the unexpected one."

"Yes," Prophet said with relish. And that was the truth, although whether it was on purpose, or whether he was wired that way, he had no idea. It probably didn't matter, but either way, it was something he'd cultivated out of necessity.

Tom laughed, seemingly with empathy rather than at him, and pressed another kiss to his collarbone, probably because Prophet had slowly started to move his hips, even as he asked, "So how did you make it here?"

"I have my resources, same as you."

Prophet frowned at him. "I'll fuck it out of you, if I have to." And when Tom shivered at the implicit promise, Prophet chuckled. "You're easy."

"A slut for you," Tom said seriously.

Prophet stared into Tom's dark eyes and knew Tom was purposely repeating those words, the same ones Prophet had uttered to him months earlier. "Good."

"At least we agree on something."

Prophet apparently *definitely* agreed with him, because as soon as Tom had uttered those words, Prophet was kissing him. Honest to goodness holding him, kissing the shit out of him. His body flooded with heat, and he was like a giddy kid, floating from the attention. And even if he didn't know anything else, he knew for sure that Prophet had come to New Orleans for him. But it didn't so much matter why, it just mattered that he was here.

The other thing he knew for sure was that sex gave them a way to tell each other all the things they couldn't bring themselves to say out loud.

Yet.

He rolled them back out from under the table, and then dragged Prophet up and pulled him into the bathroom off the laundry room. He'd noticed Prophet shivering, and while there was still hot water—hell, while there was still water, period—he figured they might as well try to get the mud off themselves. And their clothes. "Shit. Wait here."

"Where would I go?" Prophet asked wryly, and Tom wagged a finger at him. Right now, Prophet was all goddamned his, all here and present in the moment, and Tom planned to keep it that way.

Quickly, he went out naked into the storm to retrieve his bag from the ground by the door where he'd dropped it when Prophet had tackled him. It was soaked through, so he threw those clothes into the washing machine, as well as their dirty clothes scattered all over the kitchen.

Finally, they were under the warm spray. Tom reveled in the chance to clean Prophet, who seemed content to let him fuss. And Tom did, because he couldn't seem to help himself around Prophet. He washed Prophet's hair, his back, cock, ass, and everything in between, taking way more care with the other man than he did on himself.

Prophet watched him the entire time, eyes like liquid steel boring into him with a thousand unasked questions. But when Tom moved closer to check out what looked like a knife wound on Prophet's shoulder, Prophet's expression shuttered. "What?" he challenged Tom.

"This isn't from our mission." He couldn't bring himself to mention Sadiq's name.

"It's been four months, Tommy."

Four months since Tom had chosen Cope. Four months during which Prophet had simply disappeared. "Where were you?"

"On jobs."

"Where did you get these jobs from?"

"You know . . . around." Prophet motioned in the air and Tom shut the water off abruptly, the familiar agitation rising. But he wanted to give Prophet the benefit of the doubt that he wasn't pulling away. Not this soon. Plus, Tom had agreed not to push the talking while the world was falling down around them. So he'd give Prophet until the hurricane passed before he started pushing.

And he'd also make damned sure he didn't let go this time.

In front of him, Prophet shivered again, and Tom grabbed a towel and dried him off.

They each secured a towel around their waist as they walked out of the bathroom, and Tom peered into the kitchen. "We're still alone."

"They're not coming back down here tonight. Well, maybe Roger." Prophet dropped the towel and tugged his arm, and before Tom could react, he found himself naked—again—and sitting on the washing machine. Prophet moved between his legs and pulled him forward so he was balanced on his ass, clinging to Prophet's shoulders as the man kissed him.

There was nothing better than Prophet's kisses. They were as full of life and heat and as demanding as his fucking. He put everything he had into them, and the intensity flared to life between them again. It was like neither of them would get their fill anytime soon, and Prophet was right. This was so much easier than talking.

Prophet rocked against him, palmed both their cocks to stroke them languidly, his tongue still sliding against Tom's, keeping him locked into the kiss.

After what seemed like hours of keeping him on edge, Prophet broke away from Tom and went into the kitchen, then came back with a condom and lube.

Tom shook his head. "You could've mentioned that you had lube the whole time."

"Wanted to see how creative you could get," Prophet told him. He rolled the condom on as Tom watched, and then squirted some lube on his fingers.

With that predatory gaze Tom wouldn't forget if he lived forever, Prophet pushed him back slightly with a cool palm against his chest, forcing Tom's legs open. Balanced precariously, he braced himself palms down on the washing machine as Prophet slid a finger inside of him.

He tensed at first, but Prophet smiled at him, and Tom relaxed into the fingering. "Yeah, Proph. That's good."

His body buzzed as Prophet added another finger and twisted them before hitting his gland several times without giving Tom a chance to recover. His mouth fell open as the sensation of needing to come that fucking instant rushed through him.

"Not yet, Tommy," Prophet warned, wrapped his free hand around Tom's cock and squeezed the base to quell any hope of an impending orgasm. "You're going to have to find some patience."

"Maybe . . . you can let me . . . borrow . . . some of yours," Tom managed, and for that, Prophet added a third finger and simultaneously bit his nipple, and then tugged at the nipple rod with his teeth. Tom lifted his hips to fuck Prophet's fingers and within seconds, he'd almost lost control again.

Their first time tonight had been about release and relief, almost an out-of-body experience, but this time, Tom had to say that—for once—the reality was just as good as the fantasy. Maybe even better, because there was no arm's length between them. Tom had finally gotten through. Prophet was present and accounted for, staring right at Tom, daring him to notice.

And Tom had fucking noticed everything. Because Prophet was all his. Tom would set about proving that he'd never thought any differently, despite his choices.

Prophet stilled his fingers, then said, "I'm not, Tommy."

"Not ... what?"

"Pulling away. Just ... not ready to go there." He glanced over at the scar on his shoulder, then back at Tom. "But I'm here."

He was, gloriously here.

It got wet and messy and urgent. Again. Tom was panting as Prophet replaced his fingers with his cock. When he was halfway in, Tom hooked his legs around the backs of Prophet's thighs and pulled. Then groaned as his body fought to adjust.

It didn't take long before they were incoherent again. Everything vibrated around them as the storm picked up, and then the washing machine went into spin cycle and ...

"Holy fuck, Proph." Tom was thankful the wind hid his near yell as Prophet laughed and continued thrusting inside of him, filling him as they both shook from the machine.

But more than anything, Tom loved watching Prophet during sex. It was like the man was surrendering to the act, forcing Tommy to do so as well. There was no choice, and the slow buildup of the climax curled his belly, tightened his balls until he shot between them like the orgasm had been yanked from him.

Prophet came several moments later, just as Tom was recovering, pulling him into a dry climax, because the man's orgasms were a whirlwind that caught him up, slammed through him like a fucking tornado, and left him weak, out of breath, and not sure where the fuck he was.

It was awesome.

"Holy fuck," he muttered when he had the power of speech again. "Never doing laundry without this again."

Prophet laughed weakly against his ear.

Tom shuddered. "Are we just going to keep having sex so we can avoid talking about what we need to talk about?" Prophet pulled back and looked between Tom's legs. "What?"

"Just checking to make sure you still have a dick."

"Same one that fucked you through the wall while you begged for it," Tom pointed out, and Prophet's eyes grew heavy lidded with lust again. "You're so easy, Proph."

"For you."

There was so much goddamned meaning behind those two little words, and the way Prophet said them, with a slight catch in his voice . . . those two words said everything else he couldn't.

Tom swallowed hard and tried to convey the same sentiment when he simply told Prophet, "Me too."

And then Prophet smiled mischievously. "Can we fuck again so we don't have to talk? Because technically, what we just did counts."

Tom laughed. "No, it doesn't. But we can fuck anyway."

CHAPTER SEVEN

I t was more of a mutual handjob, with Tom on top of the dryer
this time, still wrapped around Prophet, and it seemed to wring
everything out of them. After a while, though, their skin began
sticking together from sweat, and Tom thought about moving.

It was only then that he realized they were almost totally in the
dark, because the door had swung closed and there was no light fixture
in the small room . . . save for a green glow that he remembered well.

Prophet was looking up at the glow stars that were reflecting off
their skin. Tom leaned in and kissed his neck. "I put those stars on the
ceiling in sixth grade." He remembered choosing the laundry room
because it was small and dark and safe. Tucked out of the way. You
could tell secrets here—or reveal them—and it would all be okay.

"Weren't enough stars in the sky for you?"

"None that were just mine. Those were for everyone—the people
I loved and the people who hated me. But these . . . these were all
mine."

Prophet didn't say anything, just threaded his fingers through
Tom's. Tom turned to trace a star pattern on Prophet's shoulder.

What were the odds of Prophet being in one of his childhood
homes—the happy one?

Whenever he'd come into the French Quarter, he'd stepped into
a different world. Being with Prophet felt exactly the same. He was
always slightly off-balance but knew that nothing truly bad could
touch him. How such an insane man had become his safe place would
probably haunt him for the rest of his life.

"So you liked it here?" Prophet asked.

Here, Tom had still been looked on with suspicion, but no one
had actively tried to hurt him. Not physically. "Yes. But Della took a
lot of shit whenever I stayed with her."

"That's the job of an adult," Prophet said, and Tom knew Prophet liked Della well enough, but he still heard anger in the man's voice. "You'd protect *you* in that situation, right?"

"With my life." Tom stared at him in the semi-darkness. "I was protecting you with my choice, Proph. You know that."

Prophet didn't say a word, but his body tensed up. He didn't pull away from Tom, but still . . .

"You're all scary calm," Tom whispered, "but I know you're so pissed at me." As much as they tried, they couldn't completely avoid this topic tonight, not unless one of them took Viagra or the hurricane ended immediately.

A long moment of silence passed. "At you," Prophet finally admitted. "At myself. You ran. But I let you. Then I ran too, and I don't fucking run. I go into the fire, T, not away from it."

"This was a different kind of fire." Tom stared at him, the glow pattern dappling Prophet's skin. Prophet, in his world. Under *his* stars. "Why didn't you want a partner to begin with? Because of what happened with John?"

"I don't work well as a team player."

"I don't buy that. I know why you had problems with *me* as your partner: my temper and almost killing that guy during our cage fight. And almost costing us our mission." He had to get it out, had to articulate it, had to say it out loud to try to absolve himself.

It never worked.

Prophet shook his head. "Your temper doesn't scare me. Not the way you think. I know tempers, but I'm worried about you."

Tom was worried about both of them. "Did you read my emails?"

"Nice change of topic."

"Proph . . ."

"Yeah," Prophet disclosed grudgingly. "All at once, two days ago. I couldn't open them before that, because I knew."

"Knew what?"

"That I'd come back. To you, for sure. And I've never done that, T."

"Even with John?" There was no malice there. The ghost of John that had hung between them four months ago had dissipated.

"It was different with John. From the time I was twelve, he was my one constant." Prophet paused, looked away as if wrestling with something he didn't want Tom to see. A long moment ticked by, and then Prophet locked his gaze on Tom, much the way he'd done that very first time they'd met, a raw, almost brutal stare. "I searched for him for two full years after everyone said he was dead."

Tom didn't say anything, just put his hand over Prophet's and waited.

Finally, Prophet said, "I told you I didn't think he was dead. I've never told anyone outside of my old team that, except for you and Cillian." Tom couldn't help but roll his eyes at the mention of Cillian. Prophet acknowledged it with a small shake of his head, but continued, "Right after I was released from the CIA's custody and the base's infirmary, I went AWOL. I basically disappeared."

"What did you find?"

"I became the man I am today because of that," he told Tom cryptically. "Everything I learned in those two years . . . they were things I never wanted to know. Things that made me better at my job. Things that fucked with my conscience more than I'll ever tell anyone. I helped a lot of people along the way. Mal said it was like my walkabout, but without the peyote." He shrugged. "Well, most of the time."

Tom crossed his arms and watched Prophet shift like a guilty teenager until he finally protested, "I was in pain. It was all natural."

"It explains so much. About you and Mal."

Prophet smirked at the sarcasm Tom had made fully evident in his tone. "You're still jealous. It's cute."

"Cute?"

"*Decent sex*?" Prophet growled back and Tom grinned. "Glad you found it funny. Gonna wipe that smirk right off your face and have a great time doing it."

"Now you're worried about the decent sex comment?"

"Too horny when I first saw you. Don't worry. You'll pay."

Tom leaned in and bit Prophet's neck again. "Looking forward to it."

An hour and several more spin cycles later, Prophet's phone beeped as Tom was making coffee. He glanced over and saw Prophet texting, his fingers moving quickly.

Prophet's back was to him, but it wasn't like he was trying to hide his phone. Tom put the coffee down in front of him and looked over Prophet's shoulder.

He tensed immediately when he saw Cillian's name and a few joking lines between the men. Still, he managed to say calmly, "Tell that stupid fucking spook to stop flirting with you."

Prophet didn't turn around, but his voice was serious when he said, "Didn't realize we were exclusive."

"If we were, you wouldn't flirt. Not like that." Tom wasn't able to take the tightness out of his voice.

To his credit, Prophet put the phone down mid-text and shoved it away. "Still can't tell if you really want me, or if you just want to make sure no one else can have me."

"It's more complicated than that."

"Not, it's not." Prophet finally turned to look at him. "Fuck, I thought it was. Thought it should be. But it's simple as hell. Scares the fuck out of me."

Tom reached out and ran a finger down Prophet's shoulder—the one with the fresh scar. "Why's that?"

"Lot of reasons. Some you don't know."

Tom gave up with the calm shit and threw his hands in the air. "More secrets? About Cillian?"

"Why don't you trust him?"

"Why do you?" Tom shot back.

"Never said I did, T. You assumed that. Sometimes, I've got to play a game."

"A flirting game? Because quite honestly, it didn't all seem to be a game."

"It wasn't," Prophet admitted. "Started before I met you. And shit, T, you and I . . ."

"I know." Because there wasn't supposed to be any Tom and Prophet. But here they were, four months later, unable to stop fucking each other. "Ten seconds in each other's presence, we're ripping each other's clothes off."

"To be fair, you ripped more," Prophet sniffed.

"You loved it."

Tom was joking, but Prophet obviously wasn't when he said, "Yeah, I did."

Before Tom could respond, Prophet held up a hand. "And we'll deal with that after we survive this hurricane, remember?"

"Such an amateur. Besides, we already broke that rule," Tom reminded him as his own phone began to buzz. He glanced at his phone and winced.

"Phil?"

"Yeah." Tom sent the call to voice mail. "Cope said he'd cover for me, but I couldn't let him keep doing that. I texted Phil and told him where I was when I hit the city limits."

"Don't fuck with a Marine, T. You'll never win."

"You really believe that?"

"I said you'll never win. Never said anything about me." Prophet grinned, then sat back in his chair like he was preparing to study Tom. "So how was Eritrea? You had a lot of downtime to write."

"I made time," he said pointedly, before sitting across from Prophet, grabbing up the coffee mug he'd given the man and taking a sip. "I learned a lot, but it was tough to go from partnering with you to training."

Prophet smiled, like he knew. The bastard.

Tom had tried to make the best of it. Had been determined to do so. And he'd listened to Cope. Trained. Tried not to let himself get bored, because bored equaled mistakes. He listened to his gut. Cope respected that. They were good partners in that Tom got hot easily and Cope was so fucking laid-back that nothing bothered him. In theory it should be a perfect partnership.

But Cope was content to work in Eritrea. He'd had his time in the military, and he was up for the risks if and when they came along, but he wasn't going to ask for them. He was Phil's go-to guy for Eritrea and typically the one who broke in the new guys, but he had no desire to run things.

"And you weren't content?"

"I was restless." Tom shifted in his chair recalling just how restless he'd been. "I spent more than half the time monitoring comms and split the other half between training and guarding wealthy businessmen. A glorified bodyguard for rich assholes. I felt like I was being wasted."

"Phil thought you were thrown into the fire too fast." Prophet took the coffee back from him and took a sip of his own. And winced at the strong chicory flavor. "What the fuck is in this coffee?"

"You'll get used to it. And Phil forgets I was with the FBI."

"Out for five years. And this is a completely different kind of job. Get trained—there's no harm in it."

"It's not my style."

Prophet took another cautious sip of the coffee. Winced again. "So what, if you can't go balls to the wall, why bother?"

"Isn't that what you do?"

"We weren't talking about me, but yes, I took intense jobs because I wanted to."

Tom asked the question he'd been dreading. "Were you looking for Sadiq?"

"Just enough to make sure he wasn't going to find me," Prophet's conceded. "He didn't know where I was, but I never stopped carrying the phone Gary used to contact me."

"Fuck, Proph—Sadiq called you?"

Prophet's jaw clenched as he nodded.

"Threats?"

"Threats. Taunts." Prophet reluctantly pulled another phone from his pocket, scanned through it, and showed Tom a picture of himself guarding a wealthy Brazilian businessman.

Tom grabbed it and stared. "You knew and you didn't tell me?"

"Tom—"

"No, fuck that. You didn't tell me—didn't want me to protect myself?"

"You were protected."

"By who? Cillian?"

"Definitely not. And Sadiq only caught your trail once, then he lost you. He's more interested in you to see if I'm with you. The less we're together, the less he's going to think that hurting you will bring me into the open."

"So I'm the one bringing the danger to you right now—the one making you vulnerable."

Prophet grew quiet for a moment, his hands wrapping around the coffee cup. "If he can't catch my scent on you, he'll leave you alone—and that's the way I want it."

"The way *you* want it. So you'll sacrifice me—us—for Sadiq? Haven't you lost enough to him already?"

They had coffee. A flashlight. A SAT phone. Everything out on the table between them. Everything they needed to help them through the storm. But nothing to help them navigate this other shit.

Haven't you lost enough to him already?

He didn't want to think about the losses—past or future. He was done with talking, was more interested in finding out if too much sex could kill them. He was just about to recommend that, to try to distract Tommy, because Tommy was doing that thinking too much thing again and—

"Weren't you worried about bringing Sadiq here?" Tom asked.

Too late. "Weren't you?"

"Fuck. I wasn't until you showed me that picture." Tom ran his hands through his still damp hair. "I get what you're saying about keeping separated. But I think we did pretty well when we were together. You know, after you blew me off and got yourself kidnapped, and I followed you."

"And got *yourself* kidnapped," Prophet reminded him. "We got out with Cillian's help."

"I would've thought of something," Tom grumbled, and there was silence again.

"I believe that," Prophet said, and Tom stared at him, almost unconsciously playing with the bracelet Prophet had tied around his wrist.

The storm had intensified. The meteorologists were predicting—with fucking glee—that the hurricane was bigger and stronger now, a Cat 3 and moving toward a Cat 4. And that goddamned bald guy from The Weather Channel was in New Orleans. Everyone knew that the guy only went to the place that was going to get hit the worst. Like a bald, douche-bag weather angel of death. Like he knew anything about survival. "How bad's this going to get?" Prophet asked.

"You've really never been through a hurricane before?"

"You say that like it's a character flaw."

Tom shrugged. Like it was.

"I've been through a tornado. I think. Near a volcano," Prophet ticked off.

Tom rolled his eyes, but Prophet could tell he was fighting a grin just the same. "You're totally lying."

"Why would I lie?" Prophet asked. "Sandstorm! Four of them. Maybe five. They tend to blend."

"Inside or out?"

"I started outside, worked my way in. Sounds so dirty."

Tom snorted.

"And thunderstorms."

Tom shook his head. "Everyone goes through those."

"Hail. Snow. Lots of snow."

"In Texas?"

"I didn't always live in Texas."

Tom blinked, probably at the realization that he didn't know where Prophet had grown up, but all he said was, "I guess the main EE office sees a lot of snow."

"Yep."

"Sore subject?"

"Been through worse." But yeah, just hearing the company's initials cut like a goddamned knife. He knew Phil had been calling, leaving him messages, but he refused to pick up. Deleted the voice mails before listening. Same with unread emails.

Tom was looking toward the window with an odd expression on his face, like he was waiting for something—and that put Prophet on high alert, since he recognized the signs of some of Tom's impending voodoo shit. And sure enough, just then, the house shook with a particularly fierce gust of wind. The ground shook—hard—and it felt like the beginnings of an earthquake.

"I've been through an earthquake too," Prophet snapped. "And that sounded like a water main."

Tom nodded in agreement, and they both went to the front window and saw . . . nothing.

"I'm going to have to go out and see if we're going to flood," Tom said.

"No way. We'll know if we're going to soon enough." He pulled a pair of night vision goggles from the box in the front hall. "Try these. It'll take a few for your eyes to adjust."

Tom pulled them on and after a minute he cursed. "There's water running down the street. Blowing, actually, but it doesn't seem to be going particularly high."

He took the NVs off and handed them back, but he still seemed distracted, darting his gaze toward the stairs. Instead of diverting his attention with more questions, Prophet looked out the window for himself and muttered, "Glad I brought a shit ton of bottled water."

As he took off the NVs and turned around, Tom touched his shoulder and said, "I didn't thank you."

"For the NVs?"

"For this. For all of this. You didn't have to do this."

Prophet swallowed. Was about to say, *Yes, I did,* when Roger came barreling down the stairs, yelling, "Prophet! It's Della—she's insisting I don't tell you, but she's got chest pains."

"Go to her," Prophet told him when he saw Tom's *Goddammit, I knew it* expression. "I'll call 911." In fact, he was already dialing the SAT phone, but Tom shook his head and took the phone instead. He dialed as he told Prophet, "I'm calling Kari—she's an old friend and a doctor. Tell her you're calling for me and Della."

He took off upstairs to Della, and Kari picked up after eight rings. Prophet explained what was happening, and she said, "I'm riding in the ambulance now—I can get to the top of the street. How's it looking past that?"

"Not great. I'll meet you and get you here."

"I'll call when I'm close. Give me five minutes."

Prophet hung up. Grabbed for the high rubber boots and a pullover that would do nothing, plus a baseball hat. Used the NVs to navigate quickly up the street. The water was spilling over the sidewalk, and there were wires whipping and sparking. He cursed the entire time.

Because he didn't mind water, but there was water and there was water.

He was buffeted by the wind but put his head down, his adrenaline rocketing at the thought of something happening to Della. He reached the crosswalk and stood there for a minute, staring up at the sky as the swelling clouds loomed like they were waiting for an opportunity to swallow the earth. A minute or so later, an ambulance pulled up, and a woman waved from the back bay. He helped her out, shouldered the heavy bags, and then told her to climb onto his back.

"If you think I'm refusing, you've got another thing coming!" she called over the wind and got on. She held his shoulders, and he jogged down the street and got them back into the safety of the house.

"She's upstairs," Prophet told Kari, took her rain gear, and walked up behind her with her bags.

Della looked pale as hell. Tom was holding the portable O2 under her nose, and she was batting him away. Kari said, "Business as usual, right?"

"Tell him to stop babying me," Della said to him.

Prophet looked at Kari with a smile. "Good luck."

CHAPTER EIGHT

Finally, Prophet pried Tom from the room, because he was obviously making Della more agitated, rather than less. Tom had refused to leave even when Kari had explicitly asked him to so she could examine Della, and Prophet literally had to pull him out, reminding him quietly that he'd called Kari purposely for this. Della gave him a grateful nod as he closed the door behind them.

This role was, at least, familiar to him. In control, taking care of things—of everyone.

Tom stood at the door for a while, and then he began pace back and forth, so much so that Roger muttered something about getting dizzy. When Tom glared, Prophet motioned for Dave to take Roger downstairs.

"Thanks for the show," Roger murmured as he walked by Prophet.

"You're lucky it's not your heart giving you problems after that," Dave told him, and Prophet snorted. Tom didn't stop pacing.

After several more minutes of that, Prophet caught him and yanked him against his body, Tom's back to his chest. Tom struggled until he realized Prophet wouldn't let him go.

"Strong fucker," were Tom's exact words and then finally, the man relaxed and leaned against him, the fight draining out of him. Prophet felt like he could actually breathe. He put his arm around Tom's chest, his palm around Tom's biceps. Rubbed the feathers of the dreamcatcher as if he could actually feel them.

"Your voodoo shit's stronger when you're here, isn't it?" Prophet asked, his cheek against Tom's neck.

"Always strong. You just fucking distract me too much when we're together," Tom shot back over his shoulder and then looked pained at what he'd said. "That's not a bad thing."

Prophet released his death grip, and Tom turned in his arms. He brushed Tom's cheek with the back of his hand. "She'll be okay."

"Yeah, I know. But one day, she won't be, and she's the only one I have."

"No, she's not."

Tom glanced at him. Sighed. "I want to believe that, Proph. I want to believe that you're here for more than a sense of obligation . . . but what if there wasn't a hurricane?"

"But there was, T."

"I'd never take you for a believer subscribing to the *everything happens for a reason* theory."

"I guess I have to remind you that you picked Cope?" Tom put a hand over his heart and rubbed. Prophet frowned. "More voodoo shit, or . . .?"

Tom glanced down at his hand and gave a small, surprised laugh. "In a way." And then he looked back up at Prophet, hand still on his heart, like it was part pledge. "Are you going to keep running?"

He put his hand over Tom's and said firmly, "I'm not running now, Tommy," the way you only could when you meant it.

"But you were."

Prophet sighed deeply and stared up at the ceiling, looking for something up there to come and save him from all this talking. Like an avalanche. "I know you think that, but you're wrong."

"Then what were you doing? Oh, right, you can't tell me."

"Dammit, not now, Tommy," he growled, fisting his hand and hitting Tom's lightly before moving away completely.

Instead of letting him go, Tom moved into him, rubbed his cheek against Prophet's shoulder. "Of all people, I should fucking understand secrets, right?"

Prophet sighed and rubbed the back of Tom's neck, wondering how he let the guy defuse him so easily. Or why. "Well, you'd think."

Tom snorted a soft laugh—the warm huff of breath tickled Prophet's neck. Prophet carded his hand through Tommy's hair, keeping him close.

They stayed like that until the bedroom door opened, and even then, Tom didn't push away from Prophet, just turned his attention to Kari with Prophet's arm still around him. "How is she?"

"It wasn't a heart attack," Kari told them. "I think it was, at most, a gallbladder attack."

"So like, really bad heartburn?" Prophet asked with relief, and she nodded.

"It's not unusual. With the hurricane, a lot of people use it as an excuse to go off their usual diet and eat crap."

"So she's fine," Tom breathed, and Prophet could feel the tension bleeding off him.

"I think she'll outlive all of us," Kari said. "Her pressure's good, O2 sats are fine. She's taking her meds regularly, and for the most part her diet's good. I think she just had too much coffee. She was trying to stay awake in case something happened to the house."

It was Prophet's turn to half sigh, half curse. Tom squeezed his shoulder. "She'd stay up if she had the entire Navy at her door."

Prophet nodded, then asked Kari, "Do you need a ride back to the hospital?"

"You know, that'd be great, but I'm not sure they'll let you through. I can call for the ambulance and meet them back up the street."

"I don't really deal well with the word 'let,'" he told her, and Tom snorted.

"I should've seen that coming," she said. "All right, big shot, let's get me back to the hospital."

"How're you going to stop the truck from flooding out?" Tom asked.

"I'll drive on the sidewalks," Prophet said.

"We're better off just walking her back."

"In this crap?"

"It's not bad," she and Tom said in unison.

"You people who live here are crazy," he muttered, but he didn't stop Kari from calling for the ambulance.

She told him, "I only did that because if you leave the house now, I know you'll be roaming the streets, getting into trouble."

"How do you know that?"

"You seem like that type," she said with a smile. A half hour later, she was packed back into the ambulance with her gear. Prophet watched the ambulance drive slowly away.

"What time is it?" he asked.

"Just before six," Tom said, stifling a yawn. "See, it's almost gone."

It was starting to get light out, even though the clouds still blocked any hope of sunrise. "It looks like the fucking apocalypse." Prophet pointed to the flooding roads, the buckled sidewalks, the street signs and other debris that had blown along the street.

"We're being a little dramatic, no?"

"No," Prophet said firmly.

"Amateur," Tom told him again, threaded his hand into Prophet's. "What now?"

"Like I said, it's my first hurricane. I'm hoping there aren't aftershocks."

"There are aftershocks, all right," Tom muttered.

"You know I can hear you, right?"

"Counting on it," Tom said. "Shit."

He pointed to the porch where Roger was frantically waving. "Della's okay," he called. "But her friend . . ."

"It's going to be like this all day, right?" Prophet asked Tom.

"Just think, you'll be a hurricane pro once this is over."

"Comforting. Really. Comforting."

His aunt was on the porch now, her feet bare, more color in her cheeks. And she had a glass of wine in her hand that Tom promptly took from her.

"Kari said red wine's good for my heart," she argued as Tom dumped it over the side railing. Roger sighed as though someone were killing him at the sight of wine going to waste, but Tom had had enough surprises to last him a good long while.

"Kari said you needed to watch your diet," Tom told her.

"Please just go to Betty's," Della said. "I invited her here, but she was too stubborn to leave her house."

"Pot, meet kettle," Prophet grumbled and ducked before Della could hit him on the back of the head.

"Aunt Della, please, go inside," Tom implored.

"Go ahead, Della," Prophet told her. "I'll go check on your friend, and Tom will stay with you."

"No, you should go together," Della urged. "We're fine here. You wired the house so we're safer than Fort Knox."

"Fort Knox actually isn't all that safe," Prophet informed her, and she smiled and patted his cheek, and Tom wondered how Prophet and his aunt had gotten thick as thieves in under two days.

"Please." She looked between the men. "You know how nervous Betty gets. It's probably just the wind, but she's convinced that people are trying to loot her house."

Tom looked at Prophet. "You up for this?"

"Are you?"

"Can't sit by and do nothing. It's two blocks down." And there was no other way to get there but on foot, and they were both already armed. Prophet told Roger to take Della inside and keep her there.

"The SAT phone number's on the kitchen table," Prophet reminded them, then closed the door and followed Tom off the porch.

Tom stuck to Prophet's back as they travelled through the flooded streets. In places, the water was up to the calves of their rubber boots, and the wind was still strong enough to make it too goddamned dangerous to be out here, and Tom hadn't felt this alive in forever . . . not since . . .

Not since the last time he'd worked with Prophet and they'd both almost died.

Some men are born to do this shit . . . adrenaline runs through their veins instead of blood. That's what Cope had told him. Before this, Tom would've thought he'd only been describing Prophet, but of course that description fit him too.

They walked over a driveway to cut through to the next block. Prophet shifted to walk behind him, *watching his six*, as Cope liked to say.

Tom liked the idea of Prophet watching his six. Almost turned and told him so when he saw the two young boys hanging onto a sign in the middle of the road as the water tugged at them.

"Son of a bitch," Prophet muttered, pushed past Tom, who said, "The current's stronger than you think."

Prophet turned to him. "Really? You're telling me about water?"

"I don't know what they're teaching in the Navy these days," Tom said with a straight face.

"Wiseass." Prophet took a rope out of his pocket—and duct tape, since the rope was stuck to the tape.

"You always travel with duct tape?"

Prophet looked at him like he was the idiot. "It's all-purpose, man. You don't carry it?"

"Ah, no."

"You might want to start."

"I'll consider it," he said, as Prophet tied a loop in the rope for a handhold and tied the other end to a fire hydrant.

"Hang on here in the middle to give me some leverage, okay? When I grab them, pull with me."

"Got it." Tom stood there, holding the rope, and watched Prophet walk through the flood, solid and steady, the water not pushing him at all. When he got to the boys, who were maybe ten, he told one to climb onto his back and hauled the other up under his arm. Tom kept a steady pressure on the rope as he pulled and Prophet walked the boys to safety.

He dumped them on the sidewalk. "Where the hell do you two live?"

They jumped at the command in his voice. Tom was glad they didn't see him do the same, but he was pretty sure Prophet had.

"Right there." One of the boys pointed.

"Go. Now."

They ran. Prophet watched until they went inside the house and closed the door, then turned to Tom and smiled suggestively. "Later, we can play commander and good little soldier."

Tom tried—and failed—to ignore how easily Prophet could turn him the fuck on by shooting back, "I'm not a soldier."

"Neither am I. That's why it's pretend, Tommy."

"Bastard," he muttered, and Prophet hooted as they got back in step and walked side by side until they got to Betty's house. Betty was Della's age, but she moved like she was ninety, and she cursed like the devil. Prophet told her he loved her, and she told him he was too old for her.

"Betty, give me a chance to prove myself to you."

"Start with the shed," Betty said. "Someone's in there, I swear it. And I'm not making you any promises."

"You smell smoke?" Prophet asked.

"Yeah. Maybe electrical," Tom said. In the distance, he heard sirens, but whether they were coming this way or not, he couldn't tell just yet.

"That way." Prophet pointed as they walked into Betty's semi-destroyed backyard. This neighborhood had taken some strong hits. The only way to get into the shed at this point was to climb over a downed tree and through a broken window. Tom handed Prophet his gun and his phone and shimmied up and over. Inside the dark shed, there were several cats who'd sought refuge, but no signs of anything malicious.

"It's all good in here," he called, more interested in checking where the smoke was coming from. He managed to step over everything that had fallen to get to the window on the other side, and saw a house on fire down the end of the next street. From his vantage point, he could also see that another tree had downed electrical wires on the corner, blocking entrance to the street because they were lying in water. He could get out through the window and walk along the stone wall of the house behind Betty's until he was past the danger. It was the fastest way. "Definitely a fire on the next street, Proph—I'm going through," he yelled.

"Tom, no, fucking wait for me. Come on, it's too dangerous."

It was—the wind had picked up again, and the rain was coming down hard—and diagonally—and Tom watched the lights of fire engines flash as they rounded the corner.

Then his gaze darted to a house that was closer to Betty's than the fire . . . Miles's house.

Miles, who'd made his life harder than it already had been when he'd been a kid.

Miles, who'd hurt Etienne so badly.

The door to the house was open—wide open. And there was no sign of anyone at the door except . . .

He looked again and swore he saw something—someone—lying on the floor inside. For some reason, his mind flashed to Etienne, lying under the bleachers, Etienne, that night in the bayou, and even though he knew it wasn't Etienne lying there, that it didn't make sense for him to go, Tom found himself propelled forward anyway. He didn't even call back to Prophet, just punched out the window, crawled through, and ran up the block, up the stairs, and into the opened door.

Before he could think, he was inside the house, kneeling next to . . .

"Miles," he said urgently, and the man's eyes, which were half-shuttered, struggled to focus. But then Miles grabbed for him, white foam bubbling from his lips. He was saying something, and Tom leaned in closer to try to hear even as he was reaching for a phone he didn't have to call 911.

Shit.

His eyes swept over the mansion's first floor, looking for something, anything, to help. It was a ghost house. What was once beautiful was now empty and broken down.

Miles wasn't letting go. Prophet would be here any second. He yelled, "We need help in here!" hoping Proph would hear him and grab the firefighters.

Miles was still frantically holding him, clawing at him, even as he mouthed something. Finally, actual sounds came out of his mouth, and Tom listened hard until he caught something . . .

"Donny?" he asked, and Miles nodded. "Did Donny do this?"

Miles just stared at him, and then he let go. As Tom felt for a pulse, a man's deep drawl said, "Son, I need you to step away and put your hands over your head."

Tom didn't have to turn toward the voice that made his stomach clench to know it was Chief of Police Lew Davis.

Son of a bitch.

He'd known Lew as both a kid dealing with a cop who hated him, and from when he'd been a deputy in the parish, and neither memory was any fucking good. He glanced briefly over his shoulder. "Lew, he needs an ambulance. He's dying."

It was only then Tom noticed the blood coming through Miles's shirtsleeves—because it was on Tom's arms now. Miles's shirtsleeves were pulled down over his wrists and halfway over his hands. Which was . . . odd, at best. He pushed a bloodied sleeve up and saw the heavy, vertical cut and the seeping blood.

Ah, fuck, this wasn't good.

"Stand up and step away from the body. Hands where I can see them, son."

Something in Lew's voice made Tom look over his shoulder again. The cop had his weapon drawn, was pointing it at Tom.

Fuck.

He stood slowly, bloody hands in the air, and moved away from Miles.

"On your knees," Lew barked and, then, into his radio, "I need a bus, and I've got a murder suspect in here." He strode over to Tom and pushed him facedown to the ground. As he yanked Tom's arms hard behind his back and placed the cuffs tightly on his wrists, Tom said, "He's dying."

He looked over at Miles, who'd stopped moving.

Lew was patting him down, pulled the knife out of his pocket, and held it up to Tom's face. "Is this your weapon?"

Tom didn't say anything. He knew better. Knowing Lew as he did, anything he tried to offer would be willfully misinterpreted, so Lew pocketed the knife, pulled him up by his arms, and walked him out of the house. And Tom was doing just fine, following Lew's directions . . . until Lew leaned in and whispered, "You pathetic piece of shit. *Bad loque,* just like your daddy always said you were. Just like your parish knows. Always figured I'd be marching you out in cuffs one day. Your daddy said he'd never been able to make a man out of you."

Goddamned pussy . . . boy, you'd better toughen up.

Bon à rien. Bad loque.

The thin hold Tom had on his control dissipated in a haze of anger. He yanked viciously against the cuffs, against Lew's hold . . . against his own goddamned past.

The cooperation was officially over.

CHAPTER NINE

After Tommy had refused to wait—the asshole—Prophet had followed the same path, through Betty's shed and across the stone wall, and he'd been about to follow Tommy down the street and into the house he'd disappeared into, until he saw the cop come out from the small alleyway that led to the back of the house with the opened door.

When the cop raced up the steps, Prophet fought the urge to follow, especially when he heard Tom calling for help just as the cop entered the house, but something stopped him.

He was glad he'd waited, or else the two of them would be in jail, and that wouldn't be in the least bit helpful.

As he watched from his place behind a car, Tommy's phone began to ring.

Cope. The partner stealer.

God, he was losing his fucking mind. Had to be the hurricane.

He glanced up and saw Tom begin to fight the tight hold the cop had on him. "Not good," he said under his breath and then, to piss Cope off, Prophet answered with, "Tom's phone."

"Who's this?"

"Who's this?" he shot back.

"Ah shit, Prophet—what the hell are you doing with Tom?"

"I'm not *with* Tom. I'm with his phone."

"What the fuck? Where's Tom?"

"Why're you checking up on him?"

"I'm his partner," Cope said, like he was speaking to a small, slow child. "That's what partners do."

"Glad you're such a Boy Scout. Making Phil proud."

"Yeah, I do. You, on the other hand . . ." Cope stopped.

After a few seconds of silence, Prophet goaded him, "Grow some balls and say it, Cope. Say it."

"Nah, too easy a dig, man. You're already on the outs. Can't kick a man while he's down."

"I'll show you down, Cope," he growled. "Your partner's getting arrested."

"What for? What'd he do?"

"Not sure." Prophet saw blood on Tommy's arms and hands as the cop led him away, and his heart jumped into his throat. Seconds later, he heard the sirens and an ambulance pulled up. The EMTs passed by Tommy and the sheriff and his men in favor of going inside the house.

Which meant the bleeding was happening *inside* the house. Prophet rubbed his forehead and just breathed.

"How can he be getting arrested if you don't know what he did? " Cope demanded. "Weren't you with him?"

"No," Prophet said through gritted teeth as Tom began resisting arrest again. Quite spectacularly too, but then, as suddenly as the struggle had started, it stopped. He thought he saw Tom glance in his direction, and he didn't know which of them Tommy had stopped for. All that mattered was that he'd stopped.

But hell, that hold on his control was tenuous at best.

"What did you do, Prophet?" Cope demanded. "Where the fuck are you two? And why in the hell are you even with him—to get him into more trouble?"

Prophet pretended that wasn't a punch to the gut. "I came to New Orleans to help his aunt, because he couldn't."

Cope blew out a breath into the phone. "I didn't know if he'd make it. Should've known he's as stubborn as you."

"Yeah, well, I guess that's why you two get along so well," he said sarcastically.

"Just when I think you're semi-human . . . forget it. So what're you going to do?"

"Get him out of jail," Prophet said simply, and then he hung up.

Cope was probably rushing to call Phil to report this. Then again, he'd been more than willing to cover for Tom. Tom had turned himself into Phil about coming to his aunt's. And Prophet had no real beef with Cope. In reality, he was a good partner for Tom. Didn't take a lot of risks, and Tom would be safe with him, if only because of the nature of the missions Phil tended to put Cope on.

But Tom's choice still smarted, and Prophet wasn't above admitting that. To himself.

He dialed Della's number. She picked up on the first ring. "Is Betty okay?"

"She's fine. Tom's not."

"What happened?"

"Some cop just arrested him for going inside a house."

"What's the address?" she asked, and when Prophet rattled it off to her, she said, "That's Miles's house."

"Do he and Tom have a history?"

"Too much of one to go into right now."

"The cop didn't seem too happy with him."

"Which cop?" Della demanded.

"Tall, dark hair with a silver patch in front, maybe mid-fifties—"

"Lew." She said it like she was spitting out something sour. "He's not easy. He's got it in for Tom. Always has." A pause, then Della said carefully, "Don't let him stay in jail, Prophet."

He wouldn't, but first he needed to do some investigating, find out what the hell had happened. "I'll take care of him."

"I know," she told him, soothing the sting of Cope's comment.

He pocketed the phone and strolled up the street to the mess of fire trucks and ambulances by the fire that was just billowing smoke now. He'd already formulated his plan. He grabbed an ME's abandoned jacket and took the black bag under it for good measure. He could slip into different identities at will—he'd started doing it as a kid and now it was a necessity in his profession. He'd always found the key was actually believing you could do the shit you were pretending to be able to do.

You had to believe it was for survival—and in this case, it was for Tom's.

I told you to wait for me, T.

He walked into the house Tom had been dragged out of in handcuffs. Two cops, an older guy and a younger woman, were standing over the body, talking in low voices with an EMT, who was kneeling next to the vic. They all looked over at Prophet.

"I'm Dr. Savoy," he drawled, because—according to the ID that had been in the pocket of the jacket—the real Dr. Savoy was visiting from Georgia. Prophet figured he was inside the house with the victims of the fire and would hopefully be there a good long while.

"I'm Sue. Guessing you're the visiting medical examiner?" the EMT asked.

"Sure, we'll go with that," Prophet said, and she laughed and quipped, "Good one. You win the hurricane," as Prophet knelt on the floor next to her and looked down at the dead man with the nondescript brown hair. Someone had closed his eyes, but his mouth was still slightly opened and frothed with white foam. "Poor fucking bastard," he murmured.

Sue obviously agreed, saying, "He needs you more than me. Bet you regret offering to come help in the middle of this. You're all do-gooders until you have to live through one of these storms."

"I'm tougher than I look," Prophet assured her, then nodded toward the victim. "Looks like an OD gone overboard." He pointed toward the slashed wrists.

The female cop indicated a small chalked circle on the floor. "Found the razor a couple of feet away. It's already bagged for you. We also recovered pill bottles upstairs."

"Can I see them?" Prophet asked. The cops glanced at each other, and then the woman rifled through the bag of evidence they'd collected and handed Prophet several plastic evidence bags, each containing a prescription pill bottle. Five in all.

"Who's the dead guy? Any one of the five different names on these bottle?" Prophet asked.

"He's a junkie," the female cop said. "Real name's Miles Jones. He probably bought or stole those pills. Wouldn't be the first time."

Prophet would check the name out anyway. As he pulled on latex gloves, he asked, "Got a license?" and she handed him Miles's wallet. Prophet went through the wallet, memorizing the man's name, address, and license number to run through his own systems.

She continued, "Place is clean. No signs of forced entry."

"So he let the killer in?"

"Lew—our chief of police—said he walked in on the crime in progress, but that it was already too late. Name of the man in custody is Tom Boudreaux."

The older cop, who hadn't said a word until now, muttered something at the mention of Tom's name and actually made the sign of the cross.

"You guys know this Boudreaux?" Prophet asked casually as he went over the body, looking for additional clues to the guy's death. The cuts on his wrists were pretty jagged, which would've required a heavy hand. If the guy had been high when he'd done this . . .

The female cop said, "Boudreaux's from around these parts. Least he was. Tried to come back but folks in the bayou ran him off eventually."

"What's the matter with him?" Prophet asked.

"Boudreaux's bad luck," she told him.

"Don't say his name," the older cop warned as he made the sign of the cross a second time, then pointed at Miles's body. "This bastard never had a chance after he got involved with the guy."

Prophet wanted to know exactly what *involved* meant, but he'd settle for finding out from Tom. After he was bailed out of prison. After he was cleared of a murder charge, for which it seemed like he might somehow have motive.

And here he'd thought nothing could be worse than the hurricane.

The cops went back to talking in low voices. Prophet listened as he snapped pictures, did a little dusting for prints on his own, which no one found strange. MEs were an odd bunch, all with their own quirks, as Prophet had discovered when he'd spent a few months undercover in a series of morgues for a black-ops mission that he never wanted to think about again. That was a whole other level of dealing with the dead.

He was almost done when he spotted the syringe under the chair in the hallway, adjacent to where Miles had been found. Level with someone lying on the ground, dying, who had maybe just enough strength to throw it out of reach.

Or he could've taken it from the murderer and done the same thing.

Prophet waited until he could grab it unnoticed and stuck it inside his glove and put it into his pocket. He bagged a few more things that might help, casually searched the house as if he had every right to do so, and came up with nothing but the fact that there was zero alcohol and not even a bottle of aspirin anywhere else, which didn't exactly jibe with the pill bottles. Addicts weren't notoriously clean and tidy. Sure, the house was in disrepair, but it was only the bottom floor that looked like there'd been some kind of struggle. The bedroom and bath were neat and clean, with towels folded and the bed made. A Bible and an AA manual were stacked on the bedside table.

As he went back down the stairs, his phone rang, another unknown number. "Yeah?"

"Is this Prophet?"

"Who's this?"

"Etienne. Della gave me your number. Before you do anything, head over to my shop." He rattled off an address and hung up before Prophet could ask who the hell Etienne actually *was*.

He told the cops he'd been called to another scene, told the EMT to send the body to the morgue, then walked out of the house and ditched everything but the evidence, picking up a police radio along the way, just for good measure.

Jesus, everyone let their guard down during a hurricane. It was a great time to kill someone or commit any kind of crime.

He tucked that away for future reference, imitated the young cop's voice on the radio to ask about Tom Boudreaux's whereabouts and learned he was just getting processed.

The address Etienne gave him was ten blocks over—he walked through the flooded streets, still empty save for emergency vehicles, even though the storm was pretty much done. He scanned the numbers once he got to the right street and saw it was a tattoo shop. Prophet stopped just short of it and stared, remembered Tom briefly mentioning his ex who gave him the tattoos.

"So it's fine when he brings up his exes," Prophet muttered to himself, looking at the *E's Ink* sign until a female voice enquired, "Looking for a reading?"

He was about to ask if that was some kind of New Orleans term for hooking but turned in time to see a pretty, dark-haired woman standing in the doorway of her shop, right next to *E's Ink*. The sign boasted *Accurate Psychic Readings*.

For the love of Christ. Being mistaken for a john would be better than this. "Not the best time," he said, suddenly anxious to meet Tom's ex.

"I'll read your palm for free." She came forward and took his hand without permission, which was normally a very bad thing. But she was a woman, so he tamped down his aggression and let her stare at his palm intently. Didn't bother telling her that Tom was really the only one who could predict his future, and it had nothing to do with his voodoo shit.

Finally, she looked up at him with a wide smile. "You're in perfect health."

"That's great," he managed, because he guessed going blind didn't count toward fucking health these days.

"And you're going to live a long life."

Again, *really* debatable.

"I see marriage and a child in your future too," she said quietly, like she knew that might throw him over the edge, and yeah, he was really the *come to daddy* type. He yanked his hand away, unreasonably angry as he stalked toward Etienne's place. She shouldn't lie to people, tell them good things when generally, good things weren't the norm . . .

"That's all people want to hear," a deep voice drawled, and Prophet looked at the smirking man in the doorway who had to be Etienne. Just had to be.

And Prophet must've been muttering out loud.

"You're not the first to come away from her saying that. People go in with an agenda and get pissed when she can't see it." Etienne was shorter than Prophet, probably five nine or so with a shock of blond crew-cut hair. He was heavily tattooed—the ink went up his neck and down to his fingers. But the tattoos were gorgeous. Different from Tommy's, but still art.

He also had a tongue piercing, which was pretty damned mesmerizing. Etienne knew it too. Add the piercing in his brow and his lip, and yeah, Tom looked tame. Until you saw him naked.

Which Prophet had. But maybe not as much as Etienne.

"What's up?" Etienne asked.

Wiseass. "You called me."

Etienne nodded. Motioned for Prophet to come further into the shop and closed and locked the door behind them. There was no power, but with the windows open and what must've been a battery-powered fan, the heat was tolerable.

Prophet leaned against one of the black leather tattoo tables as Etienne admitted, "Della called me about Tom's arrest and asked if anything'd been going on. Said you were an investigator she knew who was visiting her friend and might be able to help."

Why would Della think Etienne would know anything about Tom's arrest for the murder of some random guy from his past? And he also didn't know if he should strangle Della or hug her brilliance on that last part. She probably figured they'd get into a pissing contest over Tom—which still could happen most definitely—and had been trying to avoid it. "What's the problem?"

"I've been getting threats for the past couple of months."

"About Tom?"

Etienne shifted. "Kind of, yeah. You're the first one I've told. Figured anyone's better than the chief of police and his crew."

"There's a compliment in there somewhere, right?"

"No."

Asshole. He was beginning to see a pattern with the men Tommy was attracted to. "Did you grow up with Tom?"

"Yes." Etienne smirked. "We were boyfriends."

Was the guy trying to shock him? Or see how he'd deal with that? "Was Miles also Tom's ex?"

"No."

"How about Lew?"

Etienne snorted. "You couldn't find a more homophobic asshole if you tried. And I told Lew that when he called me about Tom's arrest."

"Must be pretty special if the chief of police personally calls you with news of Tom's arrest," Prophet saw Etienne's eyes darken. "And could you clarify if the threats are directed toward you or Tom or you *and* Tom."

"I'll take what's behind curtain number three," Etienne said.

"So you and the chief are close . . . and somehow Tom gets the short end of the stick."

Etienne's entire body tensed, but he remained otherwise surface calm. "Look, I'm not tight with Lew—or any of those cops. Lew called to rub it in. I just want to make sure Tom's all right."

That last part, Prophet actually believed, but the phone call from the chief of police still didn't make sense. "What can you tell me about Tom and his reputation around here?"

"How much time you got?" Etienne asked. His phone rang, and he glanced down at it. "Gotta take this. Give me a second."

Prophet nodded, and while Etienne spoke in rapid Cajun French, he flipped through the albums filled with sketches.

The walls were also lined with art and with pictures of people's actual tattoos. He recognized a few of them as Tommy's immediately, because he'd spent hours staring at them in person. And he'd stared, long and hard, traced them with his fingers and tongue, committed them to memory.

Etienne came up behind him, looked between him and the picture of Tom's dragon. "The next picture shows off better . . ."

"The way the tail wraps around his hipbone," Prophet finished without thinking.

"How's an investigator visiting Della's friend know what's on Tom's hip?"

Prophet glanced over at Etienne. "I'm good at what I do. You want to help me help him, you need to tell me all the shit you're holding back."

"No way. Not until *you* give up a little more about who the fuck you really are."

I fucking gave up everything already, Prophet wanted to shout. *And he gave me up.*

But instead, he walked around the shop, tapping every picture of Tommy's tattoos he saw. Eight pictures out of what had to be a hundred plus, but Prophet spotted them like beacons on a sinking ship on a dark night. He looked back at Etienne. "Good work."

"Good canvas. He drew them himself. Some I used the stencils, some I freehanded. Took a lotta years." Etienne didn't seem upset that Prophet might know Tom intimately. It actually had the opposite effect. "Lew's never gonna give him a fair shake."

"Why's that?"

"Not many people around here ever did." Etienne sighed. "Just tell him, no matter what happens, get the fuck out of here and don't come back."

"You can't tell him that yourself?"

"Better if he and I don't have contact, because I can't lie to him for shit. And that's more for his benefit than mine, all right?"

"Any idea who sent the threats you've been getting?"

"I have a general idea. Not sure if they're from Lew or the person who killed Miles. Or if they're one and the same. And no, I've got no evidence of that last part." Etienne showed him the texts, the first one dated about two months earlier. They were mostly of the standard *keep your mouth shut or you'll die* variety, but they escalated into some brutal language.

I'm going to kill you slowly. Gut you like a pig and let you bleed out while I watch. Gonna make your worst nightmare come true. Gonna make you and your boyfriend pay for everything you've done.

Prophet wanted to ask Etienne what the hell he and Tom could've possibly done, but knew that it was better to get question-and-answer time with Tom.

Etienne told him, "I'm gonna head down to the station now. I'll post Tom's bail."

"And they'll just let him out?" Prophet asked.

"It's complicated."

"Always is."

Etienne stared between a picture of Tom's dreamcatcher tattoo and Prophet. "He didn't kill Miles, and Lew knows it. They'll let him out because my father's the judge who helps Lew keep his job, no matter how many times Lew fucks up. So at least my family's good for something."

"I'll go with you to get Tommy."

Etienne smiled when *Tommy* slipped out of Prophet's mouth. "I knew you weren't a goddamned PI from the second we spoke on the phone."

"You got that voodoo shit going on too?"

"No. Just know what someone who cares about Tom sounds like."

"Let's get to the station before he gets himself in trouble," Prophet urged.

Etienne stared at him for a long moment. "Tom always had a fierce temper, but believe it or not, he's very slow to boil. Guess you know that once he gets there, shutting him down isn't easy."

Prophet recalled Tom's fight in the ring, the loss of control that seemed to come out of nowhere. But now, some of the puzzle pieces were fitting together.

On the way out, Etienne pointed to the tattoo gun and the piercing tools. "If you've got time after all this shit's over. I always did like virgins. Take your pick."

From anyone else, that line would've sounded cheesy. From Etienne, it sounded hot.

If you were mine, I'd make you pierce it.

Tom's voice, after he'd bit Prophet's nipple the first time they'd had sex. It tingled every fucking time Prophet thought about those words. He thought about how Tommy had sketched the dreamcatcher on his cast. How he'd fucked Prophet to sleep. How Doc told him Tommy had been upset when the dreamcatcher cast had been cut off.

Prophet was in so far over his head. And for someone who knew how to swim, that shouldn't've been nearly as terrifying as it was.

It was only as the police car had pulled up to the station, that what had happened started to sink in.

Prophet had seen him. Had thankfully hung back, so Tom knew it was only a matter of time before the man came to get him. But the way Lew was treating Tom, it might not matter. They sure as shit weren't going to give him bail. Or a phone call.

Miles, dead. Guilt washed over him for a moment, because there'd been many days in Tom's youth that he'd wished it upon Miles. And so many days since he'd left that he'd promised himself he'd never come back here because of Miles and Donny and the sheriff.

But if he hadn't come back here, he'd never have proven to himself how far he'd come. Although losing it with Lew showed him how far he still had to go. Didn't matter how quickly he pulled it together when he'd spotted Proph—he'd still lost it in the first place.

"Let's go." Lew pulled him out of the car roughly, nearly hitting Tom's head on the edge of the door. He'd also put the cuffs on him so damned tightly that Tom's hands had gone numb, but he didn't say anything.

"*Bad loque*," he heard one of the cops mutter as he was pulled along. Lew walked him down the steps to the overcrowded cell in the basement. Lew gave a hard tug on the cuffs before he took them off and shoved Tom inside, saying, "Guys, this is Tom—he's a *former* sheriff's deputy. Treat him as such."

There was an immediate buzz through the jailed men—a couple of catcalls, mixed with rumbles of the kind of violence that sprang up fast and uncontrollable. Violence he understood.

Bad luck. Bad news.

He flexed his hands to get the blood flowing now that the cuffs were off and put his back to the wall in the far corner. He didn't need training to tell him to do that; he'd learned at a young age that if his daddy was coming for him and there was no escape, he wouldn't get as hurt this way. Because at some point, his father would hit his fist against the wall instead of Tom and, if he was lucky, that would stop him. If he wasn't, Tom would at least get one less blow.

He pulled himself back to focus on the situation at hand. This wasn't the time to be dragged into the past, not when he was locked in this cell with fifteen other men, all in various states of intoxication and aggravation. The only air came from the large fan positioned overhead toward the open bars, but it barely moved the sticky air.

"Cop, huh?" one of the men said, his tattoos unmistakably those of a gang member.

"Not anymore," Tom said.

"So what, you're just like one of us?"

Tom didn't answer, felt the fight build inside of him, wouldn't be surprised if smoke started coming out of his ears. It had nothing to do with the men surrounding him. They would simply be the unfortunate ones to suffer the brunt of his anger.

He stared straight ahead, willed himself to stay calm. Made a mental note to ask Prophet how exactly he managed to do so.

"So, cop, what do you want us to know about you?"

Tom smiled and surrendered to the inevitable. Because you couldn't escape your fucking past, so why bother trying? "I'd rather show you."

CHAPTER TEN

Prophet waited in the back of Etienne's car, in the lot across the street from the police station. While he waited, the radio he'd lifted blurted out the news that there'd been a brawl in the downstairs cell.

And no surprise that Tom Boudreaux was involved.

"Fuck, Tommy," he muttered, punched the door of the car with the side of his fist. Watched tensely as an ambulance came and took away four men. None of whom were Tommy, which made his stomach unclench. So Tom had started—and finished—the brawl, apparently. And all he'd have to show for it would be an entirely new crop of enemies and some bruises. It also meant that there might be some assault charges pending. Which he'd find out if Etienne ever got the fuck back out here. He pondered storming the station but figured he'd make things worse.

Speaking of worse . . .

He pulled his phone out of his pocket when he heard the beep of a text that he recognized from his personal phone. Hoped it was from Tommy—like maybe the asshole could've made Prophet his one phone call—but knew it wouldn't be.

Cillian asking, *How's the bayou?*

Bayou's fine. I guess they didn't kill you.

They certainly tried. I hear your partner's in a bit of trouble.

"How the hell does he know that?" Prophet muttered. *How the hell do you know that?*

Don't bother searching your phone for chips.

Then how do you know?

Prophet, I know everything.

Fuck him, Cillian did. *Yeah, and? You gonna help him?*

I don't think I'm his favorite person. He's not exactly mine, either, since I know you stood me up for him. Although I know as well as anyone that work comes first.

Prophet nearly typed, *Tom's not work*, but something stopped him. Maybe it was for Tom's protection, or something else, but he simply answered, *Figured you'd understand.*

Seriously, anything?

Got it covered.

Good to know. Speaking of cover, please, tell Tom that, although I can appreciate his watchdoggedness, I prefer not to be investigated. Especially not by amateurs.

Ah, fuck. Should've known Tommy would do something like that. An odd part of him stirred, though, at the thought of Tommy doing shit like that for him. *I'll tell him, but I'm not his mother.*

No, definitely not that, Cillian responded. After several moments of nothing, Prophet was ready to put the phone away when Cillian texted again. *Answer me one question, though. Have you lost any sleep wondering what I was going to do to you once I got you on that couch?*

Prophet snorted, then stilled. He waited the appropriate amount of time that wouldn't trigger any of Cillian's psychological tendencies and typed, *How do you know I wasn't going to be doing that shit to you?*

Ah, yes, well . . . that's enough to make *me* lose sleep tonight.

Prophet closed the phone because Etienne was strolling back to the car, an hour after he'd gone inside. He got in behind the wheel and started the car.

"Aren't we going in for Tom?" Prophet asked.

"They already released him. He took off." Etienne tightened his hands on the wheel and blew out a breath.

"Either your family works miracles, or Lew really was busting his chops when he arrested him," Prophet muttered.

"Yeah, well, it's a lot of both, with a bit of *sometimes the truth prevails.* The ME says that Miles OD'd and cut his wrists. They're calling it a suicide." Etienne slammed the wheel with the butt of his palm.

"And you don't buy that? I saw the AA book in his room."

"It wasn't just an OD. He'd been clean for six months—the longest he'd ever been clean since he was a teenager."

"Addicts slip all the time," Prophet said. Refused to add, *They can't help themselves*, because he didn't always believe that everyone couldn't curtail their behaviors.

"There's no lost love between me and Miles. None. So if I don't believe it . . ." Etienne paused. "I can't fucking believe I'm still dealing with this shit. Should've pulled up stakes like Tom warned me to."

"Seems like he's got problems staying away."

Etienne stared at him in the rearview. "You can handle him."

"Yes."

"Do you want to?"

"I'm here, right? Can we go fucking find him before he finds more trouble?"

Etienne sighed, pulled keys out of his pocket and tossed them back to Prophet. "Those'll let you in to where he went—bet my life on it. I'll drop you off."

"I can get there on my own."

"I'm sure you can, but . . ."

"But?"

"I'm not going to be responsible for any more loss, all right? Tom needs you." He started the car and then paused. "Miles was deep into his recovery."

"What aren't you telling me? Beyond what you and Tom did when you were together that has someone threatening the hell out of you."

Etienne ignored the last part. "The rumors started after Miles's last few AA meetings."

"The meetings that are supposed to be confidential?"

"Yep. And then Miles calls me. When I didn't answer, he wrote me a letter."

"Do you have it?"

"I almost burned it, but I didn't want the bad karma."

"You people and your curses."

Etienne glared at him but didn't say a word. "He also wrote Tom a letter. I'm guessing the basics are the same. I wasn't going to pass it along to Tom but . . ." He reached into his back pocket as he drove, nearly running them off the road, and handed Prophet a sealed envelope with Tom's name on the front. Prophet stared at it, then put it into his pocket.

Etienne frowned. "Aren't you gonna read it?"

"I'm going to give it to Tom."

"You really don't know what happened to us."

"No. Want to share? Because I'm guessing you didn't bother to share with Lew."

All Etienne would say was, "It's a mess—and Lew knows all about it. The story's something that should come from Tom, not from me. But Miles confessing opened a whole can of worms. Probably for Donny too."

"Who's that?"

"Miles's best friend. Well, former. They had a falling-out years ago. He probably got a letter too."

Prophet understood Etienne's instinct to protect Tommy by not giving him more details about Miles—couldn't fault him for it, actually, since he'd been trying to protect Tom since he'd met him. Then again, it wasn't like Tom asked for it or wanted it. Which is probably why Prophet and Etienne did it. "Can I see those texts again?"

Etienne handed him his phone. "I had a friend trace them. Couldn't, because they're from a throwaway."

"Mind if I check their work?"

"Knock yourself out. Just get me the phone back when you can."

Like Prophet didn't have enough phones already, and all of them seemed to bring him nothing but trouble. Still, he pocketed it and asked, "How can I get in touch with Donny?"

"You can't."

"Okay, Etienne, enough with the cloak-and-dagger shit. I'm guessing you can get in touch with him and tell him to lay low, then? It's not like I have a lot of time to travel down the rest of Tom's memory lane here."

"Donny's not my favorite person, but yeah, I can." Etienne paused. "Tom's past is gonna come out, and it's gonna get ugly. You sure you're up for this? Because up 'til now, I've tried to keep you out, like Tom'd want, but you're a stubborn son of a bitch."

"Yeah, I know that," Prophet muttered. "And I'm not sure of anything." Etienne glanced at him in the rearview again, looked like he was going to say something, but changed his mind, shut his mouth, and drove Prophet through the flooded streets that turned to pure mud back roads of the bayou that was the source of all Tommy's pain.

CHAPTER ELEVEN

P rophet let the door swing open to the small cabin, tucked deep in the bayou, that Etienne called his studio. But he didn't walk through it. Not immediately.

He'd made Etienne drop him off down the road so Tom wouldn't hear the car coming, and obviously his voodoo-ometer was off, because he whirled around, surprised. Drew his weapon.

For a second, he kept it raised between them. Prophet stared at it and then at him, and Tom slowly lowered his arm and rested the gun back on an old table that was covered in paint, like the floor.

The little shit just stood there, surrounded by canvases in progress, looking at him defiantly. His face was bruised, his knuckles bloody, and it was hard to imagine that not more than eight hours ago, they had been fucking. And closer to common ground than Prophet could've ever hoped for.

Prophet strolled in, closed the door behind him with a slam. Grabbed a chair, turned it around, and sat, his arms folded over its back. "So . . . you and Cope."

Tom furrowed his brow. "Me and Cope?"

"You're getting along, then? You spent a lot of quality time with him."

"He's straight, you know."

"Did you hit on him without realizing that?"

"God," Tom snarled, "I want to hit *you* when you act like that with me." And yep, the brawl had made his anger worse. The place reverberated with it.

"Business as usual," Prophet said quietly. "Good to know nothing's changed."

"Right. *Nothing's* changed."

"Emphasis noted." The silence stretched between them like a lonely road. "So, did you kill your ex-boyfriend?"

"Jesus H. Christ, Prophet."

"It's a legitimate question."

"Only from an asshole. And Miles is *not* my fucking ex-boyfriend." Tom ran a hand through his hair. It was longer than Prophet was used to. A couple of months in EE did that to most operatives.

He also noted that the bracelet he was used to seeing on Tommy's wrist was gone. He glanced at the table, where Tom's gun and wallet were, and the bracelet lay there, most likely taken off when he was booked, but not put back on. "I'm supposed to call my watchdog off," he said quietly.

Tom blinked. Comprehended faster than he'd pretended to. "Is that what you're doing?"

"It's better if you stop following him."

"You're into doing what Cillian tells you to?" Tom's voice was low and dangerous.

"I'm into people not being in my business."

"Right. Just a select few are allowed in."

"I don't want anyone in more danger because of me than they need to be."

"Right." Tom's drawl was as thick as the tension.

"I didn't kill *your* ex," Prophet said, in part to change the topic. And, in part to piss Tom off. "But he did call me. Wanted me to meet him."

Tom's hands fisted, then opened. "About what?"

"You."

"Are you making this shit up?"

"Why would I do that? Figured Etienne and I should pool our knowledge and figure out why the fuck you were almost framed."

"I know why."

"Want to share with the class?"

Tom threw himself into a seat. Based on his expression, the answer was a solid no, but Prophet never let that stop him. "Not really, Teach."

"Sarcasm's my domain, not yours," Prophet informed him seriously. "Who the fuck was Miles to you?"

"Someone who made my goddamned life hell when I was growing up. Just like ninety percent of the fucking parish. Happy now?" Tom stood so fast the chair fell behind him.

"Thrilled," Prophet said dryly. "Now sit the fuck back down, because Teach isn't done."

Tom fought the urge to say *make me*, because that would make everything so much worse. His temper was already tipped and it wouldn't be hard to slam him back over that edge.

Please, Proph, don't push me there, he begged silently, but he couldn't bring himself to say the words. His stomach recoiled at the look in Prophet's eyes. Eyes, between the color of slate and granite, liquid steel, a black-bellied cloud, low and dangerous enough to make Tom's throat tighten.

So he sat, because he couldn't hide from Prophet's gaze.

Finally, Prophet stood. Shoved the chair out of the way as he slowly closed the distance between them. "You separated from me back there. That's a lot different than disagreeing on which way to go. You don't fucking separate from me. We work together."

"Thought we weren't partners."

"We were working together today. Christ, T, do you do this on goddamned purpose? Push your partners away so you can prove no one listens to you?"

"That's not fair."

"And now you're hiding out here—"

Tom stood and shoved his chair out of the way too. "I'm not hiding."

"Really?'

"Lew knows I'm here. The sheriff knows I'm here. The whole fucking parish does."

"Is that why I wasn't informed, because I'm not part of your fucking parish?"

"You don't need any of this shit coming down on you because of me," Tom said.

Prophet's jaw clenched, and he paused, like he was taking a moment to acknowledge the painful irony of those words. But then, "Did you lose it in the fight today?"

Tom winced internally. "I don't remember." His voice sounded hollow, even to his own ears.

"Let me guess—Lew put you in a cell with fuckups. Maybe even told them you used to be a deputy, right?"

Tom refused to answer, so Prophet continued, demanding, "You do know where the cops were planning on putting you if you hadn't been released, right? General population, right? Letting everyone know you were a cop *and* a Fed." Prophet sucked in a deep breath and growled, "And maybe, just fucking maybe, if you'd waited for me, you wouldn't be in this goddamned mess."

"Because you would've stopped me from running into a house with a body on the floor?"

"I think you'd have more goddamned sense, considering the reputation you apparently have in this shithole."

That definitely hit the mark Prophet had to have been aiming for. Tom placed a hand over his chest because it felt like Prophet's words had pierced his goddamned heart, and Prophet looked pleased. But he was apparently far from done.

Tom backed up as Prophet advanced toward him. But he ran out of space and hit the wall. Prophet didn't stop, his gray eyes boring into Tom's, so dark and angry and somehow freaking exquisite at the same time. His hair was longer, fell across his forehead, and Tom remembered holding Prophet in place by it earlier. When he'd been in control.

Semi-control.

He wasn't in that position now if Prophet's predatory stance was any indication. And the man moved fast, grabbing him, picking him up, and Tom struggled for just a second before Prophet growled, "Don't you goddamned fight me. Not now. Not fucking now."

Tom stopped. Prophet dumped him unceremoniously onto the bed, and Tom struggled to get a grip on anything, including himself, but then Prophet straddled him.

"I don't know what the fuck to do with you, T," Prophet murmured. "Don't know how to get through to you."

"Don't people normally say that to you?" Tom wiseassed back and instantly regretted it. Because the look on Prophet's face told him two things—he'd been right, and he'd given Prophet ideas about how to get through to Tom. He saw it in the flash of anger before Prophet's expression settled into the calm of a man who knew he was in charge and planned on keeping it that way.

Which meant that Tom was completely at the mercy of Prophet's impending wildness, could feel it shaking the space between them like a stampede of wild horses.

No one had ever tamed Prophet. Tom could only hope to possibly keep the man's interest while letting him run wild.

He swallowed hard as Prophet put his hands on the collar of his T-shirt and then ripped it in half as if it were made of paper. A clean split down the middle, and then he left it hanging there on Tom's shoulders.

Tom stilled, left his hands at his sides. Prophet hadn't commanded him to. Not with words, anyway, but it was times like this that Tom could truly see how completely badassed the man hovering over him was.

He wanted that. Craved it.

Prophet smiled then, the smile of someone who had a secret. He ran a finger around Tom's nipple, tugged the bar almost absently, as whatever plan he was concocting unfolded inside his head.

In a split second, the mood changed. Prophet eased off him, and before Tom had time to miss the contact, Prophet flipped him so he landed on his face. Prophet yanked his arms up behind his back, like he was going to handcuff Tom, but used the ends of the shirt to tie him instead, which also partially immobilized his shoulders. The bindings were tight and impossible to rip, based on the position Prophet had him in.

He heard a couple of drawers opening and closing, but Prophet still held him in place with one hand. And then Prophet reached under him, unbuttoned and unzipped his jeans and pulled them down, along with his boxer briefs—carefully, no doubt because of the piercings. And then he slowly eased Tom's hips into the air, spreading his thighs wide, which left Tom naked, open, and vulnerable.

He had no choice but to rest his cheek against the sheet, so aware of how bound he was, so painfully aware that he both hated this and desperately wanted this at the same time. He had no real way to move without throwing himself completely off-balance.

He'd have to rely on Prophet, let him take what he wanted, what they both needed.

As if to prove that point, Prophet trailed a slickly lubed finger between his ass cheeks, pressed against his opening, and Tom groaned. Tried to push against the finger and couldn't. Prophet put a hand on his shoulder to both steady him and keep him from moving, from seeking the pleasure he wanted.

Prophet's finger breached him, but it was too damned gentle. Tom tried to breathe, closed his eyes, tried to go with it. He was rewarded with a second finger and a sharp twist that made Prophet's fingertips brush his gland. He whimpered as his body demanded more, immediately.

Prophet, though, was content with setting a leisurely rhythm, taking and keeping charge. Tom buried his face into the sheets, muttered, "C'mon Proph," and was rewarded with a hard slap on his ass.

And by reward, he meant *reward*.

Tom blew out a hard breath at the sharp sting and waited for more. When none came, he begged, "Come on. You promised."

"Fucker. Not supposed to enjoy it."

But there was no way Prophet believed that. He was as intimately acquainted with the pleasure-pain continuum that Tom skated across as Tom was, because it was mapped all over his body.

As if reading his mind, Prophet reached his hand around and tugged a nipple bar hard. Tom hissed, and Prophet delivered several more hard, heated slaps. Tom wanted to reach around and grab his cock, tugged on the bonds in frustration. And the bastard chuckled. Moved his hand to play with Tom's cock piercings, a slight pull on each of them until Tom was jumping out of his skin.

And so it went—slaps mixed with tugs, until Tom was so mixed up with the sensations that he didn't know if he was coming or going. And he didn't care as long as Prophet didn't stop.

Finally, Prophet lined up behind him, dragged his cock along Tom's ass, thrusting back and forth with that minimal contact that would never be enough. Tom's skin was slick with sweat, and he'd nearly bitten through the sheets in an effort not to curse Prophet out for making him goddamned suffer.

And then Prophet was inside him, a long, not-so-slow slide that had Tom full-fledged cursing, yanking at the bindings, trying to get free and get closer to Prophet.

Prophet drew his cock out and in, the same goddamned slow pace he'd already set. A hand on his shoulder, holding him tight to the bed, the other on Tom's hip. He thrust as he pulled Tom's hips to him to make the force of his thrusts greater. Tom was trembling, inside and out. "Fucking the fight out of me?"

"Keep digging yourself deeper," Prophet told him, slapping his already sore ass, and fuck, Prophet knew he would.

Several deep thrusts had Tom whimpering. Begging. Headed toward incoherence, which was obviously how Prophet wanted it.

"Please, Proph. You know what I need."

"Yeah, Tommy. I do," Prophet said quietly.

His hips snapped against Tom, flesh slapped flesh, and their groans and curses filled the room. Tom came with jerky motions as Prophet's cock pressed against his gland, continuing to milk him, prolonging his orgasm much longer than he could ever remember it being before.

It was only after he was able to see again that he realized Prophet hadn't come. And he didn't seem to want to. He remained inside Tom, his body close as he rubbed a hand over Tom's back instead, asked, "What did the police say to you when they released you?"

Not the normal post-sex talk, but nothing was fucking normal anymore. "They told me not to leave the city limits of New Orleans or these parishes."

"Was I right about what happened to you in that cell?"

Tom glanced at him over his shoulder but couldn't bring himself to admit it. "I tripped. Down the stairs."

"I will fucking kill Lew." Prophet ran a hand along Tom's side. "Ribs?"

"Just bruised. And I'm not telling you what happened, Proph, because I don't want you to do anything stupid. I've already done enough, okay?"

Prophet ran a hand over his cheek as if he knew that was as much of an admission as he'd get for the moment. Kissed the back of his neck before muttering, "Dammit, Tommy."

"I didn't think I'd be let out."

"Etienne said the ME ruled it a suicide."

"When have you ever known an ME to rule that quickly?"

"In this town, I don't know what the fuck's going on, but your ex's family seems to be willing to lend a helping hand." Prophet paused. "Although Etienne said that this time it wasn't necessary. So what, you think Lew had an ulterior motive in letting you out?"

Tom nodded. Tested the bonds. Prophet's hands landed on his wrists, letting him know he wasn't being let go just yet.

"I want to call you fucking paranoid—and I hope to hell that's all it is—but dammit, my gut's screaming too." He shifted off Tom, pulling out of him and pushing Tom so they were both on their sides, facing each other. "Which is why you don't leave my side."

"I didn't mean to fight like that," Tom said suddenly. But he'd felt like he'd been fighting for his life, fighting against everyone and everything in this goddamned place.

He'd been fighting his past. You'd think by now he'd have realized that never worked.

"If you harnessed your temper, stayed in control when you fought, you'd be as dangerous as fuck."

"So teach me."

"You're dangerous enough already."

Tom turned to stare at him. "You going to untie me?"

"That depends."

"On what?"

"On if you're going to continue to spiral down."

Tom stared at the sheets. "Keep me tied."

Tom woke from a brief nap with sore arms, a sorer ass, face, and ribs and less of a piss-poor attitude than he'd thought he'd have.

He glanced over at Prophet, who was texting, concentrating on the screen, a small smile tugging at his lips. Without looking at him,

Prophet said, "I know you were dogging Cillian in Somalia. That you followed him to four different hotels. That you were nearly robbed and beaten twice."

"How do you know all of that?" Tom demanded, attitude newly engaged and prepared to launch, because he'd told no one that, not Cope or Phil. Hadn't emailed or called anyone from his EE phone while he'd been there.

Finally, Prophet looked up at him. And lied. "Cillian told me."

"Try again. He might've known I was following him, but I'm not that fucking transparent. Personally, I think it was just a lucky guess."

Prophet sighed. "That lead you had on Cillian? That source who was helping you track him? *Cillian* was the source who tipped you off. You were going in circles most of the time. At one point, he had you tracking me."

"Again, how do you know all these things that almost happened to me? Was Cillian following me? Why bother to throw me off the track then?"

"I have a lot of sources, Tommy."

"Maybe someday I could meet some of them," Tom shot back. "Are you working for Cillian?"

"Not for him. He had a job. A one-off. Offered it. I took it. Freelance. All mine. And for the record, he made sure you were a good three days behind me every step of the way." He paused. "That was early on, when you first got to Eritrea. And you were alone, right? Not with Cope? Zero backup in a part of the world you're not familiar with?"

Tom hung his head. Prophet stood, pocketed his phone, and knelt on the bed behind Tom. Untied the T-shirt and rubbed his wrists and arms to get the blood circulating. Tom didn't deserve that at all, but Prophet didn't seem angry anymore. He'd softened, and that made Tom feel worse. "Cillian played me. Asshole's better than I gave him credit for."

"He's good, T. Really fucking good. You need to back off him completely."

"Why aren't you? Is this about Sadiq?"

"What's your issue with Cillian?"

"I don't trust him."

"But he's not doing anything for you to trust or not to trust."

"He's looking into things for you. Anything that concerns you . . ." He stopped, feeling more than halfway foolish by saying it out loud. Putting stuff like that into an email was one thing but . . .

Prophet stroked a hand along the back of his neck—a cool touch against his suddenly overheated skin. "He was."

Tom turned to stare up at him. "And?"

A tick in Prophet's jaw, and then, "He told me John's dead."

"And I know you can't be fucking thinking about believing him."

"I have no reason to think he's lying."

"Bullshit you don't. Prophet, come the fuck on. You searched for the guy for two years, found nothing. I'm sure, even after you came back from the search, you kept looking, am I right? And in the space of what, weeks, Cillian finds his body?"

Prophet blinked at him. "Maybe it was never lost."

Tom slammed a fist against the bed. "I don't know why I bother."

"Me neither."

"Fucking impossible."

Prophet nodded, accepting that easily. Like the guy enjoyed owning it. And then he conceded slightly. "Look, I also took that job—a lot of jobs—to throw Cillian off track."

"How so?"

"If Cillian knew I was too busy to sniff around—because he's gotta know I don't fully believe him about finding proof of John's death—and he knows you can't get close to him, then he'll go about his business like he's got nothing to worry about."

"Does he, though?"

"Yep. Mal."

"So Phil knows . . ."

"Nothing," Prophet said sharply. "He can't know. For his safety. For the safety of everyone else at EE."

Tom nodded and tried to process everything Prophet had just told him. "Did I fuck things up?"

"No. It actually helped," Prophet admitted grudgingly. "Your reaction to Cillian . . . is that because you don't like the guy or because—"

"It's not because of Cillian. I just don't believe him. And neither do you." Tom pointed at him, then dropped his hand. "Let me help you find John. I want to be your goddamned partner. And I know I chose Cope—but I guess I was hoping we could still . . ."

"Fuck?" Prophet asked.

"I didn't want to lose you, Proph. That's what it was all about."

Prophet nodded tiredly. "Can we deal with one thing at a time? Your crisis is a little more pressing than a man I've been trying to find for ten years."

"Yeah. But can you do one thing first?"

"What's that?"

"Put that back on me?" He motioned to the bracelet on the table next to where Prophet had been sitting. "I wanted to, but it didn't seem right."

God, could he sound more fucking stupid? But he was done hiding, and it was the way he felt.

Prophet didn't hesitate, got up, grabbed the bracelet, sat next to Tom on the bed, and tied the thin strip of leather around his wrist. Tom flashed back to the first time he'd done so, before the cage match, when Tom had been as turned around as he was now.

But he knew a hell of a lot more now, about himself and Prophet, and he took comfort in that as he slid his hand into Prophet's. He was thinner but somehow more muscled, the look of a battle-worn soldier who used his job in lieu of a gym. "I keep getting you in trouble."

Bad loque.

"I'd follow your gut anywhere, T. That's not the issue. I'm worried about *you*."

"I know you get angry, Proph. Don't you ever fight? Just fucking lose it and start punching whoever's closest?" He realized he'd growled those words, that his hands had fisted.

Prophet, of course, had too. Reached out and physically unfisted Tom's hands. "I try not to. And when I do, I don't fight angry. Anger gives your opponent the upper hand."

"Ivan didn't have the upper hand in that cage match."

"Of course he did—you hurt him when you didn't mean to, and that shit will haunt you forever."

He hated Prophet for being right. "You took care of John like this. And you grew to resent it."

"After a while, yes. I hated feeling guilty about it, about him. But the more violent he got, the more angry he became. It escalated, and by the end, I was more his keeper than his lover. And I won't go there again. I can't. Because as shitty as it was for me, it was actually worse for John. Much worse. So that was my fault."

"You're not responsible for anyone else's—"

"I made myself responsible," Prophet interrupted, and Tom knew when to cut his losses, so he closed the subject and opened a new one.

"I'm going to clean up. Then I need to make a stop. Will you come with me, Proph?"

"Of course, T," Prophet told him without a second's hesitation. "'S'why I'm here."

CHAPTER TWELVE

Prophet followed Tom through the bramble of tall grass and other plants that lined the bayou. The heat of the day had waned as the afternoon pushed into early evening, and there was still a decent breeze, the remnant of the hurricane that had put all this shit into motion.

Granted, something good had come out of it. Someone. It hurt to watch Tom's shoulders set so stiffly as he walked ahead, like he was marching to his death. Tom wouldn't tell him where they were going, only assured him that no one would follow their asses out here.

And Prophet could see why. You could fucking die out here, and no one would ever find you.

At first, they'd driven Etienne's old Jeep through flooded roads. The sun was fighting to come out and water had receded somewhat, leaving some roads still inaccessible, but Tom knew every single back road and shortcut in this damned place.

They'd left the Jeep half a mile back.

"This is a graveyard," Prophet said suddenly as stone mausoleums suddenly loomed out everywhere between the tall grasses.

"Yes."

"Why isn't it underwater?"

"It's never flooded. It's one of the only places that doesn't."

"But the bodies are still all above ground."

"Yeah, they're shoved into these mausoleums together." Tom pointed to the nameplates on the sides as they walked.

"That's not right."

"Everyone says it's not right that this place never takes on water. It's low enough. The surrounding areas always flood."

"So what, Mother Nature has respect for the dead?"

"They say it's because there's evil buried here."

"Evil?"

"People who weren't allowed to be buried with their families. The unclaimed. Criminals." Tom's face wore a troubled expression. He'd stopped at a small clearing and Prophet came up next to him to see a small gravestone, the only one that was clearly marked and not brimming with overgrowth. Someone tended lovingly to this grave.

"That's my mom's grave," Tom said in answer to Prophet's unspoken question.

"She's all by herself."

"They have too much respect for the criminals to bury them next to her," Tom said, his voice tight.

Prophet put a hand on his shoulder, but didn't push Tom further. Everything in its time. "Do you do the upkeep?"

"When I'm here. When I can't be, I pay old man Brown to come out here and do this for me. Don't want her to be forgotten. Feel bad the rest of them are." He shrugged sadly. "I was too young to have a say where she was buried, because it sure as hell wouldn't've been here. But I don't believe in disturbing the dead unless I absolutely have to."

"How old were you when she died?"

Tom glanced at him. "She died in childbirth."

"Ah, Tommy."

Tom shoved his hands in his pockets. "Thanks for coming along. I know you wouldn't let me go alone, but that's not the only reason I asked you." He glanced at Prophet with a hint of laughter with zero humor behind it. "Correction: I shouldn't come alone. Don't say you can't teach me anything."

Prophet gave Tom's shoulder a reassuring squeeze. "Want me to give you some space?"

"Yeah. If you don't mind."

Prophet didn't, backed away to where he could keep an eye on Tommy and the area that surrounded him. He'd never been a religious man, but he'd been known to say a prayer or two. So he sent one up for Tom's mother.

Had a million questions that he expected Tommy wanted to give him answers to today. Bringing him here was the breaking of the dam. The flood of information would follow shortly.

And reciprocation would be a complete and total bitch—and Tom would definitely demand it once he got his head back on straight. But Prophet had already let him in more than he should've.

And you know that's not even enough to scratch the surface.

Finally, Tom broke away from the grave and started walking toward Prophet.

Then he stopped cold and turned to stare. The hairs on the back of Prophet's neck rose as he recognized Tom's call to voodoo. Didn't like drawing in a cemetery, but he had his weapon out, ready to cover Tom.

Tom stared north, then walked backwards to Prophet. When he got to Prophet's side, Prophet noted he'd also drawn his weapon.

"Someone's watching," Tom said. "By the shack at two o'clock."

"The law?"

"No. Definitely not."

Prophet knew when Tom's voodoo was talking. And then Tom said, "Gonna storm it."

Prophet caught himself before he groaned out loud, because what the fuck. "Seriously?"

"Yeah. You in?" Tom asked, but Prophet noted there wasn't any anger in his voice—just determination and focus.

So Prophet relented. Slightly. "Why don't you let me break in around the back?"

Before Tom could say yes or no, Prophet had disappeared. Guy was like a fucking ghost. Tom waited a few minutes then took off toward the shack at a run. Could hear Prophet's voice in his head even now.

You really have a death wish, Cajun.

But Tom barreled in the front of the shack anyway, and Prophet just shook his head. "Really?" the bastard asked. "You waited like a second?"

"You would've warned me if I shouldn't come."

"Yeah, true." Prophet pointed to the prone man on the floor in front of him. "You know him?"

Tom nodded. "How hard did you hit him?"

"Not hard enough," Prophet said as the guy started moving.

"Good." Tom bent down and searched Charlie, making sure he didn't have any hidden weapons. He pulled out a bag of what he assumed was Charlie's special homegrown weed. Prophet examined the baggie, and Tom told him, "It's good shit. Grows it himself."

Prophet raised a brow.

"It's good shit for headaches."

"Did you smoke when you were in the sheriff's office?"

"It was the only way Charlie'd give me intel."

"He's an informant?"

"Yeah. The stoner persona helps. No one suspects he remembers anything, but the guy's got a mind like a steel trap."

Prophet glanced around. "He doesn't live here, does he?"

"No. 'S'where I'd meet him, back in the day."

"He gonna talk if I'm here?"

"Yes." He spoke to Charlie in rapid Cajun French until the man's eyes focused. Well, as much as they ever did. Said he'd turn him over the FBI if Charlie breathed a word of this conversation they were about to have.

That got Charlie's attention for sure. He nodded briskly, because he always wanted to please. "I get it, Tom, but what the hell? You could just come to me. Instead, you send this asshole to—"

"What asshole'd that be?" Prophet demanded, and Charlie held up both hands.

"I'm a pacifist."

"You're stoned," Prophet said.

"He says that like it's a bad thing," Charlie told Tom. "Maybe if he smoked a little . . ."

Tom dragged Charlie to his feet. "I'd quit while I was ahead."

"Fine. Look man, there are drugs runnin' through here. Comin' down the bayou."

"Always are. Cutting into your territory?" Tom asked.

"No way, man. I'm not talking about Mary Jane. I'm talking big shit. Special K and shit like that."

"Any idea who?"

"Miles. Says he's clean, but that's bullshit."

"Figures," Tom said. He didn't offer up the fact that Miles was dead. "When's the last time you spoke to him?"

"Not since he went into that bullshit AA. I know he's still using, but he's not buying from me. So I followed him a couple of times last month. And I think the sheriff's involved."

"I'd bet on it." Tom looked out the window. "You can head out, Charlie."

Charlie nodded, tipped an imaginary hat in Prophet's direction, and disappeared out the door and into the tall grasses.

"Gotta find a better class of informants," Prophet told him.

"I think he's lying."

"No shit."

"He never lied to me before."

"And you think Charlie's not going to mention this discussion with you to the police?"

"I told him I'd turn him over to the FBI if he talked. He'll keep his mouth shut." They left the shack and walked the narrow path to the truck. He stayed in front so he could scan the area for snakes and the like. Because for a guy who'd lived in Texas . . .

"Dude, it's not the snakes that are the problem," Prophet protested. "Any alligators around?"

"There are always gators around."

"Feel free to lie to me about that shit."

He turned around suddenly and faced Prophet. "Cope's a good guy, but he's not you."

"No one's like me."

Goddamn, but he'd really missed this man. "You might be the only one in the world who can say shit like that and not sound like an asshole. Most of the time." Prophet smiled, rested a heavy hand on Tom's shoulder, which somehow managed to take the weight of the world off him. "I can't believe you came here after I left you behind. Fuck, Prophet, I'm sorry."

Prophet kept his voice quiet when he said, "Don't apologize, T. Just do me a favor—from now on, don't let your superstitions win."

"My superstitions tend to come true," Tom said quietly, but that wasn't an outright no.

Tom met his eyes quickly, then glanced down at Prophet's bare forearms. He traced his hands over them, asking, "How long did you leave the casts on?"

"Two months. Month off and then three more weeks."

Tom stared at the muscled forearms. "Good spot for tattoos."

"I guess you'd know." He thought about how he'd traced the falcon on Tom's back with his tongue last night, the wings spanning between his shoulder blades. Fierce and beautiful, and completely original, just like the man who wore it. It looked like it was rising from Tom, was strong enough to carry him with it.

Falcon.

Skull.

Evil Eye.

Nautical Star.

Dreamcatcher.

Symbols of protection, permanently etched into Tom's skin. Prophet guessed that this way Tom could always carry his mojo with him.

Even the falcon that spread its wings between Tommy's shoulder blades was significant, symbolizing freedom, something Prophet figured Tom had found once he left the bayou. But something kept pulling him back.

Maybe you never really buried your ghosts.

Maybe the only time they were truly dead and buried was when you were. And even then, Prophet wouldn't be so sure.

CHAPTER THIRTEEN

Prophet drove them back to Etienne's studio. Tom sacked out the second he hit the car and didn't wake for the half and a hour drive, even after Prophet parked.

Prophet checked the area out—it was dusk and the lights were on. Everything seemed to be in order. He opened Tom's door, shook him a little. Tom barely woke, and Prophet ended up half walking, half carrying him onto the porch. He turned the doorknob, because they'd left the place unlocked, as Etienne always did, kicked it open the rest of the way, then stilled.

"I've got to be hallucinating," he muttered. At his words, Tom roused more fully and glanced at him, then followed his gaze to the middle of the floor. "This isn't good."

"Ya think?"

"This has to be your fault," he told Tommy.

"You think I invited the alligator in here?"

"Isn't this your people?"

"My people? Are you calling my people alligators?" And then Tommy continued talking to him. In Cajun French.

"I have no idea what you're saying—you know that, right?" The alligator looked at him mutinously, and he waved in Tom's direction. "What? He's your friend—go talk to him."

"Let me go, Proph."

"No way. I'm going to . . ." He started to walk backward, dragging Tom with him, but the thing advanced.

"Prophet, let me go and don't move. We've got to shut the door behind us."

"And lock us in here with that?" Prophet asked as he took his hand off Tom gingerly, prepared to grab him again at any moment if he did something stupid.

"Yes. Because there'll be more behind it."

"You're kidding."

"You're going to argue with me now?"

Prophet leaned back without moving his feet and shut the door quietly. The alligator, which was at least five feet in length, still advanced a little, and Prophet waved his gun at it.

Tom grabbed his arm and pushed it down. "This is a message."

"And my message back's going to be damned effective," Prophet said, raising his gun again.

In turn, Tom was doing something to a length of rope he'd grabbed from a pile of crap on a table near the door. He handed Prophet his gun and his phone, then pushed his arm holding the gun down again. "Don't shoot, okay? I've got to answer it. I've got this."

"What're you...?"

The words were still floating in the air when Tom moved past him to circle the gator.

Prophet stopped breathing, completely stopped breathing, and watched as Tom's body language eased. His shoulders rolled. He looked completely confident, even as the gator moved closer. Tom jumped over it. The gator bit for him, and Prophet cursed but couldn't shoot, because Tommy was in the goddamned shot.

But before the gator could turn completely to Tommy, it closed its mouth and went to roll. At that moment, Tommy got the rope around the jaws and tugged hard. Then he slammed onto the thing's back, holding the rope fast and also using his hands to hold the strong jaws closed. The gator went into a death roll, but the place wasn't big. It only took a few rolls for Tommy and the gator to hit the wall hard, the gator on top of Tom, its belly in the air.

"Duct tape," Tom gasped.

Prophet yanked it from his pocket, held it up. "You made fun of me for carrying this—"

"Could you save the lecture for later?"

"—when it's obviously coming in handy," Prophet said triumphantly.

"Wrap it around the jaws."

"Me?"

"I'm busy keeping it from killing us. You have the easy job. It's disoriented for now."

Prophet wound the tape around the animal's mouth, muttering the whole time.

"Now tie the front arms together, then the back," Tom instructed.

Finally, once Prophet was done, Tom rolled the gator onto the floor, and stayed on its back while he pulled off his T-shirt and put it over the gator's eyes. "Watch the tail—this guy could still kill you when I roll him back to his belly."

"What? You're gonna do a catch and release?"

"No. Too big. He's considered a nuisance gator and he's gotta be put down. I wouldn't've rolled him like that if I was going to do a catch and release. Damages the nervous system to keep them on their backs."

"Thanks for the lecture, alligator man."

Tom rolled his eyes, grabbed the gator's tail, and began to pull it out of the room. "This is what my daddy does."

"Like, for sport?"

"For a living. I grew up doing alligator nuisance calls."

Prophet opened the door for him. "I thought you said there'd be more behind it."

"And you fell for it. You're easy, Proph."

Prophet followed him outside at a good enough distance, prepared to continue the conversation, at the very least, when he noticed the tall older guy waiting at the bottom of the stairs. This must be the messenger, especially when Tom tossed the gator, sent it flying. Directly at the messenger. The man seemed unconcerned, simply stepping casually to the side so it missed him.

"This place is not fucking normal," Prophet muttered.

Tom held his hand out. "Weapon."

Prophet handed it to him and Tom shot the gator cleanly, right between the eyes.

And that's exactly what he'd wanted to do, before Tommy'd decided to become the alligator whisperer.

Pretty fucking hot, though.

"Dad, this is Prophet. He's my partner. Proph, this is Gil Boudreaux."

Tom's dad stared at him. "You queer too?"

"Yes, sir," Prophet said.

"He's also a vet," Tom said, and Prophet was pretty sure he'd only done so to piss his father off more, because the man muttered something about, "Letting queers into the military was criminal."

It was a move Prophet respected, even though Tom had used him to do it. Prophet knew Gil Boudreaux's issues with his son went well beyond Tom's sexual orientation.

"He's also my partner at my new job," Tom continued, and really? Because last time Prophet'd looked . . .

Tom glanced at him, his look implying, *Not now, Proph . . . we'll discuss it later.*

The fact that Tom had called him partner, in both senses of the word, well, that was something he'd definitely need to unpack after Tom's father was gone. Didn't know if it was simply post-alligator bravado, or if Tom was trying to claim him.

The man was just a bit taller than Tom, broader too, with a paunch from drinking, plus the telltale broken capillaries around the nose. His skin looked like dried alligator hide, and his hands were giant. Prophet almost winced outwardly when he thought about the damage those hands could do to a small boy, but caught himself.

This wasn't a man you showed weaknesses to. Gil Boudreaux was definitely looking for them.

"You finally came back. Hid like a pussy for too damned long."

"I was working out of the country."

"You been by the sheriff's yet?"

"No."

"Still hidin'?"

"Jesus, do they make bigger assholes than you?" Prophet asked. When Gil advanced on him, Prophet advanced right back. "Try it, old man. Go ahead. I'm not your family, so I don't have to take things easy on you."

"I've got this, Proph," Tom said with an easy grace under pressure that Prophet wasn't sure he could ever have. He held his hands up, a silent surrender for Tom only, and he backed off.

"Heard you got arrested," Gil said to his son.

"Guess I'm finally living up to your expectations," Tom said.

Jesus, T.

Tom's father seriously growled and took a step in Tom's direction, and Tom did the same to his father.

"You shouldn't come back here. Always bring nothin' but trouble."

"You're right. And this time, trouble's not leaving until he gets to the bottom of things."

"You'd better watch yourself and that other queer with the tattoos."

Tom rolled his eyes. "Amazing you can tell us apart. And I always watch myself, but why is Etienne in trouble?"

"All I know's that his momma and daddy shoulda did the right thing and disowned him."

"Guess you should've done it too," Tom said. "Although maybe it was more fun to have a punching bag. And then an excuse to drink."

"Pushin' your luck, boy."

Tom laughed. "Luck? What luck? *Bad loque*'s all I ever had."

"Come on, T," Prophet urged, tugged his arm, pulling him up the porch stairs and into the studio, although Tom kept eye contact with his father the entire time. "Not going to get anywhere. Blood from a stone."

This was the cause of Tom's temper. The man in front of him had a bad temper too, and sure, some of that shit was inherited. But a lot of it was nurtured.

Prophet shut the door on Gil Boudreaux.

Tom had fought for his life here, just like Della had said . . . and he still was. Prophet would make sure that, this time, Tom wasn't doing it alone.

Tom went to wash up, and Prophet hung around the main room of the studio, trying to figure out how big of a liability Gil was to Tommy.

Tom *was* pissed, but he wasn't upset, not the way Prophet was for him. In fact, the whole thing, from wrestling the goddamned alligator to going purposely out of his way to goad his old man into anger, had somehow centered Tom.

And there was also no denying that there'd been a spark in Tom's eyes that he liked to see.

He glanced back toward the bathroom, where the shower was still running, then turned away to lean against the wall next to the window, where he could get a clear view of the makeshift path leading to this place. His frustration built as the wash of adrenaline and the subsequent drop-off affected his body. He was hard as hell too, because he couldn't stop picturing Tommy calmly rolling that gator, like it was nothing. His shirtless chest as he dragged the thing outside and shot it wasn't a bad image either.

It took will and force and a hell of a lot of courage to go up against a wild thing and wrestle it into submission.

Or maybe you just have some kind of alligator kink.

The water shut off, and Prophet turned his head to see Tom exiting the bathroom naked. Tom stopped short when he noticed Prophet's stare. He smirked a little and shook his head when Prophet shoved his hands into his pockets in a futile attempt to hide how turned on he was.

Looking squarely into Tom's eyes, Prophet knew what—who— he had a kink for. And the voodoo bastard knew it too.

Knew it. Liked it. Used it to his advantage whenever he could. Like now.

Because he knows you like it.

And here he'd been worried that he'd been getting too hardened the past months in the field, because he'd had to shut everything down. Now, he fought the urge to look down to check and see if he still had a dick. Except he didn't need to, mainly because he could feel it throb. "What?"

"Want me to roll you?" Tom asked.

"Not funny." But Prophet *was* rock hard. Tom stalking over to him and crowding him wasn't helping.

"You still have that duct tape?"

"Yeah. Why?"

"Come on, *bebe*. Let's play gator."

Prophet hated the way his body responded yes—eagerly—to that question.

"Think you wanna. 'M'I wrong?" Tom's drawl was thick as hell, went right down Prophet's spine, as the man's hand snaked around Prophet's waist and pushed his own hard cock against Prophet's cargo pant-clad one.

"Yes."

"'S'okay to admit you were turned on by it," Tom murmured.

"You're turned on too," Prophet pointed out, wanted to tell him to stop talking all Cajun-like, too.

"I'm not the one denying it." Tom ground his pelvis into Prophet's. "You can't lie for shit."

"Only around you."

"Good to hear you admit it." His hands curled around the back of Prophet's neck. "Wanna know the secret to wrestling alligators?"

"Yeah, sure, tell me, *cher*."

Tom smiled at Prophet's use of the affectionate word. "It's desire. The one with the most desire wins."

"Then I'm winning this one, Tommy."

"That's what you think." In one swift motion, Tom had him down, and they were rolling together, fast, with Prophet's back pinned to Tom's chest. They bumped the wall and rolled across the room again, and he didn't know what end was up.

When the world stopped spinning, Prophet was faceup, staring at the ceiling, and in the same position the gator had been in.

"Hand over the duct tape," Tom told him with a smirk in his tone. He pushed a hand down Prophet's pants.

And Prophet couldn't help but groan at the touch. "Jesus, T. How the fuck?"

"They don't teach you shit like that in the military?"

"Thinking they probably should."

"Tape," Tom ordered again, and Prophet reached into his pocket and handed Tom the roll. "Good. Put your palms together."

"You know, the alligator didn't have to listen to you."

Tom stroked his cock with quick, hard strokes that made Prophet jolt. "The alligator didn't get to have any fun, now, did he?"

"Fucker." Prophet did as Tom asked. Watched Tom wind the tape around his wrists twice. More for show than anything, but it was just enough to make Prophet know they'd be playing this game again.

Tom dropped the roll of tape, reached around Prophet's waist, and undid his cargos. Then he hooked his feet against the insides of Prophet's ankles and slowly spread his legs wide, holding them there.

"Told you duct tape has its uses," Prophet muttered, glancing at his immobilized arms.

"Gonna keep a roll on me at all times," Tom promised. "Just for this." He palmed Prophet's cock and started a rhythm that made Prophet try to escape and move into it at the same time.

Prophet groaned. "Now he listens to me."

"Never gonna forget that, right?"

"No," Prophet ground out.

"Next time, we'll do your legs too. Easier to position you."

"Next time, you'll be the one taped and bound," Prophet promised. "And over my goddamned knee."

"Proph!"

Tom's strangled cry sounded surprised, made Prophet close his eyes and shoot against his stomach and chest, hitting his goddamned chin because he came so hard.

But Tom groaned then, bucked his hips up, and rode his climax against Prophet's ass. After a few minutes, he laughed once. Then again, and said, "You're such an asshole. Can't even let me win. Have to call this a tie."

"What does this mean?"

"Means our desire's equal."

"That's not a bad thing," Prophet said. "But I still can't believe you never told me about this gator shit. There's a hell of a lot you haven't shared."

"Oh, I'm sorry. Be sure to send out invites to the pot-meets-kettle show you'll be throwing."

"I'm sensing sarcasm. I think being in Cajun country's given me some of your voodoo."

"You are an idiot," Tom informed him.

Prophet stared at the duct tape around his wrists. "I have no argument against that at the moment."

CHAPTER FOURTEEN

A shared shower and a meal later, Tom lay stretched out on the bed, hands behind his head, feeling pretty damned good.

Which meant, of course, the other shoe was bound to drop. And Prophet's ringing SAT phone sounded like the harbinger of doom.

"It's Della," Prophet said.

Yeah, same thing. "You take it. Tell her I'm fine." When Prophet raised a brow, Tom told him, "Just lie."

Prophet rolled his eyes and answered. "Hey Della, things all right? What? Okay, slow down . . ." Prophet listened intently, then mouthed a silent curse. "You're sure? Yeah, okay. Yes, Tom's here. We're fine. And no, I won't tell you where we are . . . I promise I'm taking care of him, Della. Thanks."

He hung up. Stared at Tom and said without preamble, "Donny was found dead in his house about an hour ago. Same MO as Miles."

"Suicide?"

"I think the police are starting to revise their theory."

"Which isn't good for me." Tom sat up, slammed his feet to the old wood floor and leaned his elbows on his thighs. Any tension that he'd managed to work off in the past hour was rushing back.

Speaking of tension, he noted that Prophet had paled. "Proph, you all right?"

"I told Etienne to call Donny. To warn him." Prophet's voice was hoarse.

"Shit." Tom grabbed his phone off the nightstand and dialed Etienne.

Prophet's pocket rang.

"Shit." Prophet pulled out Etienne's phone. "I took it to trace the threats he'd been getting."

"Were you planning on sharing that anytime soon?"

"We've been a little busy," Prophet shot back. "Try the shop."

Tom did, but there was no answer. "Could be that the phone lines are having trouble, post-storm . . ." He trailed off, because he didn't have to make excuses to Prophet. "Can I see his phone?"

Prophet handed it to him, and Tom scrolled through the anonymous texts. Several pages of them, going back a couple of months, and all of them making Tom's blood run cold.

"Just like him not to call and tell me about these," Tom muttered. "Trying to goddamned protect me."

"I'm guessing you'd have done the same for him," Prophet pointed out as he dialed the SAT phone. "Hey, Della, just do me a favor and get in touch with Etienne? Maybe send Roger to his shop or his house, then call me? Thanks." He hung up, waited a beat and then said, "Etienne said . . . he gave this to me." He pulled an envelope out of his pocket, and Tom stared at it. And then Prophet pulled out a plastic bag with a syringe in it. "This was at Miles's house. I think someone drugged him, OD'd him on purpose, and cut his wrists."

"Whoever did it must've known the suicide theory would wear thin after Donny." He paused. "You gonna pull Etienne from one of those pockets?"

"I wish," Prophet said. "You think something's wrong?"

"Yes." He took the envelope with his name on it, opened it quickly, and skimmed it. It was handwritten, and God yes, it was all there. Apologies for what happened under the bleachers. Apologies for their intentions that night in the bayou. Apologies for everything that happened afterward . . .

He glanced up at Prophet, who was watching him carefully but not asking any questions. "Etienne told you what this was?"

"Said it was an apology from Miles to you. Part of his making amends, as per AA. But he didn't tell me for what, just said it had something to do with you guys when you were growing up. I think it's time for you to put it all on the table, T."

"Yeah." He stared between Miles's handwriting and Prophet. "What else aren't you telling me?"

Prophet predictably cursed, "Fucking voodoo," then, "Della said . . . rumor is that your fingerprints were found on knives at both scenes."

Tom blinked.

"I tossed Miles's house—there wasn't any knife, T."

"Like I'd be stupid enough to leave one behind."

"Still doesn't negate the fact that men are dead and that things are pointing to you. You sure those guys aren't exes?"

He laughed hollowly. "Not even close. They made my life hell growing up. Things hadn't improved when I came back as a deputy."

"So the reasons you'd want them dead?"

"Too many to count."

"Shit, T." Prophet grabbed a soda, walked over to the bed, and sat down next to him. He popped the can open, handed it to Tom and asked, "What's really going on here?"

Tom took a long sip before telling him. "*Bad loque.*"

"I'm supposed to know what that means?"

"I'm bad luck," he managed.

"Well, yeah, I picked up on the translation, T. But I'm still alive."

Tom raked a gaze over him. "Yeah. You broke the curse, Proph. Or I thought you did."

"Jesus, Tommy. You can't get rid of me that easily—haven't you figured that out by now?"

Despite the trepidation in his gut at having to spill everything about his past in this parish that he'd never wanted Prophet to know, what Prophet said warmed him. He smiled, in spite of everything. "Starting to."

"Good. Because staying away from me might've ensured we'd both be fine, but we weren't happy. And I'd take happy over safe any day."

"You did that already." He set the soda down and played with the bracelet, unable to look at Prophet when he said, "I'm the seventh son of a seventh son." And then he braced for the man's reaction.

"Does that really mean something?" Prophet asked carefully.

"On the bayou, it does."

"Is another alligator going to walk in here?" Prophet demanded.

"No wonder you couldn't get a partner," Tommy muttered, finally looking at him.

"Didn't want," he corrected. "Did. Not. Want."

"Thanks for the reemphasis. Where I come from, we don't get much schoolin'," he said, deliberately slowing and drawing out his drawl.

Prophet didn't say anything. His face was set into serious lines even though he'd tried to lighten the mood a little. "So it runs deeper than just the partner thing."

Tom nodded. "Started before I was born."

"That's why your mom's in that graveyard."

"Yes."

"I know there's significance to the seventh son thing. It's a big deal, isn't it? I think there were some famous people who were seventh sons?"

"Yeah. Perry Como. Len Dawson."

"So it's a good thing, right?"

Tom laughed bitterly and threw his hands up. "Obviously, that depends on the circumstances. Depends on who you ask."

"I'm asking you. And wait, you have six brothers?"

"I have six stillborn brothers," he said, his throat tightening. He barely got out, "I'm built on the dead. Bad luck, Proph."

Prophet put a firm hand on the back of his neck. "Not for me, Tommy. Just breathe, okay?"

Tom did that, because it was easy to follow Prophet's orders, especially because they'd always kept him safe. When he'd bothered to follow them. "Sorry. Just hard to talk about."

"You were punished for something that was completely out of your control."

"Combined with the fact that I could see things, people were convinced I was bad luck. And I was. My mom, then our house burned down. Dad started drinking . . ."

"How is any of that your fault?"

"Because it can't be proven that it's not," he said fiercely. "That graveyard is where they put the disgraces. I'll be buried here."

Prophet shook his head no, his eyes blazing as his free hand went to Tom's.

Tom continued, "They say that the cemetery's built on ancient ground. That it's haunted."

"Better than alligators," Prophet said, and Tom felt the corner of his mouth pulling up into a grin despite himself.

"Asshole." Tom twined his fingers through Prophet's. "The bayou around the cemetery's where kids in my day were taken for a sort of twisted version of an Outward Bound program."

"As in, punishment?"

"Yes. Me and Etienne, Miles and Donny . . . we were sent in there together, but we were put in the cemetery, instead of outside of it. I know that was a special touch, just for me. It was supposed to be for one night."

"What the fuck did was supposed to happen from that?"

Tom glanced at him, then looked straight ahead. "My dad told me, before he let the sheriff take me, that if I survived, I was bad luck. Only evil survived evil."

"You tell me you believe that bullshit and I'll have to kick your ass."

"Someone tells you shit day in and day out, and a lot of it comes true . . ." He trailed off, then repeated, "A lot of it comes true."

"You ever think about the fact that you help more people than you hurt?"

Tom's head swam—he wavered between desperately wanting to believe Prophet and knowing he couldn't. Not about this. "Etienne and I . . . I took him to hell and back."

"He looked fine when I saw him," Prophet pointed out.

"Etienne's always fine. Like you."

Prophet let that go and moved his hand from Tom's neck, dropping it down to his shoulder, pulling him into a side embrace. Tom sagged against Prophet and stared into space. They were still holding hands. "Things got bad, Proph. Really fucking bad."

"Before or after the Outward Bound thing?"

"It started before. And afterwards, everything was just so much worse. For me. For Etienne. Even for Miles and Donny."

Prophet's phone rang, and Tom didn't need Della to tell him that Etienne was nowhere to be found.

Prophet waited, Tommy still pressed against his side, his hand slung over Tommy's shoulder, and pictured the dreamcatcher tattoo under his palm. For once, he knew goading wouldn't help—Tom would kill for that kind of distraction, and that's precisely why Prophet wouldn't do it.

Tom finally continued. "I knew the punishment existed. Everyone knew, but the thing was, no one ever admitted to being a part of it. It was a big stigma, you know? And I thought that maybe it was just a rumor started to keep us out of trouble. It was supposed to be like, an Outward Bound for fuckups. Sheriff would turn guys loose into the bayou, the west end. Had twenty-four hours to show up on the other side. It was supposed to make you a man."

"Or kill you."

"Yeah, well, you can't help but know the bayou like the back of your hand when you grow up here. But not the cemetery—not as much. But I knew my way around it. Etienne did too, because he'd visit my mama's grave with me."

"So it was you. Etienne. And the two dead guys?"

Tom nodded. "Donny and Miles were fuckups. Etienne was there because he'd just come out to his parents—and the whole school."

"Donny and Miles must've had a field day with that."

Tom opened his mouth, then closed it. Pressed his lips together tightly, and Prophet shifted, because he needed to see Tommy's face. "I'm here, T. Okay? Nothing you tell me's going to change that."

"You sure?"

"Is there anything I'd tell you that'd change it for you?" he asked before he could stop himself.

"No, Proph. No way." Tom swallowed hard. "Jesus, is this what it took to get us here?"

"Wouldn't have expected it to be easy."

"Don't think I don't remember you have some sharing to do later," Tom warned him, then cursed some in Cajun French before saying, "No lies, no half-truths. Starting from the beginning."

He could've been talking about either one of them. But for right now, Tommy was the one telling the story.

"The four of us all went to the same small high school. Came up through elementary. Etienne and I weren't friends with Miles and

Donny—Etienne and I stayed to ourselves. Me, for all the reasons I told you, and Etienne because he had a fuck-you, in-your-face attitude."

Prophet snorted. "Had?"

Tom smiled a little, even if it didn't reach his eyes. "He's toned it down a lot. He's also been an artist for as long as I've known him. He has that kind of soul."

Prophet didn't want Tom thinking about any part of Etienne's . . . soul. "You're an artist too."

"I draw a little."

"I saw the originals of your tattoos at his shop."

Tom's expression shuttered, and he stood, putting distance between them as he gave up. "I don't want to do this."

"If I don't know the background, I can't help."

Tom closed his eyes for a second, shoved his hands into the pockets of his old jeans and rocked a little on the balls of his feet. Then he stopped dead. "Miles and Donny . . . they tried to rape Etienne." He cursed again, shook his head hard, but his gaze never left Prophet's. "They *did* rape him, under the bleachers at the high school. He came out, but that's not why they did it. It's because he defended me, so it was the best way to teach *me* a lesson."

Prophet's throat tightened. He wanted to stand up and go to Tommy, but he didn't want to break his momentum, so he stayed put as Tom drew in a shaky breath. "Etienne reported it. But no one did anything, not even Etienne's parents. Della was the only adult who pushed the issue. The court wanted mediation—"

"Mediation?"

"Yeah. There wasn't even talk of prosecution. But since Etienne wouldn't drop it, and I wouldn't either, that's why we were sent on the Outward Bound thing—to work it out. See, if it'd been me they raped, it wouldn't have mattered. But with Etienne, the sheriff had an image problem. Even though Etienne's parents wanted him to drop it, he wouldn't, and so they couldn't just ignore their son's wishes so blatantly like that. And then the sheriff couldn't just sweep the complaints of the son of a judge under the rug—especially not if he ever wanted his cases before the court to get a fair shake. Didn't matter that Etienne's parents weren't happy that he came out—weren't happy that he was gay—even tried to tell him to stop 'embarrassing himself.'

And even though Miles and Donny denied everything and Etienne didn't go to the police or the hospital right away—hell, he didn't even tell me until a couple of days later—the sheriff had to do something to put an end to all of it."

"So sending you in together would accomplish what? I don't get it—did they expect you all to come out friends?"

Tom shook his head. "Look, at the time, I didn't know for sure. Figured maybe the sheriff told Miles and Donny to apologize, to beg Etienne to drop it. Or maybe he told them to threaten us into shutting up since we had no proof, and it turns out that was what he'd had in mind. But it didn't matter which one it was, because sending us all in together would prove, once and for all, no matter how it turned out, that wherever I was, trouble followed. Not that the community needed proof of that. And Etienne's parents thought it could make a man out of him." Tom pulled his hands out of his pockets and ran them through his hair as he looked around at Etienne's artwork on the walls. When he spoke again, his voice held a fierce edge. "Etienne was born a better man than anyone I knew. And fuck, we were fourteen—and holy shit, how can something that happened when we were fourteen haunt us for the rest of our goddamned lives?"

"All of this was why you'd never have won the sheriff's seat," Prophet said as the pieces fell into place.

"Yes," Tom admitted.

"But you came back here after the FBI, knowing what you were up against. And you ran. Jesus, T, it's like . . ."

"I'm my very own whipping boy?" he asked sardonically.

"You thought you deserved the punishment of trying to earn everyone's respect."

Tom hung his head, a silent concession to Prophet's words. "Even Etienne told me to go the fuck away. Not because of what it did to him. But he knew what it did to me. So you were right when you called me my very own whipping boy when we first met. Pathetic, isn't it?"

Prophet stood then, strode over to him, and put a hand under Tom's chin. "No. What's pathetic is that no one but Etienne and me could see that you've always been stronger than any of the people who tried to hurt you, physically and mentally. Your father. The people in this town. You had one safe place to turn—Etienne—but you were trying to save him too. And look at you now. No one else could've taken all that abuse. No one."

Tom sucked in a harsh breath and stared at him, like he'd never considered the possibility.

"Every time you came back, you just proved to them that you were so much stronger than they ever could be. Like you took strength from their hatred. Like you wouldn't buy into their bad luck shit."

"But I did."

"You didn't let them know that. You didn't give in. A part of you doesn't believe it, or you'd never have taken jobs that would force you to partner up again."

Tom blinked fast. Cursed. "You are so fucking good for me and so fucking bad for me at the same time."

"It's not good if you don't have the mix of both."

Prophet let go of his chin as Tom wound his arms around him, and Prophet held him while he said, "I don't want to tell you the rest of it. Or maybe I just don't want to deal with it. I sure as hell don't want to revisit it."

Prophet thought about all the things he had nightmares about. He guessed Tommy got headaches instead. It made sense. "Come on, let it out, T. Let it go and then—"

"And then it becomes your burden. And you have too many of those already."

He pulled back a bit. "You're not a burden, Tommy. Never were, never will be. You understand?" He heard how fiercely the words came out of his mouth, and he cursed inwardly. Yeah, *who's* the burden?

But Tommy didn't seem to notice. They stood together in the middle of the studio, their bodies touching, Prophet's hands on Tom's waist and Tom resting his hands on Prophet's forearms. When he started speaking, his voice was barely a whisper. "I promised Etienne that nothing would happen to him in that cemetery. I swore. Because I hadn't been there for him when he'd needed me. And at first, we separated from Miles and Donny, because Etienne didn't want to be with them. Can you imagine how cruel that is—send a boy into the woods with the guys who raped him?"

They'd been talking about it all along, but to hear it put so bluntly . . . fuck. "I'd have killed them," Prophet said softly. When he realized what he'd said, he cursed. "Sorry."

"Don't be. Because I wish I'd had the guts to kill them. But saving them—having them rely on me—was the ultimate revenge. No one ever looked at them the same. I ruined their lives because, since we were forced to keep the secret, they had to be civil to me in public. Or at least they couldn't be the assholes they normally were."

Prophet started. "What secret, Tommy?"

"Can't believe it could get worse, right? But it does, Proph," Tom said forlornly. "And this secret . . . they were afraid I'd tell it, because I was the wild card. The bad luck. The trouble. If it was going to come from anyone, it'd be me."

"Not a bad thing to be feared."

"Better to be respected."

"That's overrated."

"Well, now they're dead, and I'm being framed. You think people aren't remembering how odd it was that we came out of the woods *not* mortal enemies?"

"The firing squad around here seems smaller than you remember."

Tom laughed and looked briefly at the ceiling before settling his gaze back on Prophet. "You have no idea, Prophet. Wait. Just wait."

"What? Torches and pitchforks?"

"Keep an eye out, okay?" Tom stared out the window and then back at Prophet, as if Prophet was the only thing keeping him grounded.

"Go ahead, T. I'm right here."

He nodded. "It was just after six. The sheriff drove us to right where you and I parked and marched us into the cemetery. We each had a flashlight, a canteen, and a little food. Miles and Donny took off fast. They didn't want to be around us, and they also thought they could get someplace safe before it was pitch-black."

"And they couldn't have?"

"There is no safe place," he said darkly. "Etienne had kind of frozen when his parents dropped him off at the meeting place with the sheriff, and even after he and I were alone, he still wasn't talking. So I held his hand. That was the first time I'd ever done that—we'd been friends, but I'd always been attracted to him. Doing that there could've been the stupidest move ever, but Etienne, he told me later that he thought that might've saved him."

Prophet squeezed Tom's hand. "That's sweet."

"You're not jealous?"

"I'm trying not to break your hand."

Tom snorted. "It was over a long time ago."

"I know." He stared at Tom. "Keep going."

Tom took a deep breath and went back into the bayou, taking Prophet with him.

The dark came fast—Tom had known it would, out here in the graveyard with no lights, but knowing it and actually being in it at night were two different things entirely.

Etienne's hand was cool, even though they were both slick with sweat. It was the end of September. Muggy. They'd have been bitten alive by mosquitos if Etienne hadn't been prepared. He used the bug spray on both of them and that helped.

"We'll be all right, Etienne," Tom assured him. Tom would go to any length to make sure that was true, because his best friend had already had to endure enough shit in the past month.

"Do you think the sheriff gave Miles a weapon?" Etienne asked finally, a small shudder rippling through his body.

"I don't know." But he had a knife of his own. Wouldn't tell Etienne that. Not yet.

"We could turn around. Walk right back out. Refuse to do this," Tom suggested and Etienne laughed a little.

"You, refuse to survive? Come on, Tom—never happened."

"That's what they're trying to say about what Miles did to you. But it did. And I won't let them win like that. I won't let them brand you a liar."

"Better to brand me a rape victim? No, better to brand me a boy who gives it to anyone. I don't know what's worse," Etienne said fiercely, "the insinuation that a gay guy can't be raped, or that I'd actually willingly let Miles fuck me."

He turned to Etienne then, and he kissed him. A soft, slow kiss, the kind he'd been dreaming about doing, and in the dark Etienne shook a little and returned the kiss. Threaded his arms around Tom as

Tom put his hands on Etienne's shoulders, one hand twisting through his hair.

They kissed for at least five minutes in the dark. The only reason they stopped was that staying still in the bayou made you a target for all sorts of wildlife. And they didn't talk about it because they were fourteen-year-old boys.

"You're going to be my first tattoo," Etienne told him.

"Do I have a choice?"

"No. Not after that kiss."

Etienne's last word was cut in half by screams tearing through the heart of the swamp, turning Tom cold. Etienne simply froze and said, "That's Miles."

Tom took Etienne's hand and pulled him along behind him. They'd never been here in the pitch dark before, but they'd both been here enough that they instinctively knew the narrow path leading through the graves—made narrower by the thin beam of the flashlight Tom followed. One foot in front of the other, they followed the echoes of the screams that weren't stopping as they moved through the damp bayou floor as quickly as they could.

It took at least ten minutes of half walking, half running. The denseness of the bayou had never closed in on him the way it did then, but he needed to be strong for Etienne. Then the yelling that echoed around them, leading them in Miles's direction, came to a dead halt. And they were left in the bog, surrounded by nothing and everything.

"Tom, shit . . ."

"It's okay, E. Hang onto me," he urged, sounding far more calm than he actually was. His heart raced, because he'd already smelled the metallic tang of blood. Then he nearly stumbled over something.

Someones. He stopped short, and Etienne shone the flashlight on Miles and Donny.

Donny was kneeling on the ground, shaking Miles, whose silence was now eerie. All Tom could focus on was the blood, all over Miles's hands.

"Is he hurt?" Etienne asked as Tom grabbed the flashlight from him and trailed it along the ground farther away from them, finally hitting on something about five feet from where they stood.

"The blood's not his," Tom said quietly.

Tom's first instinct was to grab Etienne, head to the road, leaving Miles and Donny and the body behind. But he inexplicably found himself moving toward it.

He let the light travel up from the heavily booted feet, to the chest, where the hilt of a knife stood straight up like a proud soldier. A very lucky shot for Miles. Unlucky for whomever this man was.

Tom hesitated before bringing the light up to the man's face. The guy's mouth was open in surprise and his eyes . . . fuck, his eyes were open too, and appeared to be starting straight at Tom, thanks to the angle he stood at over the body.

Tom jumped back for a second, then looked again. It was no one he recognized. And for him not to know an adult on this bayou was odd. He moved closer, a hand over the man's mouth to feel for any breath, but there was nothing. Just an odd stillness.

It wasn't like he hadn't seen death before—he and his father shot alligators for a living—but this was so different. He put his hand on the guy's shoulder. "I'm sorry," he said, because he was, for all of them.

"What the—" Etienne was next to him, staring down at the body. Then he turned back and went for Donny, shoving him backwards from his kneeling position, slamming him onto the ground. "What the fuck, Donny—who'd you guys really bring that knife for?"

Tom heard the sounds of fist hitting flesh, an all-too familiar one for it to impact him.

"Is he dead?"

Miles voice. He'd pushed up off the ground and now stood next to Tom shakily.

"Yes," Tom said, from where he was still kneeling. And even if the guy was hanging on, what could they do? There was no one to call— the nearest house was too many miles away in the dark.

Tom pushed up and turned to the direction of Miles's voice in the dark. Miles, who grabbed for him, smearing something all over Tom's hands and shirt. When Tom pulled away and fumbled for his flashlight, he saw that it was blood. Then he turned the light on Miles. "What the fuck are you trying to do?"

"Listen, Tom, we gotta stick together on this."

Tom jerked away from him. "You were waiting, right? You thought it was me and Etienne coming up the pathway."

Miles blanched, and that was enough of a confession for Tom. He'd ask why, but he knew the reasons. Knew even more when he looked down at the blood covering his hands and his shirt.

They were all ruined now, and irreparably connected.

CHAPTER FIFTEEN

Tom realized he must've been silent for a while after he finished the story when Prophet ran a hand along the back of his neck and shook him a little.

"Hey, T, you with me?"

Yes, he was. Definitely *with* Prophet. He stirred in the circle of Prophet's arms. "Sorry. Yeah."

"So, the way I see it, Donny and Miles were murdered for what happened on that trip."

"Yeah," Tom repeated, but he felt disconnected from his body. Was surprised when Prophet got up, kicking his chair back, saying, "Come on, T. Let's get you to bed and get you drugged."

It was only then that the throb of migraine pain got his attention. He let Prophet guide him to the bed. "You just want to take advantage of me."

Prophet smiled. "For sure." Then Prophet propped him up, put ice on his head, and gave him his meds. "They going to stay down?"

"Maybe." He breathed, tried to force his stomach not to rebel. Let Prophet do some pressure point therapy on his hands to help with the pain. He kept his eyes closed, felt his knees go from bent to straight as his body relaxed and his mind floated away. Woke to darkness, a raging hard-on, and his hips rocking against Prophet's thigh.

Prophet was watching him, his eyes heavy lidded, his hair tumbling over his forehead. Although his eyes were worried, the mask was gone.

Times like these, Tom knew he was seeing the real Prophet. It was enough to get him through the times he couldn't. "Hey."

"Hey." Prophet slid a hand over Tom's dick, his thumb rubbing along the piercings. "Better?"

"I want it to be." But his skin was hot and tight, like he had a fever. "I want to not need you so goddamned much."

Prophet snorted lightly. "Right back at you, Tommy."

Between the pain and the incoming edges of the drugs softening his resolve on everything, he wanted to believe Prophet. Needed to know that whenever Prophet stepped in to help him gain much needed control over his temper, or helped him with his migraines, or helped him deal with his past, it was because he wanted to, not just because it was an easy way to push Tom away.

Prophet was watching him with a half grin on his face, and it took Tom a few seconds to register why. Because Tom had babbled the words out loud instead of just letting them run wild in his brain. "Shit."

"I'm here doing this—all of this—because I want to. Not because I have to. Not because it puts distance between us. I told you I'm done running. I think maybe you're the one who's still trying to escape."

"No. I don't want that."

"Then *let me*, T."

Tom was happy to pretend he didn't have a choice in the matter.

"Never fail to surprise me," Prophet murmured to him what seemed like hours later.

"That's good, right?" Tom asked tiredly, still collapsed over the man's chest.

Prophet laughed and rubbed a hand down his back. "Decent."

Tom laughed weakly. "Fucker."

"You started it."

"Wait a minute," Tom realized. "How were my meds here?"

Prophet had the grace to look sheepish. "I went through your bag. Put them in my pocket before we went out with Kari."

"In case I had a migraine down the street from my aunt's house?"

"Pressure changes. You never know . . ." Prophet trailed off.

"Thank you."

"Not done yet," Prophet said. Tom let Prophet practically carry him to the bathroom.

He leaned against Prophet under the spray, murmured, "'M'too warm, Proph."

Prophet made the water cooler, and Tom shivered as it hit his heated skin. His head throbbed from the small exertion, and he whimpered as Prophet tucked his head against his neck and rubbed his back. Realized that the damned orgasm earlier had helped the pain immensely, if only for the moments it raced through him.

"I've got you," Prophet said roughly, and Tom wanted to ask "Who has you?" but it would take too much effort at the moment, and no doubt Prophet wouldn't answer him anyway. Prophet was protecting him, which was what he did best, and Tommy realized the key to their partnership was just that—Prophet wanted to protect.

Tommy would let him, because it allowed him to protect Prophet right back.

Finally, they were both cool and far more comfortable. Prophet didn't bother toweling them off—the warm air would dry them soon enough. Tom was agreeable, letting Prophet manhandle him, put a bag of ice on his head, give him more medicine.

When Prophet led him back into the bed, Tom made a stop first, grabbing Miles's letter off the shelf and handing it to Prophet.

"It's all here, Proph."

"You sure?"

"Yeah, I'm sure," he said, then started. When he'd read Miles's letter, he'd had to break the seal of the envelope. "I can't believe you didn't read it."

"It wasn't my place."

"But it is your place to look through my bags."

"That's different."

"How?"

"We're sleeping together."

"We weren't the first time you did it." Prophet stared at him, and Tom's throat tightened as he finally realized why Prophet hadn't read it. "Shit. The video."

"Yeah, the video," Prophet echoed.

The letter in Tom's hands was somewhat equivalent to the video of Prophet that Tom had watched over and over. Granted, he'd gotten it before he'd even met Prophet, but once he had . . . he still hadn't revealed it, had hung onto that piece of Prophet's past without telling him. He'd intruded before Prophet had been ready.

Prophet hadn't wanted to do that to him, even though he could've easily justified reading it. "I'm sorry, Proph."

"It's in the past."

"Past doesn't stay fucking buried."

"For me, that will."

Prophet's words were a fierce promise as he tugged Tom to sit next to him while he read the letter about what happened that night in the bayou, a night Tom couldn't erase from his mind or his conscience, no matter how hard he tried.

Tom—

I know I'm the last person you're expecting to hear from. I'm in AA and I'm sober for the first time since high school, and I'm supposed to make amends. No, I want to. It's time.

I went into the bayou knowing that Donny had a knife. He told me what he thought we should do, and really, it was just to scare you both, especially Etienne. The sheriff didn't know anything about that. I'm sure he figured we'd try to beat you guys up, but the knife . . .

I can't even explain it, Tom. I was the son of a drunk. That's not an excuse, but I was getting beaten every night, and then I'd drink until I passed out, wake up, go to school, and bully other people to make myself feel better. And it took me a long time and a lot of mistakes to get to this place. I'm never giving up my sobriety, no matter how hard it is to face the facts that I raped someone, that I took another man's life . . . and that I'd planned to hurt you and Etienne that night.

Would I have used the knife on you? I want to say that the man surprised me—scared me. I want to say that I wasn't waiting in the dark for Etienne to come along the path toward the swamp. But I was, because raping him had made people think I was gay, and because of that, I hated him. It was all my own fault and I couldn't see that. Could only see the hatred I carried inside.

We've carried this shit around with us for too long. Looking back, I can't believe what I did—to Etienne and to you. The only way I can truly show you I'm sorry is to come forward with what I did. I realize you might get in trouble for helping the sheriff cover the crime up, but I'm going to make sure everyone knows that it was forced on you to do so. Please understand that my coming forward is the best way for me to unburden you.

—Miles

"And unburden himself," Prophet muttered as he refolded the letter. "He made this more about him than Etienne or the man he killed. That's bullshit."

"You seem to know a lot about making amends," Tom realized aloud.

"I'm an expert," Prophet said seriously. "Does this sound like him?"

"No. He was an idiot most of the time. He was also drunk and high most of the time, so maybe this *is* the real him. I'll never know now." He glanced down at the note. "It looked like he was really going to come forward."

"And so anyone with something to hide would want to shut that down. Where's that sheriff who sent you into the woods now?"

"He's dead. His son's the new sheriff."

"Jesus H. Christ, Tommy. Just . . . fuck, don't ever go job hunting without me, okay?" Tom just ducked his head against Prophet's chest, and Prophet sighed. "So the sheriff's son has a lot to lose if this comes out. Think the old sheriff involved Lew?"

Tom shook his head. "They bonded over their dislike for me, but I know Lew doesn't know what happened in the cemetery."

"I'm not ruling any of them out at this point. Tell me what the old sheriff knew."

"He found us when the sun came up because we didn't meet him at the swamp. Etienne said we couldn't leave the man's body there alone. We guarded it against the gators. So he saw the body and the blood on me and Miles. And that asshole didn't confess like he'd promised. Etienne stuck up for me and Donny stuck up for Miles and the sheriff told us to all keep our damned fool mouths shut, if we knew what was good for us. That it was Etienne's and my word against Donny and

Miles's, and that no one could prove which one of us stabbed the guy. Which meant the word of a gay artist and the king of bad luck against two normal boys."

"What about that little thing called evidence?"

"Donny got rid of the knife in the swamp. We didn't wash the blood off because we thought it would make us look guilty when, as Donny pointed out, it was an accident."

"Fuck. So the sheriff forced you to protect each other. And you did."

Tom nodded, his voice tight as he said, "He got ... gentler though. He didn't so much as threaten, but he told us the man was a transient. Homeless. It was an accident. No sense ruining any of our lives any more than they already were for an accident."

"Miles would've killed you and Etienne, T. Would that have still been considered an accident?"

He heard the anger in Prophet's voice. "Around here, at the time, yeah."

"Shit." Prophet ran a hand though his hair. "We're getting the fuck out of this place."

"Too late now." He thought back to how he'd felt all those years ago going home, showering. Sleeping in his bed and going to school. "I kept my mouth shut all these years. Watched the sheriff throw the body in the bayou."

"You were fucking fourteen. Jesus. Don't you dare blame yourself."

"Miles started up with the drugs pretty much right after that. So the letter, that's his first apology. I'm guessing he finally said he was sorry to Etienne too."

"Etienne said he did," Prophet told him.

"You'd think things would've been better after that, but everything got worse, especially for Miles and Donny. Since they left Etienne alone instead of their usual attempts to bully him and they didn't call me bad luck anymore, the rumors started. *They* were gay. *They* were cursed." Tom sighed. "That's the kind of shit that sticks with you. That's the kind of shit that ruins you."

"It didn't ruin you, T. I know that, because I know you." Prophet ran a hand over the bracelet, a reminder, and then he laced his fingers with Tom's. "So according to the letter, Miles was going to admit he killed the man in the bayou. The sheriff who covered it up is dead, so yeah, I mean, look, it's a scandal but . . . is that really motivation enough to kill?"

Tom shook his head, then stared at Prophet. "What if the man Miles killed wasn't a transient?"

"I'm guessing the gators won't be talking," Prophet said grimly. "We'll get to the bottom of it. But fuck, I hate that you went through this shit."

"I had to learn to be tough."

"You're tough enough, T." Prophet slid an arm across his shoulders. "Always were."

"Guess I'm lucky I'm not more fucked up."

"Dude, you're plenty fucked up." He played with the leather bracelet on Tom's arm. "You know why I gave you this, right?"

"Was it John's?"

"No, mine." Prophet smiled. "We all have our amulets."

Tom studied him. "Bullshit."

Prophet laughed. "John bought that explanation. So did you, for a while. It was mine, though, T. And no, I never needed an amulet. But I believed in both of you. The bracelet was just a reminder of that."

Tom's throat tightened. "It worked," he managed. "You're a fucking romantic bastard."

Prophet looked oddly pleased with himself, even as he said, "You take that back!"

"I won't tell anyone," Tom promised.

Prophet grumbled, then said, "Etienne never got in touch with you about any of this shit with Miles and AA?"

"No." He glanced at Prophet. "And no, I don't think he's a suspect."

"I didn't say anything."

"Look, the last time I heard from Etienne was right before I went to Eritrea. He told me to stay away from this place. I thought he just meant . . . in general."

"Why didn't he get specific?"

"He knew it would bring me back here," Tom admitted.

"And what about your voodoo shit?"

Tom shrugged. "Doesn't work like that. Not around here. My voodoo shit always throws off warning bells when I hit the state border. Because if I'd known that E was going to be in trouble . . ."

Was that true? Etienne had been in trouble all the time, because of Tom, because of the fact that he'd always stood by Tom and forced his parents to do the same. Etienne took up for him, and in turn, Tom made things easier on himself and on Etienne by staying away. Especially because Etienne *told* him to stay away. "Fuck, I knew something was up, okay? I knew it and I pushed it down because I didn't want to come back here."

Prophet nodded, like he'd known Tom had been lying about his voodoo shit a few minutes earlier. "Did Della know any of this?"

"If she caught wind of any of it, past or present, she hasn't said a word."

"It's all right, Tommy."

Tommy threw up his hands. "It's not, okay? You can't escape the past, Proph. No matter how hard you run, how much time goes by. You can't ever escape."

Prophet winced, then grabbed him. At first, it was a one-armed hug, and then his free hand went up to Tom's face, his palm spread, thumb caressing his earlobe, fingers sliding along his jawline.

This was past and present slamming together. And his future was the man who was holding him, which hit Tom as hard as it must be hitting Prophet. But their reunion on the grass and the kitchen wall and floor and in his bedroom . . . that told the tale.

The fact that Prophet was staying here to help him figure all of this out sealed the deal.

"I know, Tommy. I know you can't escape. That's why I didn't want to get you involved in my past."

Tom lifted his head to meet the gray-eyed gaze. "But I'm here. Don't you think I need to know, for my own sake?"

Prophet looked pained, then swallowed hard before saying, "Yeah, you do. But sometimes it's . . . I never want to talk about it."

"I get that."

"Thanks, T."

Tom buried his head against Prophet's chest again, realizing that Prophet's arms had never left him. Realizing that, in all of this, there was an implicit promise. "Not letting you off the hook though. And I'm not letting you go," he said, his voice muffled.

"Considering I'm the one actively holding you . . ." Prophet started, but his words were calm and quiet. He got it.

They finally both did.

Tom slept restlessly. The pain had returned, but he was resisting more meds, and Prophet couldn't blame him. He stayed next to him in bed, because that's how Tom seemed to sleep best, and he checked the local news on his phone.

So much going on in New Orleans still. Extra police presence, plus people coming back to their houses. Out-of-state electrical trucks, contractors, and medical personnel. It was nearly impossible to carry out an investigation there. And a killer was running around in the midst of it all.

His phone beeped. A text. Cillian. Again.

He glanced over at Tom, who appeared not to have heard the beep.

You're enjoying all the bayou has to offer?

When people stop trying to kill me, Prophet typed back.

Seems to be a regular fault of yours.

Yeah. Not sure why.

You can't even type that with a straight face.

Prophet scrubbed his face with his hand. *It's amazing how parents can fuck up their kids so badly.*

Which is why I don't plan on having any.

Prophet sighed, rolled restlessly out of bed, and he walked over to Etienne's drafting table.

You paused. You want kids.

"You and those goddamned pauses," Prophet muttered. *I didn't say that.*

You'd make a great father.

That statement slammed Prophet in the chest harder than he'd ever thought possible, and he was glad they weren't face-to-face, because there was no way he could've kept his poker face on. He threw the phone onto the table with a clatter, a silent acknowledgment that not answering was more of a tell than anything.

He figured he could lie to Cillian that someone picked that moment to try to murder him again. Whether the spook would buy it or not was up to him.

His hands shook a little, and he wanted to do exactly what he'd told Tom not to do—drink to forget.

You'd make a great father.

Don't go there, he warned himself. Doing so would mean he'd have to expose shit he'd shoved down a long time ago.

"Do as I say, T," he said out loud.

Tom's hands landed on his shoulders, and Prophet reached up to touch them.

Tom kissed his neck. "What did Cillian say?"

"Something nice," was all Prophet offered.

"I'll make a mental note to never do such a horrible thing."

Prophet snorted, then said, "You might want to call Cope."

"Why?"

"He might know you got arrested."

"Might?"

"Does."

Tom groaned. "And you're just telling me now?"

"Been busy," Prophet pointed out. "But don't worry, he blames me."

"Well, in that case, no big deal."

"Assholes, both of you."

"Gonna tell me that Cope and I deserve each other?"

"Do not even . . ." Prophet pointed at him.

"What?"

"Your accent's thicker when you pull shit like that."

"You don't like my accent?" Tom asked, attempting to make his drawl sound innocent and failing miserably.

"Not. A. Bit," Prophet said, equally unconvincingly. Tom rested his chin on the top of Prophet's head for a moment, then pulled away, tugging Prophet with him.

As Prophet turned to get up from the chair, he caught sight of a framed sketch hanging in the corner, almost out of sight. Gil Boudreaux. Younger, smiling—hard to fucking believe he ever had.

"The devil always smiles, Proph," John said from his perch on a bench across the room. "Have I taught you nothing?"

Prophet rubbed his eyes then turned to refocus his gaze on the picture. "Why did Etienne draw your father?"

"I drew it," Tom said quietly. "I was trying to find some common ground. Thought if I showed him I respected him . . ."

"You drew it?" Prophet echoed.

Tommy stared at him. "I'd wanted to give it to him on Father's Day, but we ended up fighting, and then I went back to school for summer classes."

"Let's go back to bed, T. So much less complicated there."

It really wasn't, but Prophet was willing to let them lie to themselves a little while longer.

CHAPTER SIXTEEN

Prophet would really have liked to have moved out of this place and into hiding somewhere safer, especially since Gil Boudreaux knew where they were. Prophet had no doubt that if and when Gil heard about the newest murder, he'd let the police know where to find his son.

He watched Tom sleep. Reread Miles's letter, trying to reconcile all this shit, when a sound at the door had him up and out of the small back bedroom. He gently closed the door behind him, weapon drawn.

The front door opened, and a kid walked in as if he had every right to. A suspicious, pissed-off kid who was probably somewhere in the fifteen- to sixteen-year-old range.

"Who the fuck are you?" the kid asked.

"Who the fuck are you?" Prophet asked back, although he knew the answer an instant later and softened. "I'm here with Tom Boudreaux—we know your dad. Etienne."

The kid looked him up and down. "You don't have any tattoos."

"Is that like a state crime now?"

"Should be," the kid muttered. "Have you seen my dad? I just got home from a class trip and stopped at his house to see him. There's mail from three days ago in the box. Sometimes he comes here to paint, and he gets all caught up, and I have to remind him to eat. And shower."

"What's your name?"

"Remy."

"Remy, I'm Prophet." Prophet wished Tom was awake, because a total stranger shouldn't have to be the one to break the news to a kid. "We haven't seen your dad since the night after the hurricane."

"Was he out in it? Because he likes to do that sometimes, go out and take pictures of the storm."

"No. I saw him after the storm." Prophet eyed him. "Has your dad ever just left before and not told anyone?"

Remy looked at the ground, like he wanted to say something but knew he wasn't supposed to.

"He's not in trouble. At least not with me or Tom. We're just trying to find him."

"Sometimes he'll take off, yeah. But he'll usually call or leave a note or something."

"Did anything look out of place to you in his house?"

Remy looked troubled. "I just . . . I got a bad feeling in there, so after I saw the mail, I took off for here."

"I didn't hear a car."

"Too young to drive. Legally anyway. So I hitched."

Prophet just shook his head. "Put your stuff down and grab something to eat."

Remy didn't argue. "Where's Tom?"

"He's sleeping. Headache."

"I'm not supposed to be here," Remy admitted. "I live with my mom, and she and Dad don't get along. At all."

"Will she be worried?"

"Doubt it," Remy said, and there was an honesty in his words that made Prophet believe him. "My dad's trying to get me to live with him. I mean, I want to, but the court's got to make it official."

"That's gotta be tough."

Remy smiled at him a little. Maybe Prophet was the first adult who'd told him it was okay. Sometimes telling someone to buck up had the opposite effect, while admitting something bothered you was the key to overcoming it. Or at least not letting it scare the piss out of you.

Remy munched on chips. "Are you going to tell me what's going on?"

Prophet told him about Miles and Donny, glossing over the details of the murders, and Remy stopped eating the chips. "Shit."

"Yeah," Prophet said.

"Dad told me . . . about them. About what happened." Remy looked troubled. "Tom'll find him, right?"

"We're doing everything we can. But if I don't get you back to your mom—"

"The sheriff's looking for Tom, right?"

"Kind of." Prophet hated dragging a kid into this, but Remy seemed to know the score.

"I'll go. Won't tell anyone I was here."

"I'm not letting you wander the bayou at night alone."

Remy laughed—fucking laughed at him. "Seriously? You probably don't even know how to get back here."

"Dude, I would."

"They'll want to question you, right? Because you're friends with Tom?"

Prophet wondered how the kid was suddenly smarter than he was. Remy smirked, like he knew. "Okay, fine," Prophet said. "But I'll drive you most of the way."

"In my dad's truck?"

Prophet considered the ramifications of being caught driving in a missing man's vehicle. "Anything else I could borrow around here?"

Remy paused. "Old man Jensen's down the road. He's got a pickup. And he sleeps like the dead."

"Let's go."

Prophet was just walking back into Etienne's studio around eleven thirty when he heard Tommy's phone ringing. No police cars had been around Remy's house, and the kid had texted him ten minutes earlier.

Everything's cool. No one missed me.

Prophet didn't want to think about that.

He went into the bedroom where Tom was still out like a light and grabbed the phone. The number was unknown, and he debated for a second before answering it with a brief hello, but they'd hung up already.

A few minutes later, a text came through from that same number—an address for the road just off the bayou cemetery, and then: *Midnight. Got information on Etienne. Come alone.*

Great. Just what he wanted to do. And what the fuck was with all the cloak-and-dagger shit around here? It was the bayou, not the Middle East.

Maybe it was Charlie texting him. Or hell, maybe it was Etienne, calling from a secure line and trying to trick anyone who saw his text. But whoever this was . . . they wanted Tom alone. And they sure as hell weren't getting that.

He dragged a hand through his hair. Should he try to wake Tom to talk to him about this? But he'd given the guy extra pain meds, and he was out. And he deserved to be out. Hell of a couple of days.

The less Tom went outside while the police looked for him, the better.

And tomorrow, Prophet would get them the hell out of the state. Come back here with someone else—Mick or Blue maybe—and figure this out for T.

Yeah, good plan, he told himself, tasting the sarcasm of his words.

If he headed out now, he could get there earlier than the planned meeting time. Because he wasn't going to the meeting place. First, he was going to the graveyard and then to the shack to see if he could catch anyone there. And then he'd double back to the road.

He didn't know why going to the graveyard was so important, and he couldn't boast Tommy's voodoo-shit skills, but his instincts always led him where he was supposed to be. Sometimes, it wasn't the most pleasant of places, but getting good intel rarely put anyone in the best of positions.

This was a calculated risk, and risk was the key word, because the bayou wasn't his territory. He was at a distinct disadvantage.

And you'd ream Tom for going off alone like this.

The problem was, his instinct to protect Tom from more of this shit was overriding his common goddamned sense. And still, Prophet moved forward.

He set the GPS on his phone and followed it as far as he could in the borrowed truck. But the bayou roads didn't respond to the GPS. It was like they moved in the middle of the night, when no one was watching, just to piss off people like him.

He abandoned the borrowed truck and, with a flashlight stuffed in a pocket just in case, he walked through the tall grass in the near pitch black. He'd been working on this, dealing with darkness and trying to rely on sounds and smell and touch to get him through. Because it was never too early to deal with your shit.

And it might've worked better if the makeup of the bayou made any sense, but to him, it was all just a mishmash of bog and swamp and alligators and random twists and turns that were worse than a funhouse.

Prophet had always hated the funhouse. Surprises were never his thing.

But he tracked decently, and he made his way through the winding paths, until he saw the light on in the shack where he and Tom had met Charlie. He pulled out his NVs, scanning past the trees in the distance to see if he could make out the road beyond. He hadn't heard any cars or seen any lights, so either the person meeting him wasn't there yet, or they knew the bayou well.

He took the NVs off and used that single light to guide him through the now swampy ground, his boots sinking into the mud, making walking difficult and not all that stealthy. He wondered if he'd find Charlie inside, waiting there before the midnight meeting hour.

Fucking informant piece of shit . . . if this is Charlie trying to sell Tom weed . . .

He pulled up short when he realized that the sounds of wildlife had come and gone, a loud rush past him and nothing.

Which meant they were running from a predator, because they weren't stupid.

He, on the other hand, still continued moving forward. Probably should've paid more attention to how Tommy subdued the gator rather than getting turned on by what he'd done.

On the other hand, he did have duct tape. And bullets, if it went south.

Finally, he made it to the small house. The door was locked, and he stood there for a few moments, waiting silently to see if there was any movement inside. The silence was odd, gave him the fucking creeps way more than being in the middle of the cemetery had.

He heard a car—glanced up to check the road and saw the headlights. Good. Let whoever was meeting Tommy wait. He needed to assess a few things first.

He reached into his pocket to grab the NVs, but stopped when he heard men talking and the pop of rifle shots aiming toward the bayou.

Poachers. Which meant . . .

He went to turn around in the darkness and found no beady alligator eyes staring back at him. Maybe the shots scared the beasts off. He grabbed for the NVs again, because this wasn't the time to fly blind. Before he could get them on, he felt the prick of something in his neck. He clawed for it and yanked out a dart. But even after those brief seconds, whatever medication was in there had started to work. He was dizzy. Even in the dark, he could tell his vision blurred, which was more terrifying than anything. He closed his eyes to ward off that distraction and he forced himself to stay still, to listen.

There were more gunshots and more yelling. He figured his best bet was to head to the road and try to get the poachers to help him. Because they were better than nothing.

He stumbled on his first step and realized it must've been a hidden grave. He forced himself to move slowly and quietly. And he was almost to the road, after what seemed like hours of walking in quicksand, when his world went dark.

Tom woke, alone. Drugged. In pain. He didn't call for Prophet because that would take too much effort.

But he saw the flashing lights of the cop car through the front windows of the studio, and he thanked his lucky stars the lights inside were completely out. If Prophet *were* here, he'd have already seen the commotion.

Which meant Tom had to hide.

Luckily, Etienne was as paranoid as Tom.

Tom dragged out of bed, pulled the covers up completely, smoothed them out so it looked untouched. Grabbed his weapon, wallet, clothes. Nothing stray of Prophet's was around at all. The place looked clean enough.

If they dusted for fingerprints, they'd know he'd been here, but there was no time to figure that out now.

Instead, he went into the bathroom and opened the door behind the door. You'd never find it unless you knew it was there. Etienne had painted the walls in a splatter pattern that hid any evidence. Tom crawled in, shut it behind him just as he heard the pounding on the front door.

The little room was exactly like he remembered. Etienne had left a soft blanket and a pillow. Water. It was clean, not musty as it should be. Just dark, with enough air coming in from outside, through a vent that filtered from the bathroom, not to be stifling.

He held his breath when he heard the footsteps, the sheriff shouting for him to come out with his hands up. Buried his face against his knees and said a silent prayer that Prophet would stay away from this.

When the cops left, he'd have to sneak out and find him.

Prophet woke, blinking in the marshy grass that scraped his face. He spat, his mouth full of blood and bayou, and rolled to his side.

His arms were bound tightly behind his back with rough twine. He blinked a few times in the blackness, trying to orient himself, listening to check if he was alone. But his vision was still blurry, and he hoped it was the drugs or nothing else more serious than a concussion from hitting his head when he fell.

But it didn't feel like a concussion. His cheek ached, which meant the bastard had punched him. Which was oddly personal and unnecessary.

And Tom was never going to let him live this one down.

There wasn't any light. He couldn't tell if he was by the house or the road, didn't hear the poachers anymore. But his clothes were wet, like he'd been dragged to this point. Wherever this point was.

Get it together, man. You're better than this.

John's voice, but not John's ghost. Just a memory from any one of their early training missions. And fuck, John was right.

He took a deep breath, pushed back onto his stomach and then up onto his knees. Got his balance, barely, and used the strength in his legs to stand. He wobbled for a minute, more because of the hit on the head than the muddy ground beneath him, and finally, he stilled.

That's when he realized where he was. In the middle of some kind of alligator-infested marsh. Like, there was a collection of them, just hanging out. He saw their eyes glittering in the dark, and those eyes seemed to be moving slowly closer, and he was never fucking coming back here, not ever coming back to this godforsaken state.

He bent down awkwardly, retrieved his knife from his boot, and sawed at the twine, cutting himself several times in the process, since he was forced to back away from the approaching alligators at the same time.

Finally, his hands came loose. He didn't have time for finesse or wrestling or any of that shit.

He grabbed the small gun strapped to the inside of his ankle, put two quick bullets into the head of the closest massive monster. The sound echoed in the swamp and suddenly, everything came to life for several long moments and then went deadly quiet again.

Because they'd finally recognized him as the predator. "And that's the way it fucking should be," he told no one in particular.

He stumbled along in the dark—because, to add insult to injury, the fucker who'd tried to kill him had stolen his NVs—keeping his cursing to a minimum and his weapon drawn. And then he forced himself to stop moving, to think.

When he did, all he could remember was Tommy's email.

It's hotter than hell here. Reminds me a lot of home. You know, my Cajun voodoo home. I used to spend hours tracking my way through the swamps. I could go in there blindfolded and still know where I was. Could lead myself in the dark, based on the sounds around me. The feel of the bark and moss on my fingers. How the ground felt under my feet.

Hint: walk away from the squish or you're headed into actual water. Seems simple, but people tend to panic in the dark. I don't think you would. You take action. I just fight.

Prophet took a deep breath and followed Tommy's instructions about not panicking in the dark. He just kept moving forward, away from the bayou, knowing he'd hit the cemetery soon.

He did—nearly running into a mausoleum—and realized he hadn't been dragged far. And whoever had done it had left him with his weapons. Or hadn't thought to look for any.

Did whoever it was even realize they hadn't gotten Tom?

He oriented himself in the darkness and headed back in the direction of the small shack. The light inside was off, but the sky was lightening up, enough for him to see that Etienne's Jeep was parked there.

"Tommy," he whispered and started to walk faster. He blinked hard in the still dark cemetery and saw a figure coming toward him. "Tommy."

"Proph." A whisper back.

They both kept walking toward one another, until he was able to grab Tommy. "I don't like this at all."

"No shit."

"I'm talking about the alligators. The people I can handle."

"Come on." Tom held his hand tightly and together, they walked back to the shack. Once inside, Prophet let himself collapse onto the floor.

Tom had set up sleeping bags, so the collapse wasn't terrible.

"Where've you been?" Tom demanded. "You even took my goddamned phone..."

"Voodoo shit doesn't work if you're drugged?" Prophet asked gently.

"Proph..."

"Your head okay, T?"

"Better than it was."

Satisfied that Tom wasn't lying, Prophet launched into the story about Remy showing up, and how he'd told Remy about Etienne, and then driven the kid home. And then he handed Tom his phone, showed him the text message. "And then someone drugged me, dragged me out there, and left me as gator bait. I have a strong feeling I wasn't supposed to make it out."

"You mean, *I* wasn't supposed to make it out."

"Yeah. Some wild shit—like whoever's doing this wants to see slow, painful deaths."

"You should've taken me with you."

"You helped," he told Tom, and there wasn't a trace of sarcasm in his voice. "I thought about your emails, when you talked about tracking and getting out of the bayou. So you were there, T."

"What aren't you telling me?"

Prophet paused, then figured it had to come out sometime. "I think it was your father who tried to kill me. And see, there's no really good way to say that, so . . ."

"What makes you think it was him?"

"Remember the picture you drew? The one of him smiling?"

"Yes."

"In the picture, you drew him wearing a dark-red leather sheath on his belt. And I couldn't see much, but I did see that. Pretty distinctive."

"One of a kind, made to hold his favorite knife," Tom said hollowly. "Dammit. How badly are you hurt?"

"Head aches," Prophet admitted, right before he pulled out his own phone and pressed a single button. Tom didn't question that, was too busy running his hands gently through Prophet's hair, feeling along the scalp for the knot on the left side of his head.

And Prophet let Tom fuss over him, let him shine a penlight from his key ring in his eyes.

"You don't have a concussion."

"I already knew that."

Prophet heard the shake of a pill bottle, and then Tom said, "Take these."

"Are these your horny headache meds?" Prophet asked, and Tom smiled.

"Just painkillers. I think you add the horny part yourself."

"I'll take straight Advil. Can't afford to be drugged any more than I already am. And by the way, I can alligator wrestle too."

"You wrestled an alligator?"

"What, like you're the only one who can?"

Tom stared at him. "It took me years to learn how to do that."

"I didn't have years. I had like a goddamned second before the thing killed me." Prophet looked indignant. "The other one was right behind it."

"You didn't wrestle it—you shot it."

"It's the same thing."

Tom laughed. "It's really not."

"And what the fuck—you hear a shot and you come running blindly? Have I taught you nothing?"

But Tom was fucking hugging him fiercely, like he'd finally realized the seriousness of the situation, and Prophet didn't want to deal with being treated with kid gloves, so he pushed him away. "Save it."

"Proph . . ."

"Can we figure out who's trying to kill you instead of feeling bad? That would help me more."

"Okay."

"And I need ice for my head," he muttered.

"There's no ice here."

"Right. Why are you here, T?"

"Police came to Etienne's."

"And you lost them in the bayou?"

"No. I hid while they searched. I waited until they left. I waited a couple more hours, then figured I had to go before daylight." Tom stared at him. "How'd you get here if you left me the Jeep?"

"Old man Jensen's truck."

"You stole his truck?"

"Borrowed," Prophet corrected. "Remy thought of it when I took him home."

"Did you just blame a fifteen-year-old kid for why you stole—"

"—borrowed—"

"—a truck?"

Prophet shrugged. "Little bit. Sure there's no ice around here?"

"Nothing but a bottle of whiskey."

"That'll do."

CHAPTER SEVENTEEN

"This place fucks you up," Prophet told him, several hours into the heat of the day as they sweltered together in the old shack.

Tom had taken more drugs and Prophet had finished half of the bottle of Jack Daniels Green Label and he wasn't so much drunk as he was . . . loose. More Prophet-like, if anything.

And somehow, Tom knew the guy could still fuck up an army.

"No shit." Tom held up the half-empty bottle of Jack Green. "Should I just forgive and forget?"

"No," Prophet said flatly.

"Never come back then, right? If I'd just let you handle everything . . ."

Prophet turned back to him, his granite eyes darkening. "I wanted you to go. I wanted to handle it for you, but I was wrong. I know better than anyone that anytime you have to run from something, you're headed down a dangerous path."

"I guess ghosts are inevitable."

Prophet nodded. "It's how we deal with them that makes the difference."

"Speaking from experience?"

"Yes."

"You should write that down and make it a book. You can call it *Shit Prophet Says.*"

Prophet gave him a drunken smile. "You have to get rid of this curse mentality, T. It's going to eat you up. Part of it already has. Whenever you believe the shit someone says about you, for better or worse, you become it. It gives them power. Forgive, forget, stay away—they're all parts of the same coin. Stop believing that curse shit and you won't have to do any of that stuff."

"Easy to say."

"No, not so easy. Hard as hell to do, too. *I'm* still working on it."

That admission—more than anything else Prophet could've said—broke the spell for Tom, broke the hold this damned place had on him. Because Prophet was the strongest man he knew, and for him to say that he still had to work on things— "Wait? You think you're cursed too?"

"Sometimes, T, I think we all are," Prophet said seriously.

He leaned in and kissed Prophet, then murmured, "Taste like whiskey," against the man's mouth. "I like whiskey."

"Good," Prophet told him. "I hope old man Jensen likes it too. Remy said to return the truck with a bottle in the front seat and run like hell."

Tom gave a short laugh and kept his forehead pressed to Prophet's. "I feel terrible for Remy . . ."

Prophet sighed and pulled back. "What about his mom? Sounds like there's some tension between her and Etienne."

"That's an understatement. They both wanted a kid so badly . . . Etienne was willing to do anything."

"Apparently, anything worked long enough to conceive the kid."

"Yeah, but the open marriage didn't. She's bitter. Figured Etienne would come around."

"Really?"

Tom shrugged. "Sometimes people only see what they want to."

"I hated sending Remy home to her," Prophet said. "But it's probably safest."

"Physically, maybe," Tom muttered.

"The faster we find Etienne, the faster he can fight his custody battle."

"Okay, yes." Tom pushed everything else out of his mind in order to do what would ultimately be the best thing for Etienne's son. "I'm tired of regrets. That's why I've been trying to work on things that won't let me have any."

"How's that working for you?" Prophet asked.

"Fine, until I came here." Tom held the bottle up like he was making a toast. "What now?"

"We wait until we figure out the smart thing to do."

"I think we can agree that we bypassed smart the second we kissed."

Prophet stared at him. "I think it's the smartest thing you ever did."

"I swear to God, just when I think I've got you pegged . . ." He ran a hand over Prophet's bruised cheek lightly. "Let's concentrate on how we're going to get out of this place."

Prophet held up his phone. "I called in an extraction team."

Ah, so that's what Prophet had been doing with his phone while Tom was busy making sure he wasn't like, dying or anything. "A little dramatic, no?"

"No," Prophet said calmly.

"Okay, so extraction *team* or . . . Cillian?"

"Dude, calm down. No. Not him."

"Can't be someone from EE because you're not there anymore."

Prophet stared at him. "Out of curiosity, when did you first hear about that?"

"Word traveled fast—so like, day one of Eritrea. Everyone was surprised."

"That it took Phil so long?"

"What the hell, Proph? No, that he'd do that to you. Lot of people like you, and they're pissed on your behalf."

Prophet muttered, "Kiss asses," but he was obviously pleased.

"Don't know why they like you," Tom told him, but he was smiling.

"Me neither," Prophet agreed heartily. He stretched. "These sleeping bags aren't bad. If it wasn't hot as hell, this place would be perfect."

"Guess I could turn the air on."

"There's been air in this thing the whole time?"

"You deserved a little torture."

"Maybe I even like it," Prophet said. He rolled over onto Tom and bit his earlobe while twisting one of the barbell piercings in his nipples.

Through the shudder, he forced himself to ask, "So, where were you the past four months?" before Prophet distracted him thoroughly.

"Liberating Croatia," Prophet told him seriously.

"How the hell am I ever supposed to win an argument with you?"

"You're not. Get used to it. But that was a nice try, when I'm obviously drugged and drunk with a concussion."

He threw his hands in the air. "You're buzzed."

"Can we just focus on clearing your name? Because while I'm pretty clear, you're the very definition of screwed." But Prophet was smiling as he said it. "Speaking of, aren't you gonna call Phil? You know, since you didn't check in with Cope after your arrest."

Tom shook his head. "You should call Phil."

"He doesn't want to hear from me. Trust me on that."

"What'd you do?"

"Why automatically assume it's me?" Prophet asked, and Tom stared at him. "Okay, a lot of the time it is me, but trust me . . . ah, hell, maybe neither of us should check in with your current employer."

"Better that way," Tom agreed.

"Right. So we're just fugitives with zero backup, although your aunt wields a pretty big shotgun," Prophet offered, and Tom gave a short laugh. "If my first plan falls through, we need a backup plan."

"I plan on letting you fuck me," he told Prophet. "How's that for a plan?"

"I like it. Never fucked in a cemetery," Prophet mused. "Well, there was that one time . . ."

Tom shut him up with a kiss, which was basically the way he'd wanted it. Prophet grabbed at Tommy as heat of an entirely different kind flooded his body. Then again, Tommy had always gone straight to his dick.

"For the love of all that's good and holy, do you think you two can keep it in your fucking pants long enough to be rescued?"

Tom jumped away from Prophet, who merely glanced lazily up at the big, dark-haired man framed by the doorway. "Why you gotta ruin my game, man?"

Mick looked between Prophet and Tom.

"Hey, Mick," Tom said. "I'm Tom."

"Kinda figured that one out for myself," Mick said as he walked inside.

A shorter, younger guy followed and punched Mick in the arm. "Hey, Proph! Hey, Tom, I'm Blue. Got a boat to get you out of here."

"A boat?" Prophet asked.

"Like one of those touring the bayou things with the big motor and the high seats," Blue said.

"What the hell kind of extraction plan's this shit?"

"One that involves a drunken asshole and his partner," Mick deadpanned.

"And why the fuck are you two dressed like hillbillies?" Prophet continued.

"We're blending," Mick said.

"They think we're shrimpers," Blue added, then motioned to Mick as if the man wasn't watching him. "I certainly didn't want to dress this way, but I think he's enjoying it."

"You know I can hear you, yes? He knows I can hear him, right?" Mick directed the last part at Tom, who ignored him to advise Blue, "Lose the flannel."

"Told you," Blue said, shrugging his shirt off. They all stared at the tattoos running down his arms. "Right." He pulled the shirt back up, grumbling about sweating to death, and Mick rolled his eyes and muttered something about never being given any goddamned credit.

"Can we just get the fuck out of here?" Prophet growled.

"Give him more to drink," Mick told Tom, and he was serious. Tom handed Prophet the bottle. He took it, slung an arm over Tom's shoulder, and Blue opened the door.

"We're not going to get far," Mick said as they started to walk through the cemetery toward the swamp. "There are roadblocks everywhere and police boats up and down the bayou. We can get you to a new spot, but not out of the bayou."

"Will there be running water?" Prophet asked as he stumbled against Blue.

"God, I hope so," Blue muttered. "You're kind of a princess, aren't you?"

"Remember what I told you last week at my apartment? Beat. You," Prophet reminded Blue in a low voice.

Tom had to give them credit. The airboat Mick used had a tented area where he and Prophet remained hidden while they motored slowly through the bayou. At one point, he even heard Blue talking to some of the other fishermen, introducing themselves.

"We came up from the Everglades. We're looking for work . . ."

"What the hell's he doing?" Prophet asked.

"A pretty good job of getting noticed for the right reasons," Tom whispered back. "These people can spot a stranger from ten miles out. Better not give them any reason to alert the sheriff."

Prophet grunted and took another drink. "Why can't we move faster?"

It went on like that for an hour, until the sun went down, the boat pulled into a slip, and Mick opened the tent, motioning for them to come out. Together, they moved quickly into a house on stilts hidden behind a mass of cypress trees and moss.

"Where's this?" Prophet asked.

"Two parishes over. More of a vacation spot," Tom told him.

Prophet shook his head, looked around in disbelief. "Who the fuck would want to vacation here? People keep trying to kill people."

"Don't let him drink anymore," Mick told Tom.

"There was nothing else to do," Prophet defended himself as he walked through the front door, then fell onto the couch. "Going to sleep this off."

"You do that," Mick said, then stared at Tom. "You all right?"

"Better than yesterday, yeah."

"Blue and I are going to head back to your parish to try to figure this shit out. Call if you get into trouble."

"Will do."

Blue dropped a large bag in front of Tom. "Supplies."

"Thanks."

Mick put a hand on his shoulder. "And Tom? Even drunk, Prophet can do more damage than anyone can imagine. Just keep that in mind."

Tom would add it to the stack of things to keep, because everything *was* on his mind, so much so that, once Mick and Blue left, he had no idea what to do with himself and his nervous energy.

He checked Prophet's phones and his own—no calls from Della or Etienne. Or Remy.

Jesus, E, where the fuck are you?

He and Prophet had avoided talking a lot about Etienne being missing, because they both knew what it meant. Based on what had happened to Miles and Donny . . . fuck, the chances of Etienne being found alive were slim.

The past was never really dead—Tom was living proof—but there was a difference between being haunted by it and facing judgment for it. And because he couldn't stop his mind from racing, he at least tried to stop his body, because he was about to collapse from exhaustion.

He ended up squashing himself into the corner of the couch, hoping that being close to Prophet physically would calm him.

It didn't. Too overtired to sleep, he squirmed and shifted so much he woke the guy. He looked down as Prophet maneuvered himself so his head was in Tom's lap, and he was staring up at Tom.

"Are they gone?" Prophet asked.

"Yes."

"I know they said they were going, but are they really gone?"

Tom slid his hand gingerly through Prophet's hair. The knot on the side of his head had gone down a little, but he could tell by the way Prophet moved that he was in pain. "I heard the boat."

"So we're like, stuck here?"

"Looks that way."

Prophet sighed. "I can't believe you came back here to work."

"Figured I could make a difference."

Prophet's hand came up to stroke his cheek. "Did you?"

He'd come back to stop the sheriff's son from continuing to run that same survival shit he'd barely lived through—and to stop him from torturing any young kids who were different. And he'd succeeded in the former, but the latter . . . that had been an everyday challenge, and not just with the sheriff. The community at large hadn't changed much. Maybe it had always been a losing battle, but at least Tom could look back with pride on some of the kids he'd mentored here, kids he'd made sure to help get out of the bayou and off to college—or at least to a city where they could meet like-minded people. "Yeah," he said now. "I did. But I wanted to do more. The sheriff who tortured me . . . his son Rob and I worked as deputies under a different sheriff. When he decided to retire, I didn't want to think about what would happen if Rob took office."

"And that's why you ran against him?"

"Three years running, after I saw that I couldn't change anything being his right-hand man."

Prophet raised a brow. "Robin to his Batman."

Tom snorted. "He wishes. He hated me as much as his old man had."

"How the hell did you keep your job?"

Ah, don't go there, Proph. "I did what I had to do in order to help the kids around here."

"Five years, T," Prophet said gently. "You stayed here five years and lived with this shit. Like you were punishing yourself."

When he didn't answer that, Prophet stared at him quizzically, and then sighed. "Shit, T, I didn't mean . . ."

But Prophet had hit the bull's-eye with his original question, because what had happened in the bayou was exactly the reason—the only reason—Tom had been allowed into the sheriff's department in the first place. "Look, the old sheriff made me keep a secret. The guy's son knew it—the only other person who did. It was like we were blackmailing each other. He knew I couldn't say anything, no matter how miserable he tried to make me. But he also knew he couldn't ever fire me. I figured my happiness shouldn't matter, as long as I was able to make a difference in some kid's life."

"I can't fault you for that." Prophet ran a hand through his hair, his expression tight. He didn't say anything else for a long time.

"Did *you* make a difference?" Tom asked.

Prophet must have known exactly what he was asking, because he said, "I hope so. Hard to tell when you can't fix everything."

"Maybe we should stop that shit."

"Yeah, you first, Voodoo."

"I like that better than Cajun."

"I'll note that for when I order the T-shirts." Prophet's smile was small, but it was there, and fuck, the man was beautiful when he smiled. "Did Phil send you to the shrink?"

"You know you wouldn't call Sarah that to her face, right?" Prophet shrugged, a half grin on his face and Tom conceded, "Yeah, I saw her a few times a week for a couple of weeks before I left for Eritrea. She's pretty cool. You ever see her screensaver?"

"Two guys in leather? I sent it to her," Prophet said.

"Fucking figures."

Prophet narrowed his eyes. "So, you're into leather?" Tom cursed, and Prophet continued, "Did Sarah tell you what you needed to hear?"

"I guess so. You and EE make me feel like I can do anything." Prophet gave him a slightly drunken grin, but the blush told Tom everything. He decided to push his luck a little. "The jobs you took . . ."

"Yeah?" Prophet changed from smiling to wary at warp speed.

"More dangerous than EE?"

"Ah, Jesus, T. Compliment me and then use it to get stuff out of me? That's . . . a good technique." He shook his head. "Okay, fine. Regarding the danger—I'm used to flying without a net."

"What does that mean?"

"Means I took black-ops jobs in between EE jobs all the time," Prophet told him. "Some Phil found out about and some he didn't."

"You need to be spanked."

Prophet paused to consider this, asked, "Will you be wearing leather while you do it?" and then his stomach growled. Loudly.

"Way to break the mood. Wait here."

"I wasn't going to get up and cook," Prophet called after him. "Check for leather in the bag."

Tom shook his head as he rifled through the supplies Blue brought . . . and dammit all to hell if he didn't find a pair of leather cuffs in there. He pocketed them, pulled out a couple of sodas and sandwiches, and brought them back to the couch. Prophet sat up next to him, started eating.

"Are you going back to EE?" Tom asked.

"No," Prophet said sharply.

"I know Phil regrets letting you leave."

"Yeah? Did he tell you that or put it in the company newsletter?"

"EE has a newsletter?"

Prophet glanced at him sideways. "Just a Christmas one. Make sure to get him the picture of you in your Santa boxers."

"You've got a Santa kink?"

Prophet stared at the ceiling and mouthed a silent prayer. "I'm not going back to EE."

"And I'm guessing you don't want to talk about what happened."

"You are correct, sir."

Tom frowned.

"Fine," Prophet huffed. "Look, out of everyone, Phil knows me. Knows who I am and what I do. He can't promise to be okay with that and then suddenly turn around and punish me for it. I'm too old to change. And too old for broken promises, T."

Tom didn't say anything, just stroked a hand through Prophet's hair. The betrayal was evident, from the set of Prophet's shoulders to the look of cool granite in his eyes.

"Don't," Prophet warned.

"Okay."

"You're thinking it."

"But I did the same fucking thing Phil did, Proph."

"No, you didn't," Prophet said evenly. "You didn't sign on for me."

"But I wanted to after I met you. That has to count."

"It does," Prophet told him. "And I don't want to talk about me and EE anymore."

"I get that, but . . . I thought you were supposed to take over?"

"Things change."

"So you really didn't come to my aunt's house because Phil asked you to?"

"He didn't ask me. Even if he had, I did this for you, T. Get that straight—for *you*."

Prophet paused. "Your aunt put me in her will."

"Yeah, right." But he didn't discount that possibility, because Prophet had a way of getting under your skin. And Tom had stopped minding it, because embracing it was much easier.

Prophet rubbed his palms along his thighs, and his expression was one that Tom was beginning to understand all too well. The man was restless. Caged-lion restless. But the problem was there was no place to go.

But there was something to do. He pulled the leather cuffs out of his pocket and Prophet's eyes widened. "You don't want to talk, this is your other option."

For the briefest of moments, he swore Prophet would say no, was even beginning to curse himself for bringing up binding Prophet's wrists. But then Prophet's eyes darkened, and his cheeks flushed a little when he said, "Jesus Christ," and then, "Use me, Tommy."

It was part order, part plea. Watching Prophet carefully, Tom opened the cuffs, the ripping sound of Velcro reverberating around the room. Prophet swallowed hard as he stared at the bindings, but then he moved his gaze up to Tom's eyes and stood his ground. Tom's cock hardened in a rush, piercings rubbing against his jeans. Prophet glanced down between his legs, but he was waiting—so still, maybe the most still Tom'd ever seen him.

"Stay there," he told Prophet, and the man gave the briefest of nods, trusting him. He moved behind Prophet and tugged at the bottom of his shirt, murmuring, "Take this off."

Prophet did, without turning around, kept his hands at his sides. Tom ran a hand over his back, tracing the muscles, planning tattoos he could put over the smooth skin. Prophet usually shuddered whenever Tom did that, and this time was no exception.

He grabbed one of the man's forearms and brought it behind his lower back. Wrapped a cuff around it and closed up. The metal chain between the cuffs clinked softly in the quiet room, as he did the same to the other wrist, then pressed a kiss to the back of Prophet's neck. He walked back around and faced Prophet for a long moment, before putting a hand on his shoulder and pushing down. "On your knees."

His voice sounded husky to his own ears. Rough too, and his throat was thick—with lust, with a million other emotions that only intensified when Prophet sank down as ordered and tugged at Tom's zipper with his teeth.

Tom threaded his hand in Prophet's hair and pulled him back. Pulled his own zipper down with his free hand, slowly, exposing his piercings one by one as he freed his cock. "That what you're looking for?"

"Yeah, Tommy," Prophet murmured. "Fucking let me."

Tom guided Prophet forward by his hair, and Prophet licked the head of his cock, then sucked it into his mouth up to the ridge, swirling his tongue around and down, just enough to flick the first piercing.

Tom jolted, because Prophet had taken him in several creative ways, but not like this, on his knees. And what made it hotter was the way Prophet watched him, submissive, and yet the look in his eyes told Tom he was still in goddamned charge. Tom was more than happy to let him be right, even as he showed him how wrong he was.

Prophet pulled back a little, a wicked look in his eyes as he looked up at Tom. He licked slowly along the ladder of piercings, and then he paid special attention to each one, tugging the barbells between his teeth until Tom hissed or groaned and tightened his grip on Prophet's hair warningly. Each time, Prophet would comply, letting his dick go, and he'd wait patiently, and each time Tom brought his mouth back to his cock, he was rewarded with the tug and pull, lick-suck-twist motion. His pain-pleasure center intertwined to where Tom could barely pick out which was which. He knew he just wanted more.

Prophet's tongue cushioned the piercings as he took Tommy down his throat, as far as he could. Tom's hand slid into his hair, then tightened, holding Prophet there, and he moaned at the sucking, wet heat, his hips jerking with zero rhythm. Prophet hummed around his dick—or maybe he was laughing at how Tom had almost lost it, and that didn't matter because *oh yeah*, that tingled up his spine. Watching Prophet's lips stretched around his cock, knowing they'd be red and swollen afterwards, and that he'd still kiss the shit out of him made him moan.

God, he needed this release—they both did. Because as much as this was about sex and pleasure, it was also about need. And they both showed their need for each other so well this way.

He held Prophet in place, using the man the way he'd asked. Thrusting into his mouth, fucking it, and when Prophet groaned around his cock, Tom held fast to his hair, bucking harder.

And Prophet was bound. For him. He wasn't fighting the cuffs at all, and the sight of this strong man surrendering, watching him with an unrelenting gaze even as he took everything Tom had was too much. And when he came in a hot rush, he didn't even consider pulling out of Prophet's mouth—and Prophet's mouth sucked him in too tightly anyway. He clutched Prophet's hair as he shot down the man's throat, and Prophet kept his eyes looking upward at Tom the entire time. Locked and loaded by his gaze, like the goddamned first time they'd met.

"You always have to have the last word," Tom croaked, after his body stopped shuddering. Mostly.

"I didn't say anything," Prophet protested with a smirk, sitting back on his heels. "And you're still hard."

Tom sank to his knees and kissed Prophet, tasting himself, reaching between their bodies to pull down Prophet's pants, just enough to get to his cock. He kept Prophet kneeling as he palmed the hot skin of his cock and stroked, swallowing his surprised groan.

He kept his mouth on Prophet's, muffling the cursed protests that really weren't protests at all. Jerked him harder until Prophet stiffened and shot between them, biting Tom's lower lip in the process. Even after he released it, they stayed together like that, foreheads pressed together, lips touching, the sound of their ragged breaths filling Tom's ears.

Prophet shivered slightly and said quietly, "Get them off, T."

Tom wasted no time in ripping the cuffs off and throwing them aside. He rubbed Prophet's wrists for a few seconds, before Prophet brought his arms around and hugged him.

He ran his hand through Prophet's hair again, massaging the man's scalp, the way he knew Prophet liked. As if in agreement, Prophet groaned, low in his throat, and closed his eyes.

With one hand running through his hair, Tom trailed the other to the back of Prophet's neck to rub the knotted muscles as they made their firm return back to earth.

The trip away had been good while it lasted. He sighed and Prophet murmured, "We'll figure this shit out, Tommy."

"For the first time, I believe that."

CHAPTER EIGHTEEN

One minute, Prophet was in a drowsy sleep, the alcohol diluted by food and time, sex and sugar, and the next, he was staring up at his wrists.

They were tied together with rough rope, which was looped around a metal ceiling beam. He was half-balanced on a chair, his toes aching from trying to keep himself from hanging and putting pressure on his arms. His shoulder had nearly popped out when he'd fallen asleep.

He looked down and the room was the same room where he'd been sitting with Tommy. But Azar was there too, for just a second, before walking away with his weapon drawn.

"No. Fuck. No," Prophet heard himself say, but his voice was nothing more than a hoarse whisper.

"I'm ready—just fucking do it!" John shouted and Prophet steeled himself, because he knew Azar hadn't been bluffing when he'd threatened to kill John if Prophet didn't tell him everything he knew about the man he'd killed, the man who knew how to build nuclear triggers. Two shots and Prophet kept staring straight ahead, refusing to give any of them the satisfaction of seeing his heart breaking.

He and John had been captured by Azar two days earlier. They'd tried to fight the terrorist's men off, but there'd been too many of them. Even then, Prophet knew immediately that their classified mission had been compromised, that they'd been set up.

That there might be no way out.

But Prophet would keep pushing, because that's what he did. It was the only way he knew how to operate. The most effective way to live. Because it got rid of the people in his life who couldn't handle it, couldn't handle him, and it gave him a chance to keep everyone at arm's length until he figured out which group they fell into.

Tommy hadn't been wrong about any of that.

Jesus Christ, you are so fucking broken.

He blinked, and he was in the house on the bayou again, standing by the kitchen sink, scared to turn around. Last he'd seen, Tom had still been sleeping.

Tom, who might eventually get to the same point Phil had.

"I didn't get to that point," John said. Prophet glanced to the right, where John sat on the counter.

Why *hadn't* John?

Because John had been family, lover, teammate, best friend. Because, despite all of that, John had never let his guard down, no matter how much he'd pretended to let Prophet in.

John was great at pretending. But Prophet never pretended he was anything other than what he was. Because what was the point of being close to someone if they couldn't know exactly who the fuck you really were?

"Incoming!" John called. "Take cover!"

Prophet blinked, and the desert loomed in front of him again. He moved back to cover Hal and . . .

"Hey, Proph, you all right?"

Tom's voice was calm. Low. Like he wasn't sure Prophet was all there or not and fuck—*fuck*—had Tom seen the whole damned thing? Fuck. Prophet should've know that as soon as he made himself vulnerable to Tommy, his own mind would start working overtime.

He turned and met Tom's concerned expression. Thunder boomed over the house.

Thunder. Not explosions.

"At least you're not completely crazy," John told him, but Prophet refused to tear his gaze from Tom, because Tom was what was real. Because Tom was here for him in a way John never could've been. And as unfair as that was, he'd long ago gotten rid of any illusions where John was concerned.

He blinked again and he was kneeling next to the couch with an arm over Tom, holding him flat and protecting him from the incoming enemy fire.

Tom, not Hal.

He eased up on his grip, allowing Tom to turn slightly. He put his forehead against Tom's thigh and the man put a gentle hand on the back of Prophet's neck.

"How often do these happen?"

"Way more since the last case," he admitted. "You're a heavy sleeper for someone who was in law enforcement."

"Not as heavy a sleeper as you might think," Tom said quietly.

Prophet's eyes watered, and he blinked it away. Still couldn't bring himself to look up when he said, "Sadiq killed Chris to taunt me. Sadiq hurt you to taunt me. All because of what happened on a mission ten years ago. Do you see why I wasn't meant to have a partner?"

"You went through hell during that mission, Proph. I still don't know exactly what happened, but I could see it when we were captured. You relived it then. I guess you've never stopped reliving it and I wanted to help—"

"You did."

"I still want to. You can't be alone forever."

"I can try."

Tom shook his head. "It worked for like, four months before you tackled me and let me fuck you."

"I thought you were an intruder," Prophet pointed out as he lifted his head.

"You always let intruders fuck you?"

"Isn't that a hot fantasy?"

Tom laughed a little, then sobered. "Can you talk about any of what causes the flashbacks?"

"No. Not any more than I've already told you."

Tom sighed, obviously frustrated.

"Look, you already know enough to get you in trouble. In fact, you're already in trouble with Sadiq."

"I know what I just saw had nothing to do with Sadiq."

"It had *everything* to do with him."

"Christ, Prophet, we are so fucked up." Tom slid to the floor next to him. "I can't help you unless I know what your burden is. And I want to help you. Let me in, Proph."

No one—*no one*—had ever said that to him. "Just saying that means more to me than you'll ever know."

Tom's hand was still cupped around the back of his neck, rubbing slowly. "Then that'll have to be enough for now."

And, because Tom didn't push, Prophet would let him in further than he should, further than he'd ever let anyone in . . .

As soon as they figured out Tom's mess.

When Mick and Blue checked in via secured line a couple of hours later, they hadn't found any trace of Etienne. Etienne's parents had filed a missing person's report, and the sheriff had found a small bloodstain in the grass behind his house, which was being tested to see if it matched Etienne's blood type.

"And Tom Boudreaux is most definitely a person of interest," Mick added.

Tom groaned and put his head on the table next to the phone. It was Prophet's turn to rub the back of his neck, and damn, it felt good.

After Prophet's flashback, they'd showered. Had sex. Showered again. And now, Prophet was decidedly sober and apparently ready to take on this case.

"Anything on Miles and Donny?" he asked Mick now.

"I ran that syringe you pulled from Miles's house. It was ketamine. Same thing found in both Miles's and Donny's bloodstream. But man, it was a giant hit for both. Not the way an addict like Miles would normally take it, and based on reports, Donny wasn't an addict at all. So even though the coroner's reports for both aren't ruling out suicide, they're also not ruling out murder anymore." Mick paused. "Look, we all know it was definitely murder."

"And I'm the number one suspect," Tom said, his head still down, voice muffled. "They'll say that Miles and Donny were afraid I'd expose their secrets. They'll twist around the AA rumors that Miles was going to spill and instead say they were nervous about what I'd say."

"So what, you conjured up a hurricane and came to town just to kill him?"

Shit. He lifted his head.

"What?" Prophet asked.

"I, ah . . . I told Etienne I was coming to town," he said. "I'd made a tattoo appointment."

"For when?"

"I made it before I went to Eritrea. It was supposed to be last month. But then shit came up and I didn't ask for the time off and . . ."

"And Miles had the letter ready for you. Because he wanted to hand it to you in person—maybe he told Etienne that. Maybe he asked Etienne to bring you here for that, and that's another reason Etienne wanted you to stay away."

"And what, Miles told his AA group all that?" Tom asked.

"Things in confidential meetings depend on addicts staying sober enough to keep their mouths shut," Prophet said gruffly, and Tom stored away the fact that this wasn't the first time Prophet discussed addicts as if he had intimate knowledge of the subject.

Mick's voice floated up from the phone. "Could Etienne be involved in this?"

Tom did not want to consider that. But he'd have to.

"Has Etienne ever run before?" Prophet asked.

"No, that was me." He paused. "Etienne would get really caught up in his work—he liked quiet when he drew or painted. And if he couldn't get it in his studio because we were there . . . who knows? But Proph, I can't see him dropping out of sight just when all this was going down."

"Sometimes that's when people do. When Etienne talked to me while you were in jail, he seemed to know that the sheriff would come down hard on him too. Maybe the blood wasn't his. Maybe he's hiding until it's safe to come out."

Tom really hoped so. Another death on his conscience would be unthinkable, beyond the fact that Etienne was a good man. A great man. He'd done his share of tattoos for pure fun and profit, but most people didn't know how much time he spent in hospitals, helping women who'd had breast reconstruction, who'd lost eyebrows to chemo. He helped amputees, decorating their stumps and their prosthetics so that way, when people stared, they'd really have something to stare at. "He's got to be okay, Proph. He fucking saved me, more times than I could count when we were growing up."

"Then he will be," Prophet said simply. "He was as worried about you as you are about him. I don't think he'd leave you. And he seems like the kind of guy who'd admit to what he'd done."

"So we're not looking at him for the killing?" Mick asked.

"We're just looking *for* him," Prophet clarified. "He's got a kid he's trying to get custody of."

Mick was silent as Tom racked his brain, trying to think of where Etienne might've gone. They'd had several haunts when they were younger. But when they got old enough not to care that people knew they were together, they hadn't needed them anymore.

"I'm sure the sheriff's already been to Etienne's house," Tom said.

"So now we'll go," Prophet told him.

"We can't leave here, remember?"

"We can't—but Blue can be our eyes."

Tom realized that, despite all he'd heard about Blue and his conquests, you couldn't fully appreciate what he did until you saw him scale . . . anything. Like fucking Spiderman.

And Blue couldn't help it. One minute, he was there on the ground, the next, he was on the roof. Or in a tree. And he and Prophet were viewing it from the front row, or, in this case, a camera attached to Blue's NVs.

Mick looked lethal. Blue was far more dangerous. It would be easy to underestimate him.

At least there was no police tape anywhere, so technically, they weren't breaking two laws. Just the whole illegal entry one.

"You know, there's a spare key under the rocks in the back," Tom said again.

"Key?" Blue acted like the word was foreign. He slid inside an opened attic window in the dark and scanned the room.

Tom recognized the paintings. Etienne kept a small cache in his attic, pieces he didn't really like anymore but couldn't bear to part with.

"It's quiet," Blue said. "Cool."

That was the way Etienne always kept it.

"It's clean. Just a layer of dust—maybe four days old," Blue said.

"Which matches his disappearance," Tom agreed. The man hated dust and clutter.

"Great place," Prophet commented as they watched Blue go down the stairs and turn into the master bedroom. He went first to the dresser.

"Check the top right drawer," Tom told him. Blue did, pulled out Etienne's wallet. "Shit."

Blue opened it. "Cash and credit cards here. License too. Plus a watch and a wedding ring."

Prophet looked at Tom.

"Not mine," Tom told him.

"He didn't really marry Remy's mom," Prophet said.

"Kinda did, yeah."

"Hello, you two—can we gossip later?" Blue asked.

"I wouldn't have to gossip if you could find me something," Prophet grumbled.

Blue put his middle finger up in front of the camera he wore.

Tom turned to Prophet. "So you're not the least bit jealous of me and Etienne?"

"I do a great job of hiding it, don't I? Unlike you."

"You like when I don't hide it."

Prophet smiled in agreement.

"Bastard," Tom muttered, and then he semi-froze.

Prophet asked, "T, what's wrong?" just as Blue announced, "I hear footsteps."

"Blue, get the hell out of there," Mick told him. Tom watched as the camera attached to Blue gave him a dizzying shot of Blue basically jumping out of the window and finally coming to hang on the rope about halfway down. There were sirens in the distance.

And even though that was happening a couple hundred miles away, he couldn't help but look around.

Prophet's phone beeped. He looked at the number and frowned. "Shit. Gotta take this." He pressed a button and said hello.

"Who's this?" A female voice over the speakerphone.

"Who's this?" Prophet asked back, his concern clear on his face.

"I found this number in my son's phone. Did you take him, you bastard?"

Prophet looked at Tom. "Remy's mom?" he mouthed, and Tom nodded, the tension tightening around his head like a vise.

Tom was about to say something to Blue when he heard a voice behind them say, "You didn't have to go through all this trouble to find him. I could've helped."

Tom watched Prophet's expression harden for a second before going neutral, and Tom knew that face well by now. There was a threat.

He turned, saw Charlie holding a gun pointed at the back of Prophet's head. "Charlie, what are you doing?"

"You'll both have to come with me to find out," Charlie said.

CHAPTER NINETEEN

All Tom could think as he stared at the man he'd thought of as a laid-back stoner with the memory of an elephant was, *Get him talking*. "What the hell, Charlie?"

"You'll find out soon enough."

"I'm not going fucking anywhere with you, asshole," Prophet told him, then grabbed his neck and yanked a dart out. "What the fuck? Ah, not again. Dammit."

"Shit, Proph." Tom went for him, but Charlie waved his gun. The real one he held in his left hand—the dart gun was in his right.

"If you don't cooperate, you can be sure you'll never find Remy in time to save him," Charlie told him, and Prophet muttered, "Fuck," even as he stumbled a little. Tom grabbed his hand and Prophet gave it a squeeze, almost like he was telling Tom to do what Charlie wanted. Which had been Tom's plan too.

"Disconnect that." Charlie pointed to the computer and Tom reluctantly pulled the wire, cutting them off from Blue. "I knew your friend wouldn't come along all peaceful like. And since he came in your place last time and survived the alligators, I figured I'd give you both another shot at this."

Charlie, *not* Gil Boudreaux. A small victory, but still... "At what?"

"You'll find out soon enough. In the meantime, you wrestle him into the car for me, all right, Tom?"

"We can leave him here. He's got nothing to do with this," Tom said through gritted teeth. Prophet was passed out on his shoulder. He put two fingers against the man's neck, reassured by the steady—albeit slow—beats of his pulse.

"He'll be fine. Unless I have to give him another dose."

"He's already passed out."

"What matters to me is your cooperation," Charlie said, and Tom suddenly saw the man clear as day, like the curtain had been lifted.

Charlie hadn't changed, like Tom had thought the other day. No, *Tom* had changed. He'd finally gotten his head out of his own shit enough to be able to see that Charlie had *always* been lying to him.

He noted for a brief moment how ironic it was that he'd been upset that none of his partners trusted his voodoo shit, when really, he managed to ignore it a hell of a lot. And fuck it all if he didn't want to tell Prophet he'd been right about that too.

But the thing was, Charlie hadn't known about Tom's involvement with Miles and Donny. Not until . . .

Charlie had been watching Tom try to put the pieces together, and when he started, Charlie gave him a round of applause, hitting the corner of the hand he held the gun with. "Give the deputy a prize for making a connection. I heard the AA rumors about Miles too. That he was going to admit to something big."

"I'm not a deputy. And why would you care about those rumors?"

Charlie waved the gun at Prophet. "Get him in the car. Don't try anything, Tom."

"Can't we just talk this out, Charlie?"

"Maybe we could've, if you'd shown up in the marsh, instead of your friend here. But now it's complicated."

Tom got moving, because he didn't want to risk Remy's life, or risk Charlie shooting Prophet and then be forced to leave him there.

Leave no man behind didn't just pertain to military men, but by going with Charlie, the chances of escape were tougher. Unless he was taking them into the bayou, in which case, Tom definitely had the upper hand, because Charlie had only lived here for five years.

He hoisted Prophet up and over his shoulder, because the guy was out. Deadweight. He walked out of the house, and Charlie pointed to the trunk of the car. Tom had no choice but to put Prophet back there. And stuffing a big guy like Prophet into the back of the small trunk wasn't easy—he winced when he jammed him awkwardly on his side.

"Now handcuff him. Behind his back," Charlie said, tossing him the cuffs. Tom maneuvered Prophet's arms carefully behind his back, making the cuffs loose enough for his circulation.

They'd never hold Proph for long anyway.

Charlie had him cuff and chain Prophet's ankles too. Made Tom close the trunk and then handcuff himself to the passenger's side door as Charlie blindfolded him. But not before he caught a glance of a red knife sheath on the floor by Charlie's feet. Briefly, he considered the fact that Charlie might've killed Gil Boudreaux, but decided that his father was too goddamned mean to be taken down that easily.

"You don't have to do this," Tom told him.

"You trying the psych bull rap on me, deputy? Oh, right, forgot, you couldn't keep that job. What, did your favor from the sheriff run out?"

Tom's gut tightened. He rubbed his wrists together so he could feel the leather bracelet. "How do you know so much about it?"

He felt the prick of a needle in his arm and fuck, he wouldn't be able to track where Charlie was taking them. The blindfold wouldn't've been an issue, but the drugs . . .

He only managed to fight unconsciousness long enough to hear Charlie's nonanswer.

"You haven't figured it out by now?" Charlie asked as he started the car and jerked it through the tall grasses.

Prophet groaned. His mouth was cotton and nasty, and he blinked through his blurred vision. His arms were jacked up behind him, but hey, at least he wasn't hanging from them.

"Seriously?" Tom asked, and Prophet realized he'd said that last part out loud.

"Gotta be grateful for the little shit, T," he managed, and that's when he realized that they were sitting back-to-back, tied to chairs and each other. "Guessing we're alone?"

"Charlie's been gone for half an hour, at least."

"The kid?"

"No sign of him," Tom said grimly. "And I don't know if Blue or Mick got picked up by the police."

"Shit." He'd told Mick to grab Blue and get the hell out of there if anything bad went down. Whether they'd listen or not was another story, but even if they weren't hours away, neither of those men knew the bayou. Not like Tom or Charlie. "Any idea where we are?"

"We're in an old boathouse. There are a few of them left along the swamps near the cemetery in my parish—he could've easily taken the time to drive here because he blindfolded me. And he fucking drugged me."

"I think he dropped me at some point. Feel like I was slammed into concrete." Prophet rolled his neck a little, trying to orient himself.

"I carried you."

"You dropped me?"

"It was into a padded trunk, not the ground." Tom was working on the ropes and Prophet moved his fingers to help him.

They had to play this safe and slow. With Remy's life on the line, Prophet's usual methods of just slamming the hell out of Charlie wouldn't work here. "This is going to require your touch, T."

"Yeah," Tom muttered, because Prophet wasn't talking about the ropes. "If we corner him, he's not going to talk. That's what this whole thing's about—making all of us pay."

"What'd he tell you?"

"He heard the AA rumors about Miles and what happened on the bayou."

"Why the fuck would he care?"

"I have no idea," Tom said, as he helped Prophet try to get the ropes as loose as possible. They didn't get far, because the ropes were a mix of thick braided twine and thinner rough rope tied in intricate knots from hell. Charlie had obviously learned his lesson, because he'd stripped Prophet of his weapons, including the knife he usually kept in his boot.

Tom struggled against the ropes. "I thought sailors were supposed to know knots."

"Kidding me with that shit, Tommy?"

Charlie strode in then, looking so pleased with himself that Prophet wanted to smash him. "Have you figured it out yet?" Charlie asked, and Prophet bit his tongue to keep from saying anything that would make the situation worse.

And he had a strong feeling it was going to get worse anyway, especially when Charlie pulled out what looked like an old-fashioned cattle prod.

"I want to help you, Charlie, the way you always helped me," Tom reasoned, and Charlie smiled, like he was an equally reasonable human being. And then reached out and stuck the cattle prod right into Prophet's side, where his shirt had ridden up.

The electric heat seared his bare skin and for what seemed like forever, his entire body was suspended in a twist of pain. When it left, he was still vibrating, his brain scrambled and his entire body came down in one big shudder.

He was aware of Tom cursing, yelling at Charlie to "cut it the fuck out!"

"We're playing my game now, Tom. All those years I helped you out . . . I had no idea who I was helping."

Prophet spat out, "You were saving your own ass, Charlie, because you were dealing. Last time I looked, that was illegal." Charlie held the prod against Prophet's side again. Prophet tensed, waiting for the jolt.

"Charlie, don't," Tom said. "What happened in the bayou wasn't Prophet's fault. It's mine, okay?"

"That's what Miles said too, right before I killed him," Charlie said, pulling the prod back, and Prophet leaned back in relief. "Right after he confessed what he'd been talking about in those AA meetings. Because I'd been looking into my father's death for years, but there was nothing."

"Your father?" Tom asked quietly, and oh fuck, this wasn't good. "That was your father who—"

"That was my father you killed!" Charlie yelled and stuck Prophet with the cattle prod again, triggering it this time.

When he could focus again, he heard Tommy begging. "Come on, Charlie—use the thing on me. I'm the one you want to hurt."

"Exactly. You're the one who I want to watch suffer." Prophet drew in a stuttering breath, and felt Tom still trying to free their wrists.

"Where's Remy?" Tom asked. "Just let him go. He's got nothing to do with this, Charlie. Don't ruin his life the way ours were ruined. If you do nothing else, have some goddamned compassion for the kid you once were."

"It's too late for that," Charlie said.

"You fucking bastard," Prophet muttered. "Why not go after the sheriff who put kids in danger to begin with?"

"Why not shut up?" Charlie told him, moving around to face him.

"I've found that's never really gotten me anywhere," Prophet told him seriously.

"Are you fucking trying to get another round of electric current?" Tom asked, obviously going for the distraction. Anything that pissed Charlie off enough to keep him talking, even torturing, was better than killing them.

"Gonna happen anyway. Might as well do something to earn it," Prophet said, and was rewarded with another long prod. "Fuck. Me."

Even as he jerked, Prophet could feel Tom loosening the ropes enough so he could easily pull his hands out when the time came. Prophet breathed through the pain as Tom finally asked over his shoulder, "Is Remy dead?"

The asshole checked his watch. "He will be soon. He was bleeding out the last time I saw him."

Tom sucked in a hard breath. Remy had to be close for Charlie to know that. And since this was symbolic, then he'd have to be keeping Etienne and Remy close by.

It was a risk, but . . .

"I know, T," Prophet said when Tom squeezed his hand urgently.

"You know what?" Charlie demanded.

Prophet jumped him then. Slammed him to the ground with an unnecessary force that felt really fucking good. Tom grabbed the gun as it slid across the room and held it on Charlie.

"Take us to Remy," Tom demanded.

"It's too late," Charlie told him.

"It's never too late," Tom said in a voice so fierce Prophet knew he meant it.

Prophet put his fingers on the pressure point along Charlie's neck. A quick squeeze dropped the man to unconsciousness. Then he emptied Charlie's pockets—flashlight, phone, knife, car keys.

"Did he have a GPS in his car?" he asked Tom.

"I didn't see one. I didn't hear him use one either."

He scrolled through the GPS capabilities on Charlie's phone. Just because the man hadn't needed to use it tonight didn't mean he hadn't been planning this.

"You found something?" Tom asked as he hauled Charlie to one of the chairs and tied him.

"Old GPS coordinates, not too far from here."

"Let's go."

Prophet let him take the lead, and Tom followed the coordinates through the thick bayou grass, the swamp sucking against his boots with every step. It was like quicksand around here . . . and they had no lights. He closed his eyes and just pictured Remy, and then he called out softly, "Remy, it's Tom. Where are you?"

He was greeted with the night sounds of the bayou. Prophet was right behind him, so close he could feel the heat off the man's body. And he was back here again, fourteen and trying to find someone in the dark.

He pictured the cemetery to his right. When he'd walked home in the daylight with Etienne, they used to take the pathway that led down to the swamps instead of veering off toward the main road.

He took a few steps, reaching out to let the big cypress trees guide him as he trained the flashlight on the ground, until he was walking without having to think. And then he stopped and heard someone crying softly. "Remy?"

"Tom?"

Remy's voice. Weak. He and Prophet moved forward in tandem, until the light shined on Remy, who was half-lying, half-kneeling next to Etienne.

Shit. Tom knelt next to Etienne, because Prophet was already next to Remy. He touched Etienne's neck, although it was obvious before he felt the cold skin that the man was dead, even if he hadn't seen the spread of blood over Etienne's chest.

He blinked tears back but didn't have time to process anything because Prophet was calling him urgently. "Tommy, I need your help. He's bleeding out fast. Knife wound to the chest."

He closed Etienne's eyes and moved over to help Remy.

"Remy, can you stay with us?" Prophet asked and Tom was amazed when he heard, "Tryin'. Hurts."

"I know, Remy, I know," Prophet muttered as he used his own T-shirt to try to staunch the flow of blood. "This is gonna hurt, but I have to put pressure on it, okay?"

Tom heard Remy's soft "okay" as he dialed in an emergency with Charlie's phone and stayed on the line until he heard the sirens in the distance.

"Ten minutes out," he said softly.

Prophet's mouth twisted, because that could be too long. In the darkness, Tom mourned his friend as Prophet held Remy practically in his lap, murmuring something only Remy could hear, because Remy was murmuring back. Prophet kept pressure against Remy's chest in what seemed like a futile attempt to stop the bleeding. Tom could smell the metallic tang, and he was surprised it hadn't brought out any predators.

He turned slowly, saw several pair of eyes glittering in the dark behind them. They weren't moving closer, but Tom pulled his weapon in case they advanced.

"Do not even tell me there are alligators stalking us," Prophet said quietly.

"Okay, I won't."

"Tommy's an alligator whisperer," Prophet told Remy. "We'll be okay."

Remy made a sound between a laugh and a cough, and Tom caught the gurgle. The sirens were closer, and Tom could make out lights along the far end of the swamp.

"My . . . dad . . . ?" Remy asked softly.

Prophet waited a beat. Then confirmed, "Yeah."

Tom's chest squeezed.

"Charlie . . . tried to kill me. Dad . . . stepped in front. I tried . . . to help him. But Charlie . . . he said . . . I didn't deserve . . ."

"You're going to make it, Remy," Prophet told him firmly over the sirens. "You hear me? You fucking deserve to live."

Tom swore he heard another gurgle from Remy, but then everything was drowned out by the fast-approaching sirens. Tom shined the light toward them so they didn't get missed, or run over. Prophet stood with Remy and he started walking toward the sounds, while Tom walked backwards, watching the glittering eyes fade behind them.

Eight hours later, Tom was sitting in the waiting area outside the ICU, forcing Prophet to eat something. Remy'd had surgery, but he hadn't woken up yet. Remy's mom had banned them from the room, but she couldn't force them to leave the hallway, and Prophet refused to do so.

When Remy's mother had kicked them out of the room, Tom had gotten in her face until Prophet had pulled him away.

"What the fuck, T?" Prophet had asked, and Tom stared over his shoulder at her until the door closed completely. When Tom turned back to him, he'd said, "So Etienne was right to try for custody."

"Yeah." Her mother lioness act made him sick—she was covering her own ass, rather than being truly concerned about Remy.

Unlike Prophet, who seemed beside himself with worry for Remy. So Tom did what Prophet usually did for others—he mothered the man. Blue and Mick had done the same, until they'd gotten a call from EE and had needed to leave. Tom hoped Phil hadn't gotten word of what had gone on around here, but, as Prophet pointed out, Phil always seemed to know everything.

The state police had Charlie in custody, and they'd taken statements from both Tom and Prophet. And they were waiting to take one from Remy too. They'd talked to the sheriff—the only other one who knew the story besides Tom—and he'd talked about what happened all those years ago, while simultaneously smoothing things over. Tom figured the truth was finally out, so he had nothing to hide. And he couldn't be certain, but he was pretty sure the cops who talked to him had some sympathy in their eyes instead of the usual suspicion.

He'd still need a lawyer though, because even though sympathetic, the police told Tom not to leave town.

Two hours later, Tom put down his coffee, because he just knew Remy was awake. Finally. He stood and Prophet raised his head to stare at him. Seconds later, there were shouts coming from Remy's

ICU room. Several nurses and a doctor ran past them into the room and both men advanced toward the glass doors to get a better view.

Remy looked to be thrashing wildly, his legs slamming the mattress, and Jesus, it looked like a seizure.

But then Remy calmed down a bit, and a nurse came out and motioned to them.

They didn't stop to question anything, just rushed into the room. Remy's mother glared angrily, but the second Remy saw them, he stopped writhing.

"He's all right?" Tom asked the nurse.

"He's lost a lot of blood, but he's been slowly stabilizing. Woke up on his own, so I always take that as the best sign."

Tom watched Remy grab for Prophet's hand, and Prophet took it and held it, half-kneeling against the bed, talking to him in a low, soothing voice.

A minute later, Prophet turned to face the room. "He wants the rest of you out for right now."

"I'm not leaving him alone with you two," Remy's mother snapped, but Remy managed, "Leave, Mom. I need to you go."

"Ma'am, we do need to get him calm, so if that helps," the doctor told her.

She pressed her lips together firmly before saying, "I'll give them five minutes."

The nurse and doctors weren't leaving though. As they worked to check Remy's vitals, Tom moved closer to the bed. Remy was hooked up to monitors that beeped every second. He looked pale and young . . . so fucking fragile.

"What do I tell the police?" Remy asked him now, and Tom swore his heart broke in two.

"No more secrets, Remy. You tell them everything you know."

"But won't that . . .?"

"Don't you worry about me," Tom told him. "Prophet'll make sure we're both okay."

Remy seemed satisfied with that answer, even as Prophet shot Tom a sideways glance.

And then Remy said, "I told him to stop. That it'd happened when my dad was fourteen and that he'd never killed anyone. I told him my dad was sorry about it and that he'd suffered too. I told him my father was a good man." His voice broke a little, but he pushed on. "Charlie told me that his dad had been a good man too, and that it was time to ruin my dad's life, the way my dad had ruined his." Prophet hadn't let go of Remy's hand at all, or maybe it was the other way around. "Will you guys stay when I talk to the police?"

"Of course," Prophet assured Remy, and then continued to hold his hand while he drifted back to sleep.

"You okay?" Tom asked him.

Prophet shook his head. "I don't get it, Tommy. Why did Charlie have to hurt this kid."

It wasn't a question, and he was grateful for that, because he didn't have an answer, beyond his own guilt. He could see the pain in Prophet's eyes too, and he put a hand on the man's shoulder. "I talked to Charlie every week for years. I had no fucking clue."

"Sometimes, our mind blocks us from shit it's not sure we can handle. Besides, you were the one who said that your voodoo shit didn't work like that." Prophet paused. "It was Charlie who put me in that marsh, right?"

"Yes. He had my father's sheath in his car." He paused. "I called home. Hung up when I heard his voice."

"Well, at least your father didn't try to kill me."

"You really know how to lighten a situation up."

Prophet smiled a little. "I try, T. 'S'all I can do." And then he glanced back at Remy.

"He's going to be okay."

"Damned straight he is." Prophet touched his hand to Tommy's. "Stop the guilt shit, okay? None of this is your fault. I need you to believe that."

Tom wanted to, desperately, and so, at that moment, he did.

CHAPTER TWENTY

They dragged themselves back to Della's twenty-four hours later, after Remy's condition had been upgraded to good—she welcomed them with hugs, and then she yelled at them for scaring the crap out of her.

"And I'm making us a big dinner tonight—no arguments," she said after asking about Remy.

"None," Tom told her.

"Good. Roger and Dave are helping me. You two, go . . . shower." She crinkled her nose. "How long were you in the swamp?"

"Too fucking long," Prophet called over his shoulder, already halfway up the stairs. Tom followed him into his old room at the far end of the hall.

Prophet's bags had already been here, and someone had brought Tom's up here too and placed them next to each other. Prophet just grunted and headed to the bathroom, stripping as he walked.

Tom grabbed clean clothes from both their bags, threw them on the bed, and went to join Prophet. Neither of them was up for anything more than getting clean. Tom couldn't remember the last time he'd been so sore.

"You think your wrists are okay?" he asked as he soaped Prophet's back and neck.

"I don't know," Prophet said honestly. He stared down at them like they could give him the answer. Made fists and then stretched them out. Tom was going to offer to massage them for him when a knock at the door pulled his focus.

"I'll get it." Tom grabbed a towel and went to open the door. Dave was there with a tray.

"Della figured you guys would need something to tide you over before dinner," he said.

"Thanks, Dave."

"Good to have you guys back here safely," Dave told him, then mouthed, "I like him," as he pointed toward the bed where Prophet had now deposited himself with his iPad.

"Me too," Tom told him.

Dave shut the door behind him, and Tom slid the tray onto the bed.

"Smells good," Prophet said as he made some kind of hand signal.

Tom was about to ask what the hell he was doing, but when he sat next to Prophet, he saw exactly what was happening.

Prophet was Skyping with Mal.

Mal the psycho. Mal, who he guessed was better than Cillian, except that was like saying a gator was safer than a rattler. He and Prophet were both signing quickly—looking intense and serious— although he knew Mal could hear. The wicked looking scar across his throat had taken away his ability to speak, probably severely damaged his vocal cords. His survival was no doubt something of a miracle, or a testament to the fact that psychos were harder to kill than most. So either Prophet was just comfortable signing with the guy, or he didn't want Tom to know what they were talking about.

Mal glanced in his direction then made a hand motion to Prophet that certainly didn't seem like it came from any ASL dictionary.

"What's that mean?" Tom asked Prophet.

"Just saying hi."

"Yeah, because he's the friendly, pop-in-for-a-chat kind of guy," Tom muttered, fighting the urge to give the screen the finger, then giving in and doing just that.

Mal smirked and cut the screen off in reply.

Prophet smiled. "Everyone has that urge with Mal."

"What does Phil see in him?" Tom asked and immediately felt guilty, because the guy had saved Prophet's life when he couldn't. "Forget it. Sorry."

Prophet cleared his throat. "Mal doesn't *exactly* work for EE or Phil."

"What does that mean?"

Prophet shrugged and actually succeeded in looking innocent. But Tom wasn't buying it, especially when Prophet came back with, "Mal's like, you know, extra help."

"Like for an after-school project?"

"If it involved C4 and a machete, yes."

Tom opened his mouth and closed it. Shook his head like that might be able to stop the crazy, and still had to ask, "Phil has no idea you call him?"

"I'm, uh, kind of forbidden to call Mal."

"But you still do it."

"Well, yeah." Prophet looked at him like he was the crazy one. "Figured what Phil doesn't know won't hurt him."

Tom tried to digest that, thought about the fact that Prophet had called Mal instead of Phil when he'd been shot. Which meant Doc was complicit in this whole Mal thing too. "I thought Phil knew everything."

Prophet considered that. "He hasn't killed me over it yet."

"He might be biding his time."

"Maybe. But look, he'd kill Mal first, and that would give me time to run."

Suddenly the iPad screen came to life, and Mal shot Prophet the finger.

"I knew you were still listening, you asshole!" Prophet shouted.

Mal signed something back to him.

"You hurt yourself using that word?" Prophet asked.

Mal signed something again, pointed at Tom, and Prophet just shook his head.

"What did he say about me?" Tom demanded.

"You don't want to know."

"You're right."

"Told you," Prophet said, looking quite pleased with himself. "Don't say I never tell you anything."

He signed to Mal, and Mal cut the screen again. This time, so did Prophet. He pushed the iPad onto the nightstand and pulled the food toward him.

Della had prepared some fried shrimp and other seafood. She was probably making gumbo and had bought too much, as always.

They ate directly from the tray, not bothering to scoop anything into bowls. Tom asked, "Will you finally tell me what you were doing for the past four months?"

"Can't say." Prophet said around a mouthful of shrimp. "Can't remember if I'm allergic to this or not."

"You're kidding me, right? Yeah, you are. You're trying to distract me rather than tell me anything."

"I tell you what I can."

Tom put his hands out toward Prophet as if to say, *I rest my case.* "I can't fucking protect you if you don't tell me shit. If I don't know who—what—I'm protecting you from."

Prophet stared, and Tom waited for the joke, the snort, the wiseass comment, because he was well aware that was he repeating Prophet's earlier words to him, but was also aware of how stupid it was to try to protect a man who was a weapon.

But Prophet didn't say anything. Instead, he reached out and grabbed the front of Tom's shirt and pulled him close. Gave him a kiss that tasted like cocktail sauce, and then pulled away, grinning.

"That's not getting you out of my questions."

"We almost died in that godforsaken bayou. That should get me out of any kind of interrogation for at least a week, if not more."

"You owe me."

"I owe you?" Prophet asked incredulously. "I saved your ass like three times. Three and a half."

"You can't save someone's life by halves," Tom told him. "And I helped save us. And I saved you from the alligator."

"I could've just shot it the first time." Prophet sighed. "You really want to do this now?"

"What I don't want is to not be able to get in touch with you until the next natural disaster."

"And that wasn't all my fault, Tommy. But fine." Prophet pushed the tray away, propped his head on the pillows, and crossed his long legs. "What do you want to know?"

"Start anywhere."

"I was born in a small town—"

"Why'd you go to work for the CIA?"

"I had no intentions of working for the CIA, but the Agency had other plans for me." He rubbed the back of his neck. "They saved me from a court martial."

"And beat the hell out of you," Tom muttered, and then realized what he'd said. "It was the goddamned CIA in that video." The video he'd gotten before he'd ever met Prophet had documented an interrogation Prophet had endured after he and John had been captured by Sadiq's brother, Azar. In that video, Prophet had pinned his interrogator under the table, nearly breaking his neck in the process. But something about what Tom had watched on screen had never seemed right to him.

"I figured you had to realize it wasn't Azar in the video at some point," Prophet said.

"It felt like CIA," Tom admitted. "Where's the agent from under the table now?"

Prophet gave a small grin. "Still hating me."

"At least you let him go."

"It wasn't an easy decision. Bastard kept me tied down for four days. Wouldn't let a doc come see me. Wouldn't feed me. So you treat me like an animal, don't be surprised when I bite."

He spoke the words calmly, but there was tension in his neck.

"They run through guys like toilet paper," Tom said, and Prophet glanced at him strangely. "Sorry, just an expression Ollie—my mentor at the Bureau—used to say."

An odd expression crossed Prophet's face for just a second, so briefly that Tom could easily talk himself into believing he'd imagined it. So he did. And then Prophet told him, "Well, you're not there anymore. And he's right."

"How do you know Mal?" he asked, and Prophet sighed. Shifted a little. "And if you tell me to ask him . . ."

"He was on my team."

"Mal was a SEAL?"

Prophet nodded. "We came up through BUD/S together. Training for SEALs," he added.

"I know that." Tom crossed his arms.

"What? I answered your question."

"Minimally," Tom pointed out, and Prophet rolled his eyes. Rubbed his wrists.

"I'm not giving you Mal's history."

"Was Mal on your team when all this happened with John?"

"Yeah."

"Where are the others?"

"You know . . . around." Prophet waved in the air like the men would magically appear. Tom even looked over his shoulder, a slight chill running through him, but he shook it off.

"So, still in the Navy?"

"Nope."

"CIA?"

Prophet snorted. "Definitely not. They're a little bit . . . wanted. Well, I guess it depends on what country they're in and what names they're using," he added, almost helpfully, like that made things better.

"And that doesn't bother any of them?"

"We were trained for that shit. Picked for it because we're good at it. Because we loved it. That doesn't stop. It's like, when we got too good, no one liked that. Well, tough shit."

There was way more to this. "Do any of them work for Phil?"

"None of them work for Phil. I don't either," Prophet added, with a gleam of anger in his eyes.

"Do they not work for Phil because they're looking for John?"

Prophet didn't answer.

"Tell me this—if your team is still so close and loyal—" Prophet didn't argue with that. "—then why didn't any of them show up to save you from Sadiq?"

Prophet's jaw twitched, and he stared at Tom.

"The Irish guy with the skullcap," Tom said slowly. "What the fuck, Proph? Are they around us, all the time, like ghosts? All those texts . . . I thought they were EE or Cill . . . but your team . . .?"

"What do you want me to say?"

"You want me to be your partner—your partner—and you won't let me in."

Prophet shook his head. "It took a murder charge to get you to open up to me."

"Tit for tat?"

"Tommy, I have a team. A past. A lot of shit I can't talk about. I know you want to try to help, but you can't."

"If you took over EE, would you hire any of your boys?"

"I'm not taking over EE."

"If you were allowed to partner with your old teammates, would you?"

"Yeah."

"So much for being anti-partner."

"They saved my life."

"Thought you saved your own life when you forced the CIA to release you," Tom challenged him. "Guess it depends on what version of the story you tell?"

"Guess so." Prophet said, his voice quietly frustrated. He stalked off and Tom let him.

"Guess I pushed it too far," he muttered to himself.

A voice with a tinge of an accent said, "You did. You should really leave him alone."

Tom froze. Didn't turn around right away. "Leave him alone, as in forever?"

"Depends. Will you pull that shit constantly?"

Tom did turn then. Same guy, same skullcap, standing by the window. "You're damned straight I will. For one thing, he's my partner. I take that shit seriously. For another, I'm already involved. Sadiq knows who I am. So for better or for worse, I'm a part of this. So no, I'm not going to leave him alone. Maybe you can start telling me what the fuck's going on?"

The guy grinned. "I can see why he likes you."

"I'm not liking him much right now."

"You and I both know that's not true. Look, I can't hang out here. I shouldn't even be here."

"Then why are you?"

"Sadiq's guys are sniffing around. Getting a little close."

"And you're sniffing around them, looking for John?"

The guy's eyes flashed. Tom was pushing his damned luck all around. "Tell Proph I'll be in touch. And if anyone besides him asks, you never saw me."

Before Tom could say anything, the guy was gone out the window in a jump to rival Blue's.

CHAPTER TWENTY-ONE

Prophet came back into the room about twenty minutes later, carrying another plate of shrimp. He glanced warily in Tom's direction, like he was bracing himself for another round of interrogation.

Yeah, well, he can fucking deal with it.

"Your friend was here. You know, skullcap guy."

Prophet's brows raised. "King was here?"

"He didn't take the time to introduce himself."

"Why isn't your voodoo shit working, Tommy?" Prophet asked as he grabbed for his iPad and hit some buttons.

"It was. I just didn't know your team would be stalking me."

But Prophet was talking to the screen, demanding, "Were you here the whole fucking time? Because I almost got eaten by alligators."

Tom heard King's voice, noting the accent was a little thicker, more of a brogue, almost. "Do you think I would've just sat there and watched you nearly get killed by alligators?" King hummed. "I mean, I'd like to think I wouldn't have that, but . . . no. No, I think I would've saved you and not waited."

"You're such an asshole."

Prophet cut King's cursing off and threw the iPad on the bed.

"So I don't get it—these guys just . . . hang around, waiting for you to get into trouble?"

"Kind of, yes."

"How many of them are there?"

"King. Mal. Ren. Hook."

"And you repay them, how?"

Prophet managed to look vaguely insulted. "Sometimes I save their asses too, and they have to pay me back somehow."

"For Mal," Tom said. "How do you repay Mal?"

"Mal likes favors."

"Favors."

"Yeah." Prophet raised a brow.

"Like sexual favors?"

"It's complicated."

"Wait a minute, after Mal helped when you got shot—"

Prophet waved him off.

Tom decided that, as much as he wanted to know, it was better right now that he didn't. Still . . . "One day, you're going to answer my questions about Mal."

"Yeah, one day." Prophet smiled, and Tom got hard.

"You're baiting me into fucking you."

Prophet had the nerve to look offended by that. "I don't need to bait you into fucking me. I don't need to bait you into me fucking you, either. If I wanted to fuck you or you to fuck me—" Tom found himself flipped onto his stomach on the floor, with Prophet's dead weight pressing him. "—I'd do this."

"This is your idea of seduction?" Tom managed.

Prophet jerked him onto his side and cupped his cock, which of course, had long since betrayed him. "You seem not to mind."

"What was this conversation about again?" Tom asked.

"If you're not with me, you're in less trouble . . ."

"No, it wasn't. And you don't know that I'm in less trouble, not for sure. Besides, it's too late. I'm involved."

Prophet moved off him with a curse.

Tom rolled over. "You're so fucking impossible."

"It serves a purpose."

Tom grabbed him by the back of the neck. Knocked him down and rolled him, using Prophet's own body weight and struggle against him.

"Tell. Me. About your team. Why all the secrecy?"

"They're around. I talk to them, but we all work better alone. Keeps us out of trouble."

"Because if you work together . . ."

"The CIA tends to get involved if we get together," Prophet said. "We've been ordered not to. By the CIA. And I can't fucking tell you anymore about that piece of it. Not without risking them, so stop. I wouldn't risk you like that."

Tom nipped the side of Prophet's neck with his teeth.

"You like marking me," Prophet noted.

Tom sucked hard where he'd bitten, then asked. "What've you been doing?"

"Stuff." Prophet's voice was hoarse.

"Well, while you were doing stuff, I was in Eritrea, trying to contact you."

"Except when you were chasing me thinking it was Cillian," Prophet pointed out.

Tom rewarded him by sliding his tongue along his neck, then biting his earlobe. Prophet shivered. "Not fair, Tommy."

"Were you working with Cill?"

"Definitely not."

"And your team isn't working together."

"Well, when you see King, Ren isn't far behind."

"I didn't see Ren."

"You never will, unless he wants you too. He and King are a matched pair."

"Of what?"

"Can't pry them apart."

"I thought none of you were supposed to work together."

"We're not. But there are psychos who are the exception to every rule."

Tom put his hands to Prophet's face. "Talk to me, Proph. What do you do?"

Prophet looked into Tommy's mismatched eyes and finally told the man exactly what he was goddamned best at.

"I go after the guys the CIA and the military leave behind, the ones they tell, 'we will disavow any knowledge of you if you're captured.' When that happens, I don't fucking forget them." Neither did his SEAL team. It wasn't a particularly glorious or high-paying job most of the time, but it wasn't a thankless one either. "I also help their families, because civilians shouldn't have to suffer because their spouse or parent signed up for all that shit."

"How did that become one of your specialties?"

"My first CO . . . his brother was a POW." One long, whiskey-soaked night, Prophet, LT, and LT's brother—who was blind as a result of his capture, but Prophet didn't tell Tommy that—had talked about . . . everything. That conversation still reverberated through Prophet's life, affecting everything he did, most of the choices he'd made.

Tommy was the one choice off the path he'd started down that night.

But right now, Tom was watching him. Waiting. He knew there was more. That goddamned voodoo shit.

He drew in a deep breath, trying not to worry about what Tommy's reaction would be, and not succeeding. "I also guard the men and women we call specialists," he explained. "Typically, the knowledge they possess is dangerous enough that we want them on our side. But if they fall into enemy hands during transport and that knowledge is compromised . . ."

"What happens, Proph?" Tom asked.

"If I can't stop the situation, I have to take out the specialist." His heart beat a thousand miles an hour as he waited for Tommy to judge him for that.

"I can't imagine," Tom started. "How do you know you'd be able to handle that?"

Prophet stared at him. "You're thinking it was a way for me to punish myself or something? These jobs started before John and I were captured, T."

"So?" Tom asked quietly, and Prophet ignored that in favor of answering Tom's original question, sans the double meaning.

"Look, with a job like that, especially with the specialists, the most important thing is a conscience. People think you don't need one—shouldn't have one, because that would make it easier. But it shouldn't be goddamned easy. And when you can't feel anything, that's when you've turned into the walking dead. And I've seen too many walking dead men in my time. I never want to become that."

"And you didn't."

He'd come so damned close, though. He took a breath, but he wanted to get this out fast. Because he never liked talking about it. "After Azar and the CIA, I lost myself for two goddamned years. And Phil found me. Pulled me up and out. To this day, he doesn't know much more than what kind of job I'd been doing and that I was looking for John. He knew enough then not to ask about it. Still knows enough now."

"Sometimes not knowing any better gets you further," Tom said.

Damn, the guy was smart as fuck. "When Phil first tried to recruit me, I resisted. But Phil told me I was wasting my talent."

"You, resisting?" Tom drawled. "Say it ain't so."

"I resist until I get all the facts," he protested, but Tom shook his head slowly.

"You try to make it impossible to love you."

He stared up at the man. "Tommy, I don't fucking have to try. This is just me."

"I know. I fell for just you."

"Give it time, T. You'll regret that." No self-pity, just a truth he believed.

"Like Phil?"

"Yeah, just like that," he muttered. "Took him longer than most."

"So what do we do now?"

"You go with Cope."

"We are not back here again, are we?"

"No, we're not. This has nothing to do with us—I want to fucking *be* with you, Tommy. I just can't work at EE anymore. You can, and I don't want you giving that up."

"You can't or won't?" Tom pressed.

"Same thing in my world," Prophet said. "It's good work. You like it."

"I like working with *you*, Proph. We're a fucking good team, and you know it. And I know you're going to keep taking black-ops jobs. I won't let you do that alone."

"Sadiq will take any opportunity to use you against me. He already has."

Tom persisted. "We're effective together."

"We're fucking scary together."

"We can grow old fighting crime."

Prophet obviously didn't hide his expression fast enough, because Tom asked, "You worried about growing old? We can retire."

"Yeah," Prophet said wistfully, and how was he going to share his impending blindness with Tommy?

You've already told him way too fucking much.

"What are you worried about?"

"That I'll hurt you," Prophet said honestly. "That I'll get you hurt."

"Same here, Proph. But I can't stay away."

The tension was running high between them, good tension of the *what the fuck do we do now* variety. Tom watched Prophet carefully, trying to gauge his mood by the color of his eyes. Dark gray meant danger, lighter with a tinge of blue meant happy, even peaceful, if only for mere moments. But now the mood ring colors that were Prophet's eyes weren't helping, because he'd gotten caught up in their sadness. "Why does me not being able to stay away upset you so much? It's not supposed to."

Prophet nodded, and his voice was rough with emotion when he said, "I'm okay with putting myself at risk, always have been. But I can't keep pulling people into my shit."

Tom put his arms around him and just held him. "No one's ever taken care of you back, Proph. You have to fucking let me."

"I don't know how," Prophet said, and Tom sighed internally, because that wasn't a *no*. Not by a long shot. "I can fuck up a lot of things," Prophet muttered.

"Not this."

Prophet didn't even look up at him.

"Come on, Proph. Don't do this."

Prophet stood, paced around the bed, and stopped in front of the window King had entered from. "You want to be my partner outside of the job too. But T, being a partner's the same all the way around. Still gotta learn to work together. In sync, not just trying to put the other one in to a bubble and going all out to save him. If we listen and work together, we don't need that shit."

"So we listen and work together—" Tom started, but Prophet held up a hand.

"As it stands now, you count on me. I watch your back. I spend so much time worried about you, I get us both into trouble. I won't go back there and let that happen again. You're scared I'm going to get hurt. I'm fucking terrified of the same thing, but there's something you can do about it. And you won't."

"So I'm supposed to go work with Cope and you're going to disappear, just like the rest of your team's been forced to do?" Tom demanded.

"For a little while, yeah."

"And what about us?"

"Tommy—"

"No, don't. Don't use that name in one breath and tell me you're leaving in another."

"It would help a whole hell of a lot if you'd understand."

"It would help a whole hell of a lot if you'd let me help."

"You can't. I can't bring you any further into this than you already are. I can't do that to anyone, T, but especially not to someone I . . ." He trailed off, shook his head. "I can't."

"Won't."

"In this case, they're the same exact thing."

"How long?"

"I don't know."

"It could be years?"

"Yes."

"Why did you come here then?" Tom demanded.

"Because I missed you."

"But only for the sex, right? That's the only thing I'm allowed to help you with."

"Did you ever consider that you're a shitty partner, and that bad luck has nothing to do with it, Tom?"

"Fuck you very much," Tom growled. "I don't need this shit."

Tom's head ached under the weight of Prophet's words. They'd hit the mark, the dart in the bull's-eye, and while Prophet meant them, he hadn't completely said them to wound.

He'd spoken the truth and that made Tom's world spin. Because he'd never trusted himself enough to be an effective partner—and that's exactly what Prophet had been trying to show him the entire time.

But that familiar anger rose up, and he couldn't get a handle on it fast enough. "Go home, Prophet. You still have one of those, right? Go to your spook or Mal or Doc and fuck your way through whoever you need to."

"Right. Me leaving like this clears your conscience. Makes all this so much easier on you." Prophet leaned in. "I'm staying. Gonna watch all your secrets tumble out onto the floor. Watch it get messy and ugly. And you know what? Afterward, I'll still be here, because I'm done running from us."

CHAPTER TWENTY-TWO

After spending two days in Etienne's studio feeling sorry for himself, Tom manned up and emailed Phil. And then he showered and dressed for Etienne's memorial service.

He wasn't invited, so technically, he'd be going after the fact. And it was hot and crowded and horrible. And he swore he saw Prophet there, but when he blinked, he couldn't find him again in the crowd.

When he'd visited Remy in the hospital, the kid had sworn Prophet hadn't been there, but Tom knew better. Remy had been released that morning, but he'd heard rumbles that Remy's mom wouldn't let him come to the service.

Tom needed to keep Della involved in that. He'd given Remy Della's number—and he'd make sure Della knew it. When she was speaking to him again.

Now, he said a prayer for his old friend, his heart heavy for the way this had ended. For being the only one to escape. But Etienne would've forgiven him, because the man always had. It was time for Tom to forgive himself.

He stopped at a bakery first, then drove to Della's. Prophet's truck was still in the driveway. He was still there, as promised.

When Tom walked through the front door, the house was warm and smelled like paint. He followed the scent, walked through the kitchen and back into the rarely used formal dining room. Prophet was painting—rolling the walls, the fan lazily blowing the hot air around the room. Prophet was caught up in the mindless work, his shirt soaked with sweat, his hair caught in a green bandana, the muscles in his arms standing out with the slickness of his skin.

What Prophet was thinking was anyone's guess.

"How long have you known I was here?" he asked finally, and Prophet froze.

He hadn't known.

Fuck.

Tom didn't hesitate to move forward. Prophet still hadn't turned around. Tom pried the roller from his hand, put it down on the tray, and turned Prophet around.

His eyes were glassy, and he was probably headed down the dehydration route. Of all people, he had to have known he was pushing it.

Which is exactly why he was doing it. Keeping busy. Refusing to give himself time to think. Or to feel.

Tom shoved a glass of iced tea into his hand, and Prophet drank greedily. Tom got a towel from the kitchen, soaked it, and brought it over to Prophet. He started by wringing it out over Prophet's head, then wiped down his face and neck.

"'M' fine," Prophet rasped.

"Yeah, as fine as I am."

Prophet glanced up at him. "I'm supposed to order you the fuck out of the house if you show."

"You can try."

"You like taking care of me," Prophet murmured, like he'd finally come to terms with it.

"Could say the same thing about you." He paused. "Phil said he didn't give you the choice. If he had . . ."

"I don't think I would've been able to let you go," Prophet admitted. "And I'm not the type to hold anyone against their will. Problem is, I've got a lot of past. It's never really going to be over. And you were relieved that I walked away."

"Yeah," Tommy said hoarsely. "I didn't want that, but fuck, Prophet . . . my luck . . ."

"Fuck that—has nothing to do with luck."

"Guess we both ran."

"I ran toward you," Prophet said indignantly.

"Took you months."

"I know," Prophet said, his voice softer.

"Don't do that again. It's too late to pull any more of that shit," Tom said fiercely and Prophet lifted his head to gaze at him.

Finally, he said, "What shit?"

"The 'I don't want a partner' shit. You don't have to work for EE, but that doesn't matter. I'm helping you from now on. Got it?"

Prophet stared at him for a long moment. "So what, I'm stuck with you?"

"Looks like it."

Prophet shook his head almost sadly, like he felt sorry for Tommy now. "Just don't look under the tarp in the office and you'll be fine."

"Trust me, I have no interest in going near it. But I'm not letting you go. I mean it."

"I know that."

"Do you really believe it?"

"Yes." He glanced over at the donuts Tom had brought. "You trying to seduce me with those?"

"Yes. Is it working?"

"Yeah."

Prophet's smile wasn't big, but it was enough.

"Fucking love making you smile, Proph." He stroked through the man's wet hair. "Love the fact that you came here for me. Weren't ordered to. You just came. For me."

Prophet didn't deny it. Ran his tongue over his lower lip before biting it, like he was trying to hold something back.

He straddled Prophet and tipped the man's head up with a hand under his chin. "Been waiting for this."

He kissed Prophet, and Prophet groaned against his mouth, hot and sweet. He curled his hand around the back of Prophet's neck as he tongued the roof of Prophet's mouth. It was slow and sensual, unrushed. Hot, wet, and sticky. When he pulled back, he held into Prophet's lower lip between his teeth for just a second before letting it go. Prophet moaned softly, then noted, "You've got a lot of making up to do with Della. She's really pissed at you."

"You. Drive me. Crazy."

Prophet gave a smile. "Short trip."

Tom opened his mouth. Closed it. Then, resigned to his fate, leaned in and kissed the hell out of Prophet, letting Prophet's mouth work its magic, until all he could think about, all he wanted, was reduced to the man he held.

The man who held onto him just as tightly. And after they'd exhausted themselves kissing, made lazy by the heat and the reunion, they were both content not to rush into ripping each other's clothes off.

Finally, Tom pulled back. He was still holding one of Prophet's hands, and now he turned it over and traced a few of the lines he found.

"What, you're a fortune-teller now too?" Prophet teased.

"I've been to enough of them. It's a rite of passage around here."

"Do you know if they're bullshitting you?"

"I like to think so, but I don't know for sure."

"The one I saw next to Etienne's shop . . . she told me everything was great."

"And it's not."

"Did anything great happen since I saw her?" Prophet demanded.

"This isn't bad," Tom reminded him. "I haven't visited one for a long time. When I was thirteen, that same woman told me I'd end up with a man whose name began with E." He stopped cold when he saw Prophet's face. He'd schooled it quickly, but not quickly enough. "What?"

"Nothing. Just dizzy," Prophet lied, and Tom let it go for the moment. "Did you know you were gay then?"

"Long before that, but I didn't go around telling people. I was surprised the fortune-teller saw that. And I already knew Etienne, had a crush on him—and then, by the following year, he was the guy I thought I'd be with forever, like you do when you're in love for the first time." Prophet actually growled a little, and Tom couldn't lie that a little jealousy on that end was completely satisfying. He was about to continue when something stopped him, and he stared at Prophet for a second before asking, "What's your real name?"

Prophet stared back at him.

"Name," Tom repeated.

"There go those orders again."

"You said it makes you hard."

"No, mine make you hard," Prophet corrected, his mouth quirked slightly to the side, like he was holding back a smile. And failing. "Name's not a big secret."

"Then why can't I find it on any EE paperwork?"

"Why were you searching through my stuff?" Prophet demanded.

"For the record, I couldn't find a single trace of your personal files in EE's offices."

"That doesn't answer my question."

"You haven't answered mine either."

"Fine," Prophet huffed. "My name's not anywhere for security purposes. When I was in the military and the CIA, I got banned in some countries under my official passport name."

"How many people know your actual first name?"

"It's not a secret."

Tom glared at him. "Then who calls you by it?"

"No one."

"Does anyone know it?"

"My mother, I think."

"Proph, seriously?"

"What's it going to change? If it doesn't start with E, what's it going to change?"

"Absolutely nothing," Tom told him.

"It's Connor," he said, and Tom grabbed him and kissed him. Because it didn't fucking matter. All that mattered was that Prophet was here with him.

As if in agreement, Prophet kissed him back hard, then tugged Tom's lower lip with his teeth, sucked it hard, and dragged it away before sliding his tongue along Tom's.

"You can really get off on just kissing, can't you?" Tom murmured when he pulled back.

"Oh yeah." Prophet ran a thumb along his bottom lip, brushed knuckles over his cheek, and suddenly, just like that, he knew Prophet was lying.

He pushed off Prophet's lap and stared at him. He fisted his hands to stop them from shaking.

Prophet pulled his wallet out. He handed Tom an ID card, and Tom shook his head. "I can't find a single instance of your first name anywhere and the entire time it's been on your driver's license?"

"You're all so busy digging, you forget the obvious." Prophet still held out the license to him, and Tom still refused to take it. "You wanted to know, babe. Not the time to freak out about it. Especially when your voodoo shit turns out to be right."

"Fuck," Tom whispered, finally grabbed the card. He stared at it through a sudden haze of tears even as he muttered, "Son of a bitch."

You'll end up with a man whose name starts with E. And he'll rip through your life like a tornado. Then again, a tornado can handle a volcano.

Prophet's real name was Elijah. Elijah Drews.

His own fucking personal tornado.

Tom blinked. "Yeah, so Prophet works."

"That's only part of where it came from."

"What's the other half?"

Prophet's smile lit his face. "Maybe I'll tell you after you fuck me."

Tom's breath caught. "Fair enough."

EPILOGUE

The police department unexpectedly cleared Tom and Prophet to leave the state twenty-four hours later. Just in time for a message for Tom from Phil himself, demanding his presence in EE's offices first thing the following morning.

In sixteen hours.

"We'll make it," Prophet told him.

"I'm gonna need Dramamine," Tom grumbled. But true to his word, Prophet pulled into the EE lot four minutes before Tom's scheduled meeting with Phil. They'd barely stopped, they looked like hell, smelled like fast food, and Tom was changing his shirt on the walk into the building.

They hadn't really discussed anything about this on the ride. They'd listened to music, talked about movies and other things unrelated to killing and shooting, and now Tom realized he was nervous. And it wasn't about what Phil would tell him. It was because he and Prophet were back where they started . . . at EE.

It's different now, he told himself firmly. And he forced himself to believe it, because Prophet did.

If Prophet didn't, they wouldn't have made this drive together.

"What do you think the New Orleans police told Phil?" he asked Prophet now, stopping him from opening the doors to the main floor.

"Whatever he did, he owes someone there now," Prophet noted. "And there's going to be a hell of a lot of paperwork. But hey, we didn't do anything totally illegal."

"Very comforting."

"Yeah?"

"No."

Prophet shrugged, stuck his hands in his jeans pockets. Tom knew he didn't want to go inside, but he refused to let Tom go in alone.

Now, Prophet opened the door and walked in behind Tom, and the busy office seemed to come to a complete standstill.

"Uh-oh," Prophet sing-songed under his breath.

"Incoming," Cope mouthed as he passed them, and Tom swore the ground rumbled under his feet. He looked up to see Phil marching out of his office, his posture Marine rigid. The hallways cleared in seconds as everyone took cover.

Everyone except for Tom.

"You are in so much goddamned trouble," Phil started as he got close. But before he could take the final steps closing the distance between them, Prophet stepped in between them.

Like a goddamned human shield.

His back was to Tom and the tension was palpable—thick and uncomfortable. Tom wanted to pull Prophet from the line of fire. But he didn't.

"Leave him alone." Prophet's words were calm, but his stance wasn't.

"You don't tell me what to do," Phil said, his voice and stance equal to Prophet's. Which was really fucking dangerous.

"You don't tell me either," Prophet told him. "And this one isn't his fault."

"Let me guess, it's yours."

"No, it's not his." Tom stepped out from behind Prophet to stand next to him.

"Well, look at that—I finally get you two assholes to work together, but it's against me and my rules." Phil grimaced, then turned to Prophet. "Are you here to ask if you can come back to work?"

Tom held his breath, but Prophet looked Phil in the eye and said, "No," without a trace of rancor or regret.

That startled Phil, but Tom wasn't sure if the head of EE had shown it in his expression, or if Tom just knew. Either way, Phil shook it off quickly and said, "Then wait here, because Tom doesn't need a bodyguard. Tom, my office, now."

Tom was surprised that Prophet simply nodded and let him go, but he was glad. He didn't need any further tension between Phil and Prophet clouding what he needed to do.

He followed Phil down the hall and into his office. Phil shut the door and motioned for him to sit and he did. Faced Phil across the desk. Waited.

"I know why you disobeyed a direct order," Phil said finally.

"I know why you gave me one. You knew I wouldn't listen. You knew it, and you did it anyway." Phil didn't deny it. "You do that a lot."

"Not to you."

Tom blew out a frustrated breath. "If you like it when we don't follow the rules—"

"I like operatives who can think outside the box. I don't need people blindly following my orders, Tom."

"You need to stop fucking with him." Phil stared him down, but Tom wouldn't buckle. Not on this. "You want me to work here, I'll work here. But you need to stop fucking with Prophet."

"You're good for him."

"So were you."

Phil's expression tightened. "I know you want to help him with whatever shit he's got going on. I don't want to know about it. I can't. Just go with him. And then bring him back to me, Tom."

"And what's he going to think I'm doing if I suddenly have time off from EE to help him?"

Phil pointed to the monstrous pile of folders on the corner of the desk, an evil glint in his eye. "Paperwork. From running roughshod around little things called laws. And bringing two other operatives in on the job. Who, by the way, are still denying everything."

"That wasn't all my fault."

"No, but I'm guessing you'll take all the blame for your partner, now won't you?"

Yeah, he would. And Phil had known it before they'd walked back in here. "Yes, sir."

"Fuck the 'sir' shit. And one more thing."

"What's that?"

"Your boxes and your Harley are here."

"Why?"

"You were evicted."

"For what?"

"They were suspicious that you were never there," Phil said. "You're welcome to stay in one of the upstairs rooms until you find time to look for another place."

When he walked out, he noted Prophet's office—his and Prophet's—was exactly the way Prophet had left it.

Prophet was sitting in the office chair by the door, where Tom had left him. Except he had two boxes of pencils and a giant bag of red Twizzlers.

"Did you raid the supply closet?"

"Natasha gave them to me. Apparently, they tend to miss people who do shit like fuck with the office supplies." A small smile tugged at the corner of his mouth.

They walked out to Prophet's truck together, and once they were on the road, Prophet asked, "Well?"

"I got evicted."

"No shit?" Prophet asked. "Where's your stuff?"

"Upstairs in EE's living quarters."

Prophet turned and started driving back. Tom didn't question that, just continued, "He wants me to stay at EE."

"Work with him, T. Someone needs to keep an eye on the place."

"And what're you going to do?"

"What I need to so we can both stay safe."

"Now you get romantic."

"That's romantic?" Prophet asked. "Maybe I'm better at it than I thought."

"He's kept your office the exact same way. Looks like no one's been allowed to touch it."

"Great. Like I'm dead and it's my memorial."

Tom sighed. "It's not like that."

"Like I've retired."

"Like that'll ever happen." He paused. "Just do me a favor? I've been telling you this from the start, but get your eyes checked."

"I get regular physicals."

"Okay, but . . ." He stopped, shook his head. "Enough. Let's go celebrate."

"The fact that you were evicted?"

"I wasn't evicted as much as let out of my lease. She thought there'd always be someone there to do stuff like mow the lawn."

"You were like her houseboy."

"Shut up."

"I could use one."

"A houseboy?"

"Yeah. You'd fit the job well."

"What's the pay like?"

"Negotiable. Like always." Prophet turned to stare at him once he'd pulled back into the EE lot. "You know this isn't going to be easy, going forward."

Tom didn't know if he was talking about them, or the shit with Sadiq, or the fact that Prophet would be working black op jobs, or all of the above. But if and when Prophet went looking for Sadiq, Tom had to follow. He had orders.

And he would've done it without them.

Get ready for Mal and Cillian's adventures!

DIRTY

EXTREME ESCAPES, LTD

DEEDS

SE JAKES

Coming to Riptide Publishing
January 13, 2014!

ACKNOWLEDGMENTS

These books are such a labor of love, and they're not created in a vacuum, so, as always, I have many people to thank.

For Sarah Frantz, the most gifted editor I know. For Rachel Haimowitz for all the opportunities she's given me. For LC Chase and the gorgeous covers and layouts. For everyone at Riptide for making my publishing experience insanely wonderful.

Thanks to Nerine Dorman for the Afrikaans translation. And to SC, MN, and JD for their many stories and insights.

As always, thanks to the readers who hang out with me on Tumbler, Facebook, Ask SEJ, and Twitter too. You guys are so awesome—thanks for taking this journey with me, and for loving these guys as much as I do.

Last, but never least, for my family. For everything.

ALSO BY SE JAKES

Catch a Ghost (Hell or High Water, #1)

Men of Honor Series:
Bound by Honor
Bound by Law
Ties That Bind
Bound by Danger
Bound for Keeps (EE, Ltd.)

Standalone:
Free Falling (EE, Ltd.)

Hell or High Water Series Coming Soon:
Daylight Again
If I Ever

Dirty Deeds Series (EE, Ltd.) Coming Soon:
Dirty Deeds
Dirty Lies
Dirty Love

ABOUT THE AUTHOR

SE Jakes writes m/m romance. She believes in happy endings and fighting for what you want in both fiction and real life. She lives in New York with her family and most days, she can be found happily writing (in bed). No really . . .

She spends most of her time writing, but she loves to hear from readers, so you can contact her the following ways:

Email: authorsejakes@gmail.com
Website: sejakes.com
Tumblr: sejakes.tumblr.com
Facebook: Facebook.com/SEJakes
Twitter: Twitter.com/authorsejakes
Goodreads Group: Ask SE Jakes

Enjoyed this book? Visit RiptidePublishing.com to find more edge-of-your-seat romantic suspense!

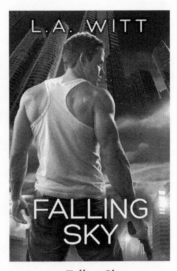

Gravedigger's Brawl
ISBN: 978-1-937551-53-7

Falling Sky
ISBN: 978-1-62649-040-6

Earn Bonus Bucks!

Earn 1 Bonus Buck for each dollar you spend. Find out how at RiptidePublishing.com/news/bonus-bucks.

Win Free Ebooks for a Year!

Pre-order coming soon titles directly through our site and you'll receive one entry into a drawing to win free books for a year! Get the details at RiptidePublishing.com/contests.